SAVAGE RISING

REDEMPTION HARBOR SERIES

Katie Reus

Cover art: Jaycee of Sweet 'N Spicy Designs
Editor: Julia Ganis
Author website: http://www.katiereus.com

Publisher's Note: This is a work of fiction. Names, characters, places, and incidents are either the products of the author's imagination or used fictitiously, and any resemblance to actual persons, living or dead, or business establishments, organizations or locales is completely coincidental.

Savage Rising/Katie Reus. -- 1st ed.
KR Press, LLC

ISBN-10: 1635560225
ISBN-13: 9781635560220

eISBN: 9781635560213

For Arabella.

Praise for the novels of Katie Reus

"...a wild hot ride for readers. The story grabs you and doesn't let go."
—*New York Times* bestselling author, Cynthia Eden

"Has all the right ingredients: a hot couple, evil villains, and a killer action-filled plot.... [The] Moon Shifter series is what I call Grade-A entertainment!" —Joyfully Reviewed

"I could not put this book down.... Let me be clear that I am not saying that this was a good book *for* a paranormal genre; it was an excellent romance read, *period.*" —All About Romance

"Reus strikes just the right balance of steamy sexual tension and nail-biting action....This romantic thriller reliably hits every note that fans of the genre will expect." —*Publishers Weekly*

"Prepare yourself for the start of a great new series! ... I'm excited about reading more about this great group of characters."
—Fresh Fiction

"Wow! This powerful, passionate hero sizzles with sheer deliciousness. I loved every sexy twist of this fun & exhilarating tale. Katie Reus delivers!" —Carolyn Crane, RITA award winning author

"A sexy, well-crafted paranormal romance that succeeds with smart characters and creative world building." —Kirkus Reviews

"*Mating Instinct*'s romance is taut and passionate ... Katie Reus's newest installment in her Moon Shifter series will leave readers breathless!"
—Stephanie Tyler, *New York Times* bestselling author

"You'll fall in love with Katie's heroes."
—*New York Times* bestselling author, Kaylea Cross

"Both romantic and suspenseful, a fast-paced sexy book full of high stakes action." —Heroes and Heartbreakers

"Katie Reus pulls the reader into a story line of second chances, betrayal, and the truth about forgotten lives and hidden pasts."
—The Reading Café

"Nonstop action, a solid plot, good pacing, and riveting suspense."
—RT Book Reviews

"Exciting in more ways than one, well-paced and smoothly written, I'd recommend *A Covert Affair* to any romantic suspense reader."
—Harlequin Junkie

"Sexy military romantic suspense." —USA Today

"Enough sexual tension to set the pages on fire."
—*New York Times* bestselling author, Alexandra Ivy

"*Avenger's Heat* hits the ground running...This is a story of strength, of partnership and healing, and it does it brilliantly."
—Vampire Book Club

"*Mating Instinct* was a great read with complex characters, serious political issues and a world I am looking forward to coming back to."
—All Things Urban Fantasy

PROLOGUE

Zac moved through the quiet hallway of the high-rise bank. Half a world away from home, this was his last job.

That was what he'd been telling himself for the last five jobs, however. But then the CIA would offer him another contract and he'd take it. Sometimes the contracts involved "liberating" something, but more often than not lately it was taking out a target.

There had to be more to his life than this. He just wasn't sure he was ready to walk away yet. Because what else was he going to do? It was a hell of a thing to be skilled at. And work kept his mind busy—except when he was alone. Then his mind couldn't seem to shut off.

One of his best friends had recently been killed by a cartel, even if they'd never found her body. He'd been consumed with thoughts of her murder but there had been no one to blame. Not one individual he could go after. Because if he'd had a name, that person would be dead. He mentally shook off that thought. He didn't have the headspace for that now. Not if he wanted to get out of here in one piece. Distractions got a person killed.

Get your head in this, he ordered himself.

The bright lights of Hong Kong glittered in the background from the windows of every open office door he passed. Normally he wasn't hired to work in Asian countries because he was white and tall. He tended to stand out.

But he'd been called in specifically for this job. The powers that be wanted an outsider. Someone not connected to the region and not likely to work it again. He fit the bill and had been available on short notice.

At the sound of an elevator ding in the distance, he froze for all of a second before ducking into a nearby office. The place was supposed to be empty tonight except for one person. His target.

Tense, he backed up against the wall behind the office door, pulling it as close to his body as possible. He could see through the crack well enough. Faint footsteps sounded in the distance along with laughter. Of someone young and female.

A moment later the words became clear. A little girl chattered to a woman, mostly in English. Through the crack of the open door, he saw a dark-haired little Asian girl and a dark-haired woman—Caucasian, not Chinese, however—pass by him. From the file he had on his target he knew that the guy had married an American woman and for now they were living in Hong Kong. But they would be moving to London soon enough.

Well his target wouldn't. Maybe the family still would. Not his problem though. This had to be them. They must be coming to visit the man.

He quietly texted his contact. For most jobs he went completely dark, but he occasionally took a burner phone with him in case. Because every once in a while, there was an "in case." *Family is here. Not sure how long. Going to abort for now.* He could just take the guy out on the road, which would be trickier, but doable.

The response was almost immediate. *Take them all out.*

He blinked once, stared at the message. The target deserved to die. That was never in doubt. He'd seen the man's files. He knew the dark things he'd done. That wasn't why Zac had been hired to kill him, however. He'd been hired because the man had betrayed his handler. He'd been working both sides—and double-crossed the CIA. Because of his betrayal, four good agents had been executed. That alone was enough for Zac to go after him.

But kill his family? *No.*

Again, the response was immediate. *This needs to happen tonight. Do it.*

Zac's finger hovered over the keypad. He was tempted to text him back, telling him to go to hell. Instead he pocketed the phone and slipped back out into the hallway. As he did, a little toy car rolled out from the only office with the lights on.

He stilled against the nearest wall. The little girl raced out, her long black hair flying behind her as she did. Scooping it up, she smiled to herself and looked in his direction. Because of the shadows she must have not seen him because no alarm crossed her face.

God, she was so young. Maybe eight? He didn't know shit about kids but she was young, small and innocent.

And his contact wanted him to end her life as if it were nothing? "Wrong place, wrong time" was exactly what his contact would say. Screw that.

When she skipped back into her father's office, he hurried back the way he'd come, sticking to the shadows and avoiding the security cameras. This building definitely wasn't as secure as it could be. Someone else would eventually do the job but it wouldn't be tonight.

And it wouldn't be him.

Once he was on the crowded street he sucked in a sharp breath, his senses going into overdrive.

A blast of warm, stale-smelling air rolled over him as he moved past a restaurant. Then he was inundated with jasmine incense, exhaust, and too many foods to sift through. He hated the smell of Hong Kong. It only made him miss home more.

Even if he didn't technically *have* a home, Redemption Harbor, South Carolina would always be where he considered home.

As he passed a garbage can, he dropped the phone into it and kept walking. Instead of heading back to his hotel room, he stopped at an all-night cell phone store and picked up another burner. He sent his temporary number to Brooks, his best friend, and to Mercer—one of his closest friends and also the man who'd recently lost his wife to cartel violence. He'd send it out to the others later. For now he needed to grab his false ID, money and get out of the country.

He was surprised when moments later the phone rang. Mercer.

He answered immediately. Since Mary Grace—Mercer's wife—had been murdered, he tried to be available to Mercer as much as possible. "Hey, I wake you with that text?"

"No."

"What's up? You okay?"

"Yeah. I mean, no. I'll probably never be okay again but...something's going on with Brooks and Colt."

"Colt?" he asked, sidestepping a cluster of teenagers taking a picture of themselves. Colt was supposed to be on vacation or some bullshit. Not that he'd really believed Colt would take one, but he'd assumed the man was working another undercover op.

"Yeah. He stopped by and left Brooks to babysit me while he goes out of town. He's borrowing Brooks's family jet too."

Colt worked for the CIA, something Mercer wouldn't know. He might suspect though. And if Colt was using a private plane instead of one of the many resources at his disposal, he was up to something. Zac cleared his throat. "Do you *need* someone to watch you right now?" he asked carefully in reference to the "babysit" comment. Last time he'd seen Mercer the man had been deep in the denial stage. Not that Zac blamed him. He didn't want to believe Mary Grace was gone either.

Mercer cursed. "No, Jesus. I'm not going to kill myself. Though...I've thought about it."

"Hell." Yep, he was getting out of here tonight.

"Just being honest. Something's going on with them. Colt left and Brooks is being cagey. Won't leave my house. I hate to ask but I need you—"

"I'll be there as soon as possible. Give me a couple days. I'm not in the country." He turned left at the next street, heading for the nearest bus stop. He might not care for the overpowering smells here, but they had the best public transportation he'd ever used. Since he'd basically just given the middle finger to his current contract job, he needed to find another way home. While he was almost a hundred percent sure no one would come after him for ditching this job, he wasn't going to tempt fate. Besides, the man who'd hired him knew his rules. Then he'd gone and asked him to break his biggest one. He'd never killed a kid and he wasn't going to start now. He had some of his soul still intact.

"If you're sure—"

"Shut up with that. Yeah I'm sure. You're my friend. My *family*." The family he'd chosen.

"I just don't want to inconvenience anyone." Mercer's voice was low, quiet.

And Zac felt like a complete and utter shit. "You could never inconvenience any of us. *Ever*. I know you're torn up. But we all lost her. We all miss her." His voice cracked on the last word. And Zac couldn't even say her name. Couldn't say *Mary Grace* out loud. Losing her had cut a hole right through their entire group. There were seven of them who'd been friends since they were kids, and while most of them had moved away from Redemption Harbor once they'd grown, their bond ran deep. She'd been like a sister to the rest of them. "And if you think for one second you could inconvenience me, then I've been a shitty friend the last couple months." Which he was pretty sure he had been. Hell, he shouldn't *be* on this job. He should be back home, with Mercer.

"Savage—"

"I'm on my way."

"Don't tell Brooks you're coming, okay?"

He paused but said, "Okay." Out of everyone, Brooks was more like a brother to him than anyone else. Even more so than any of the guys he'd served with in the Corps. It felt wrong to not tell him he was coming home, but for Mercer he'd do it.

Even making the decision to head that way felt right. As if he was supposed to be there right now. He'd never believed in fate or any of that shit, but deep down, he knew he had to get back to Redemption Harbor. Right now.

CHAPTER ONE

—When the past comes calling, don't answer!—

Seven months later

Olivia frowned when she heard her doorbell ring. It wasn't particularly late, at just after eight o'clock. But for her lifestyle, it was. She'd just put her daughter to bed and was cleaning up the kitchen from their arts and crafts evening of glitter and glue. A little over six years ago she couldn't have imagined this would be her life. Couldn't have imagined she'd *love* this as her life.

But love it she did.

Valencia, her daughter, was the best thing that had ever happened to her. Before Valencia she'd had a chip on her shoulder, had been out to prove to the world—aka her parents—that what they represented was bullshit. That she could live her life on her terms, any damn way she pleased. Because of that, she'd made mistakes. A lot of them. But her daughter wasn't one of those mistakes.

Nope. She'd saved Olivia's life.

Setting the bottle of purple glitter on the granite-top kitchen counter, she wiped her hands on her yoga pants and made her way to her foyer. When she peeked through the peephole, ice filled her veins, sharp and cutting.

Kyle freaking Neely stood on the other side of her door. Blinking once, she looked again. Nope, not her imagination.

Her lights were on and he no doubt knew she was here. Ignoring him wasn't an option. No, it would just make things worse. There was only one reason a man like this would be here. Only one she could think of, anyway. He wanted her for a job.

She'd just tell him no and be done with it. But she needed to be smart about it. Because he was a very dangerous man. She took a few steps back and called out, "Coming." Hurrying back to her kitchen, she quickly texted her neighbor.

Ex showed up, can you come over in five minutes to interrupt us?

Kyle wasn't her ex but her neighbor wouldn't know that. None of her neighbors had actually met her ex. She'd moved into this neighborhood as a single parent. And she wanted someone to be aware that she wasn't alone right now. Kyle wouldn't make a move against her with witnesses. No, that wasn't his style.

She heard another knock and the tension in her shoulders spread.

As soon as she got a positive response from her neighbor she tucked her cell phone into the back of her yoga pants and calmly walked to the door. She forced her steps and her breathing to remain even. Because a man like Kyle sensed any weakness.

When she'd been young, she'd been dumb enough to do a couple high-end heists with him—before she realized what a psycho he was. Then she'd learned that he'd tortured and killed one of the guys he'd recruited for a job because he'd suspected the man of being a Fed.

Steeling herself, she opened the door. And immediately realized her mistake. He wasn't alone. Another man lurked in the shadows of her porch, a silent threat if there ever was one.

She kept her focus on Kyle, and raised an eyebrow. "Been a long time."

His gaze swept over her, mostly clinical, a little disdainful. Probably because she wasn't like he remembered. Body type, yeah, she hadn't changed much. But instead of the sexy leather and lace she used to wear she had on yoga pants and a gray T-shirt that said *Tired as a mother.*

Olivia placed a hand on her hip. She needed to put on a calm yet annoyed persona. He was invading her personal space. No matter what, she couldn't let on that she was afraid of him. "Can I help you with something?"

Without responding, he shoved past her. Maybe she shouldn't have opened the damn door.

"Well come on in, then," she snapped, glad her voice didn't shake. You had to stay strong in the face of predators. Even if she was trembling inside, she'd never let him see that. Nope.

The other man strode forward too so she stepped in front of him. "You stay outside," she snapped. "I don't know you and you're not coming in my house."

The guy, dressed similarly to Kyle, paused, then looked over her shoulder at Kyle. Expression grim, he stepped back. "I'll wait in the car."

They both had on dark slacks, button-down shirts and jackets. All custom made, of course. Kyle was about six feet tall, lean and elegant. The other guy was a couple inches shorter and stocky. Pure muscle. The kind of guy who looked like he could crush a skull with his bare hands. She was glad he left, though she still wouldn't let her guard down. Kyle was too devious for that.

Fear lanced through her as she thought of her sleeping daughter upstairs. And she was glad she'd been smart enough to text her neighbor. She could keep Kyle talking for five minutes.

"I need you for a job," Kyle finally said. He slipped his hands into his pockets, watching her closely.

"I've been out of the game a long time." Well over six years. Ever since she'd found out she was pregnant she'd stopped running high-end heists and left that life behind. No more cons, no stealing, just an honest life with her daughter.

"I know. I wouldn't be here if I had anyone else. But my guy fell through. I need someone I've worked with before—so I know you're not a narc—and I need someone with your skill set."

She shook her head. "Kyle, I've been removed from that life for so long."

"Exactly. No one knows you. And I know you keep in shape. And you've kept up with climbing...despite your sloppy attire." His lips curved up slightly, again with the look of disdain.

She bristled at his words, then paused as they set in. How the hell did he know she'd kept up with climbing? He must have been watching her. Olivia wanted to say no again, but knew better. So she crossed her arms over her chest and pretended to feign interest. "What's the job?" Maybe if she got a better feel for it, she could sabotage it without him knowing.

He shook his head and actually tsked at her. "You know the deal. No details until later."

She paused, trying to think of a way out of this. "Fine. I'll think about it."

He took a menacing step forward, but she made herself stand her ground. She was only a couple feet from the front door. Not that she would run, not with her daughter to protect. But she was also closer to the stairs—which led to her daughter's room. The most primitive sensation filled her as she faced off with him. If he tried to move past her to the stairs, she would attack. And he'd have to kill her before she let him up there.

"That sounds a lot like a 'no,'" he murmured, his voice deceptively calm. Nothing about him seemed menacing, but she knew him. Had seen him beat one of his partners within an inch of his life because Kyle thought the guy had stolen from him.

"I said I'd think about it. You just show up out of the blue and demand I work with you again. I have responsibilities now."

He leaned down, his expression darkening. "Let me make this clear. I'm not asking. I'm telling. I need your skills. And if you go to the cops..." Without turning away from her, he slid his hand into his jacket pocket. Then he placed something in her hand.

A picture of her daughter. Leaving school, wearing her pink and green unicorn backpack.

Her temper spiked inside her like lightning. Without realizing she'd even moved, Olivia struck out, her palm slamming across his perfectly chiseled cheek. Pain ricocheted through her hand and up her arm even as he lifted his own arm, backhanding her.

With no time to block herself or brace for the attack, she stumbled and slammed into the banister, her eye catching on the newel post. As she hit the bamboo wood floor, Kyle's boot connected with her ribs once.

Hard.

Sucking in a sharp breath, she couldn't even cry out as the pain receptors in her side exploded.

The doorbell chimed and Kyle froze above her, looking as if he was ready to murder her.

"If you hurt me, I can't do the job," she managed to wheeze out. "Dumbass." She shouldn't antagonize him, but seriously, this fool wanted her to do a job with her specific skill set—which included potentially rappelling off buildings. She couldn't very well do that with broken ribs.

The doorbell chimed again and Kyle stepped back. "I'll be in touch." Kyle turned on his heel, heading toward her kitchen.

Relief flooded her system, making her even shakier. She didn't want her neighbor to see Kyle's face. A moment later she heard the back door slam even as someone started pounding on the door.

"Olivia!" It was Luke Anderson, her neighbor—also a retired cop. She didn't like involving law enforcement, or former, as it were, in anything. But he'd been the only option.

"Coming," she managed to call out as she pushed herself up off the floor and wiped damp palms on her pants. As she steadied herself on her feet she saw her daughter at the top of the stairs, her favorite stuffed unicorn under her arm, dark eyes wide and filled with tears. *Oh, hell.*

Since Valencia didn't have on the sound processors that worked as part of her cochlear implant system, Olivia signed that everything was okay, and for Valencia to hold on before she turned to the door.

Wincing as she pulled it open, she wasn't surprised to see both Luke and his wife, Claire. In their fifties, both were retired and lean in the way lifetime athletes were. Luke had a gun tucked under his shirt and Claire was holding a tennis racket in one hand. Olivia wanted to laugh and cry at the same time at the sight of the tiny blonde-haired woman and her weapon of choice, but just stepped back as they both barged in.

Seconds later, Valencia was racing down the stairs and jumping into Olivia's arms as Luke said, "What happened to your eye? Is...he still here?"

Great. Olivia figured she'd get a bruise but was hoping nothing would show just yet. She ignored the pinch of pain in her ribs as her daughter squeezed tighter. *Just suck it up,* she ordered herself. "He went out the back. I need to talk to Valencia before I answer any questions." Her daughter's face was buried against her head, and comforting her was Olivia's top priority.

Both Luke and Claire nodded as Luke said, "I'm going to make sure your house is secure."

Grateful he would do that, she carried her daughter to the living room and sat down, Valencia still clinging to her. Leaning back slightly, Olivia started signing using American Sign Language.

Are you okay? she asked her daughter.

Who was that? He hurt you!

A bad man. And he's gone.

Valencia's eyes filled with tears in response.

Shit. Parenthood didn't come with a training manual, and right about now she really wished that it did. *He won't hurt me ever again. And we're going to be taking a trip to see Aunt Skye and Uncle Colt soon.* She'd come up with the plan all of sixty seconds ago and really hoped it was the right choice. Because ignoring Kyle Neely was not an option.

Olivia's college roommate, Skye, had once worked for a branch of the government. Olivia wasn't sure which one, but she could make some guesses. Now she ran a consulting firm with her husband. They were the only two people in the world Olivia could turn to for help. The cops or any form of law enforcement were totally out. Cops couldn't do shit against a man like Kyle Neely. She had no proof of what scam he was running, who he planned to steal from, nothing. And even if she did, narcing him out would make her daughter and everyone close to her a target. Not happening.

When will we leave?

Olivia hated to pull Valencia from school and speech therapy but she couldn't stick around a second longer than necessary. She needed distance, and fast. *Tonight.*

Okay.

And I need you to go with Mrs. Claire, just for a few minutes while I pack your bag.

No!

Sighing, Olivia simply nodded. *Okay. Will you stay down here while I pack your bags?* Normally she wouldn't ask her daughter, but she'd just been traumatized. Olivia wanted to give her some choices right now. And she wanted to talk to Luke alone and explain—as much as she could—why this wasn't a big deal and that she'd be leaving for a few days. Most likely longer. But she wouldn't tell him that.

Can I have ice cream?

She stifled a laugh. God, that was so her daughter. *Yes. With sprinkles and chocolate syrup.*

That earned her a small smile. But fear still lingered in Valencia's gaze and Olivia had once sworn that would never happen. That her own past would never touch her daughter.

After kissing Valencia once again, she left her in Claire's capable hands and went searching for Luke—who she found making sure the windows in Valencia's room were secure. Man, she'd really lucked out with her neighbors. And she hated lying to them. But she had no choice.

"Hey, Luke."

"House is secure but I think you two should stay with us tonight. And I'm going to be calling a detective friend of mine since that jackass hurt you—"

Half-smiling at his tenacity, Olivia held up a hand. "Slow down. I'm not talking to a detective or anyone else."

He crossed his arms over his chest, frowning. "Why not?"

"Because it will make things worse." So much worse. "But I will be leaving for a few days to visit a friend of mine. A friend who works for the FBI." A little lie, but she needed Luke to know they'd be safe and to back off. "This thing is complicated, and before you argue, I'm not involving local law enforcement. I'm simply not. I need to leave tonight and I'd like to ask you for a favor."

He eyed her for a long moment, watching her carefully. "What did your ex want?"

"I can't tell you."

"Is it about your daughter?"

"No!"

Sighing, he let his arms drop and she knew she'd won. "Okay, then. You'll call me when you arrive where you're going?"

"I will."

Doing this would go against all his cop instincts, but he was a good judge of character and maybe he realized she wasn't backing down on this. He couldn't force her to do anything and he hadn't seen her struck by Kyle so he wasn't even a witness. He didn't even know who Kyle was or where to find him. "What's the favor?"

"I need to borrow your car. Just to get out of here. I'll drop it somewhere safe and let you know where it is."

"I'm driving you wherever you need to go." The set of his jaw was firm.

And she knew it would be pointless to argue. "Okay. I have another vehicle ready to leave town. But we might be followed so I don't want to take my car."

"Yeah, I figured that since you wanted to borrow my car. I have something that will fix that."

"What?"

"I'll call a buddy of mine, have a couple of patrol cars drive down the street. Anyone trying to monitor your house will leave and your ex won't recognize my car when we head out. He won't know to follow us."

She blinked once. "That's...a really good plan." Better than hers. "Thank you... Why are you doing this?"

"Because you're a good mom and a good neighbor. And Claire and I adore you guys. I know you're holding something back, but that's okay."

At his words, tears sprang to her eyes but she blinked them back. "Thank you," she murmured.

"What about Martina?"

"She's still in Florida, but I'm going to call her as soon as we're on the road." Martina Cruz had been Olivia's nanny growing up, but she'd been more than that. She'd been the mother Olivia had never had. A hell of a lot better parent than her actual mother had been. Now she lived a block away and was Nana to Valencia. She was the only other person who Kyle would think to target. Olivia was so damn grateful Martina was out of town right now on vacation in Fort Lauderdale.

"Good. We'll pick up your mail for you and I'll keep an eye on the house."

"Thank you."

"So you already have a backup vehicle waiting for you?" His words were dry.

She nodded, but didn't expound. She'd wondered when he'd ask about that. Some habits died hard. Deep down she'd always worried that a day like this would come. Because normal people didn't map out escape routes and have backup vehicles stashed. But she'd done just that. She even had go bags ready for her and Valencia. Despite what she'd told her daughter, she didn't have to pack much. Because one bag was already ready to go.

"One day you and I are going to have a conversation about all this," Luke said.

"I know."

Sighing, he closed the distance between them and wrapped an arm around her shoulders. "Let's get going. I'll put in that call. You get Olivia's stuff together."

"Thank you." Swallowing back the wealth of emotions threatening to overwhelm her, she put her game face on. She'd jumped off forty-story buildings before. She could and would face this.

No way was she letting the garbage of her past touch her daughter or anyone else. She just had to figure out a way to get Kyle off her back. And that meant getting to Redemption Harbor.

CHAPTER TWO

—Running on caffeine and dry shampoo.—

Olivia kept her sunglasses in place as she waited in the lobby of Redemption Harbor Consulting. Gage, a man who worked with Olivia's friend Skye, had gone to find her.

Valencia gripped Olivia's hand tightly. Her little girl hadn't spoken much since waking up in the car an hour ago. Not audibly or through signing. It worried Olivia, but right now she was trying to keep it together and not freak out. She didn't have that luxury.

"I miss Nana." Valencia's voice made her jump.

"I miss her too," she murmured, looking down at her daughter. Small for her age, even small for being part-Korean, Valencia took after Olivia's mom and looked more like she was four than six. And right now, she appeared even more fragile. It broke Olivia's heart, making her more determined to fix this problem. She wasn't going back into the life she'd left, but she also wasn't letting her daughter get hurt because of her past choices.

At the sound of murmuring voices, she looked up to see Skye and her husband Colt moving quickly out of a hallway onto the dark cherry wood floor of the lobby. Tall and muscular, Colt tightened his jaw when he saw Olivia. He looked fierce and angry, but she knew it wasn't directed at her.

Skye, a force of nature, moved like lightning toward them and Valencia dropped her hand, running at the other woman full speed. Olivia knew she should have called first, but she'd been so determined to get here and it had been so late. Then...she'd simply lost her nerve. She was about to drop a lot of information on her friend and ask for help she wasn't even sure Skye could give.

In jeans and a black T-shirt, Skye was casual, but there was a lethal air about her. Always had been. Even when they'd been in college. She'd always been aware of exits and everyone in a room. It was like she just took all the information in without trying or being conscious of it. Like breathing. Olivia used to quiz her for fun, testing her memory, and Skye was never wrong.

"What happened?" Skye demanded, holding Valencia in her arms. With auburn hair, lightly bronzed skin thanks to her father's Spanish heritage, and striking eyes the color of the Mediterranean on a clear day, Skye was stunning and intimidating. Having grown up living in the United States and Spain, she spoke multiple languages, including ASL.

The question was expected. Olivia was wearing sunglasses inside—to hide the bruise forming on her eye—and she'd shown up unannounced. Before she could answer, her daughter signed to Skye, telling her that a *bad man hurt Mommy.*

Yeah, that about summed it up. "Can we talk about this in private? I was hoping maybe..." Olivia's voice cracked and she inwardly cursed. This was no time to get emotional. But lack of sleep was making her edgy. She'd told her daughter that everything would be okay, and if Olivia started crying, she looked like a liar. And she would probably scare her. Not acceptable. "Maybe Colt could watch Valencia so we could have a few minutes to talk, just the two of us?" she asked.

Skye nodded then signed to Valencia, asking her if she minded hanging out with Uncle Colt, something that Olivia appreciated.

Valencia shook her head then cautiously moved over to him. Not because she was afraid of him, but likely because she didn't want to be separated from her mom. Olivia's hands balled tight at her sides. If she ever saw Kyle again she was going to do more than slap him.

Relief flooded her as Skye wrapped an arm around her shoulders. Olivia was actually an inch taller than her but she leaned into the hold, needing support right now. If Skye couldn't help her, she wasn't sure what she would do.

"Who hurt you?" Skye asked, leading her into a sleek conference room. The same cherry wood floors seemed to be standard throughout the building. Skye had shown her some of the "before" pictures, and this gleaming, high-end interior was nothing like the warehouse it had once been. And some of the security features she'd seen were incredible. Video cameras and sensors were everywhere. The kind of body sensors it would be very difficult to beat if you were trying to break in.

"Well...this won't be a short answer."

"I've got time. You hungry, thirsty?"

Her stomach was balled too tight to contemplate food. "No, but thank you." She cleared her throat and took off her sunglasses. When Skye sucked in a sharp breath, she winced. "It's not as bad as it looks." With her coloring, the bruise had gone to the purple and blue stage almost immediately. She'd cover it up with makeup later, but that hadn't been as important as getting out of the house.

Skye's blue eyes narrowed a fraction, but she simply nodded. "You need ice?"

"No."

"Okay, tell me what's going on, then."

"I'm going to start at the beginning—which is before Valencia was born. After college, I made some stupid choices."

Ugh, there was no way to say this other than just to blurt it out. She'd delved into her life of crime after college and had never told Skye about what she'd gotten into. "Because of my upbringing and my education in art history, I've always had a good eye for antiquities. My ex-husband—who was just my boyfriend at the time—was running cons, stealing from the wealthy. People who could afford it. At least that was what I told myself at the time to justify his actions. I've always been good at blending in, getting into places I don't belong, thanks to an 'education' from one of the security guys who worked for my father."

She briefly smiled at the memory of Stan Hill. In his fifties at the time, he'd been lean, fit and wily. He'd been the one to teach her to crack her first safe.

"Anyway, I mentioned my knack for cracking safes and recognizing valuables and my ex brought me in for one of his heists. During that first job his crew was about to pass up two ugly but very expensive pieces because they didn't know what they were worth—until I told them. It quadrupled their final take. After that, I started working with my ex full time for a few years. We started running our own jobs and I learned a few tricks on my own." Hell, she'd learned a lot on her own, had outgrown Heath—her ex—as a fellow thief had once told her.

All of it had been such a rush. Finding a target, planning the heist, stealing from rich assholes just like her parents, or corporations who could afford it. God, she'd been so deluded. All self-righteous about what she'd been doing. But she'd just been a criminal, stealing because she thought it was a way to say a giant "fuck you" to her parents. Basically she'd been an entitled jerk and she never wanted to go back to being that person. Didn't even want to associate with people from her old life.

A tight, heavy ball settled in her stomach. "I'm not proud of what I used to do," she murmured, looking away from Skye for the first time since sitting down. Shame made her cheeks heat up. She wished she could go back in time and shake some sense into her younger self. Luckily she hadn't been in that life for long.

"I'm not going to judge you." Skye's voice was so matter-of-fact.

Olivia looked up, saw no recrimination in her friend's eyes. It made this a lot easier, even if she still judged herself. She took a deep breath. "Okay, then. Well, my ex-husband, Heath, who I'll just call asshole, somehow got hooked up with a man named Kyle Neely. Neely is smart. He sets up one job a year. A big one. Big enough that the take can set you up for years. We worked two with him. It had been a unique year for him apparently because he did two jobs. Both were too big to pass up. Long story short, Neely is scary. I watched him beat someone almost to death and I heard through the grapevine that he killed someone he suspected of being law enforcement. And last night he showed up at my home and told me I'd be working a job with him. He's not giving me a choice either." She motioned to her face even as she said, "He threatened Valencia."

Skye's eyes narrowed. "What kind of job?"

"No idea. He keeps everything very compartmentalized and he won't work with someone he doesn't know. He's never done jail time because he's smart."

"You've never done jail time."

She snorted. "Yeah, because I got out of that life when I was relatively young. It was right after college—which is why you never knew about it." No way would she have told Skye anyway. Because no matter what she tried to tell herself, what she'd been doing had been wrong—and she felt a lot of shame for that.

"What happened to your ex?"

Olivia lifted a shoulder. "No idea. He signed over rights of full custody and I agreed he'd never have to pay child support. He, uh..." She glanced over her shoulder even though the door was closed. She'd never told her daughter this—and never would. Olivia looked back at Skye. "When we found out Valencia was Deaf he decided that it was 'too hard' for him to deal with. He said our lives were perfect before her and she was going to screw everything up. He was a weak, selfish man-child. I was just too young and stupid myself to realize it."

"Asshole is too nice for him." That deadly glint she'd seen before was in Skye's blue eyes. It matched the edge to her voice.

"I know. But I got Valencia and I lost a loser, so I call it a win. And...I told him if he ever came back and tried to disrupt my daughter's life I'd turn him over to the cops. I've got evidence linking him to a couple crimes." And she didn't feel an ounce of guilt over it.

Skye's eyebrows lifted.

Olivia just shrugged. "He's selfish enough to have come back later and tried to blackmail me for my skills and use my daughter against me. To him, she'd be nothing more than a bargaining chip. I took that away. I never wanted the stink of him to touch her."

Skye nodded once, almost as if in approval. "You think he's behind this? Or working with Neely?"

"No. The only reason we were even brought in was because of my skills. My ex was...a con. But small time. He liked to run card games, count cards, pick pockets, that type of thing."

"So what are all your skills, *exactly?*"

"Simply put, breaking into places, taking things that don't belong to me, and getting away clean. I'm really good with safes in particular."

"Huh…I probably shouldn't be surprised at your past. Not with your job."

Ugh. She needed to call work and tell them to cancel all her upcoming contracts. That was going to be a pain in the butt, but they'd just have to deal with it. She worked for a boutique security firm that was hired by large corporations to crack their own security and point out flaws and weaknesses. She got to use her skills and make her own hours. And it didn't matter where she lived because they provided transportation to all her jobs.

"So why not go to the cops? Why come to me for help?" At Skye's question, the panic was back and it must have showed on her face because Skye sat forward slightly. "I *am* going to help you. I just wanted to know why you thought of me."

"First, no cops because, come on. They can't do anything. I have no proof against Kyle. And…he gave me pictures of Valencia leaving school as a not-so-subtle threat. He's been watching me. No idea how long either. And to answer your second question, in college you put my name on that SF86 form. When I was interviewed by a couple uptight government agents in plain blue suits asking all sorts of questions about you, I knew you were getting some sort of clearance. So I knew you worked for the government. And then with the whole 'you're alive' thing seven months ago and no real explanation with why you'd 'died' then come back to life other than working on something to do with national security…I figured you'd know the right people. Or you'd be the right person to help. And okay, the last time I visited…I overheard two of your guys, Brooks and Gage, talking about a job they'd done helping someone. And everyone I've seen who works here looks kinda scary. It's clear they've all got training. Military or government, I'm guessing."

Skye nodded. "Okay, I figured that was why no cops...and I am the right 'people.' Everyone here is. In a minute I'm going to let you talk to Gage—our computer genius. He'll want to know every little thing there is about Kyle Neely and we're going to rip his life apart. From there, we'll figure out a way to stop whatever it is he's doing. Or get him arrested for whatever crime he's planning. You and Valencia will have to lie low for a little while, but we'll make sure this doesn't come back on you."

Olivia leaned forward, letting out a long, pent-up breath. "Thank you. I...just, thank you so much."

"No thanks needed. We're going to take care of you. That means you get home cooking tonight, and you'll stay at Brooks's estate. You already know that he has horses and a giant pool so Valencia will be in heaven. The ranch is incredibly secure and—"

Olivia burst into tears. They just rushed out and she couldn't stop them, even when she heard Skye moving toward her.

"Don't cry!" Her friend's voice was panicked, which just made this even more embarrassing.

"Sorry...been holding all this in since he showed up at my house." Taking a deep breath, she wiped at her cheeks as Skye crouched in front of her.

"We're going to stop this guy. And he won't know you were behind it either." She was starting to say more when Olivia's phone rang.

The specific ringtone told her it was Martina, sending a waterfall of relief coursing through her. "I need to get this. It's

Martina and I've been trying to get a hold of her." The only reason she hadn't been going into total crazy-pants mode was because she knew Martina, her surrogate mother and friend, was on vacation and hopefully having a great time. She'd be safe from Kyle.

Skye simply nodded and stood back, leaning against the shiny wood table as Olivia answered.

"Hey, glad to hear your voice."

"I told you not to be stupid." Kyle's smooth voice came over the line.

The bottom of Olivia's world dropped out. "What the hell have you done with Martina?"

Next to her, Skye jolted upright and pulled out her phone and started texting at a rapid speed. Olivia tuned her out as Kyle continued.

"Nothing. Yet. But you called the cops. What did I tell you about that?"

"I didn't call the cops! My neighbor is a retired cop. When he came over and saw the bruise on my face I told him it was my ex-husband who'd done it before he ran out the back. My neighbor had some patrol cars drive around the area looking for him." The story was close enough to the truth that if Kyle had been scanning police radios or had a contact at the local PD—which she doubted—it would be believable.

"You left."

"You show up out of the blue, *assault* me and demand I work with you! All while my daughter was at home. Hell yeah, I left." When she felt Skye's hand on her shoulder she glanced up.

Keep him talking, she signed using ASL.

Olivia nodded even as Kyle said, "Did you tell anyone about our conversation?"

"Where's Martina?" she asked, putting the call on speaker and setting the phone on the table in front of her. She knew Kyle wouldn't tell her, but if Skye wanted her to keep him on the line, she could do it.

"Secure. And before you go all hysterical, I haven't hurt her."

"I want to talk to her."

"No, but I'll send you a video of her. Now, did you tell anyone about our conversation?"

Skye nodded then started signing, telling her how to answer.

Olivia raised her eyebrows at Skye's instructions, but nodded back as she answered. "Yes."

There was a long pause. "Who?"

"An old friend. Not law enforcement. He's like...us." Olivia hoped that Skye knew what she was doing by telling her to feed Kyle this bullshit information. She'd come here for help so she was going to trust that Skye knew what she was doing. "I was scared, so I went to him about you."

"A friend?"

"More than a friend."

"I should kill your *other* friend right now."

Panic punched through her, but she kept her voice steady. She didn't need Skye to tell her what to say for this. "If you do I won't work with you and you know it." If he was desperate enough to kidnap Martina, then he needed Olivia badly. She would use that to her advantage. Because as long as he needed her, Martina would stay alive.

"So you're working with me now?"

She nearly snorted at the stupidity of his question even as Skye started signing to her again.

She said as Skye instructed, "You've given me no choice. But I'm bringing my friend with me. I did some jobs with him back in the day." That kept things vague enough.

"If he's a cop or Fed—"

"You really are stupid if you think I'd ever put Martina in danger. This guy...he's got a thing for me," she said, following Skye's orders. "Always has. It's why I ran to him. I knew he'd help."

"A thing?"

"He's in love with me. Or thinks he is. More like obsessed." She raised her eyebrows at Skye, who just shrugged and kept signing. "He dropped everything for me."

Another long pause. "I'm going to test him. If he doesn't have the skills I need..."

"Yeah, I know." Her partner would be killed.

"I'll be in touch." The call ended before she could respond.

"Damn it," she muttered. Nausea filled her as she sat back. Her friend, a woman she considered a mother, was being held by a psycho because of her.

"You did great."

It sure didn't feel like it. "He didn't say *yes* to anything."

"Yeah he did. If he plans on testing your guy—"

"My imaginary guy...who apparently is obsessed with me?"

"It's the only reason a man would drop everything for a woman. Okay, that's not true, but a man like Neely will understand the reasoning. It will make sense to him that you turned to someone, a man, for protection. And that's all you need, for him to believe you. For him to see you as weaker."

"You came up with that stuff pretty fast."

Skye lifted a shoulder. "It's what I do. And he's on the hook. He didn't say no to your partner, and—"

Olivia snatched up her phone as a text message came through from an unknown number. A video. She pressed play. Martina, sitting in a chair—not bound, at least—with a plain pale blue background. A wall. She looked at someone off the screen then nodded before looking at it. She smiled, appearing as if she was trying to be brave, and Olivia bit down on a knuckle to stop from crying again.

"*Mi pequeña.* I'm okay and haven't been hurt." Then she started reading off headlines of what was likely the day's news. Olivia would check as soon as possible. "Take care of our angel, Valencia. And do what's right for *her.*"

The video ended and Olivia shoved out a breath. "She doesn't want me to do anything for him."

"Yeah, I caught that," Skye said. "I don't think your old buddy got that, or he'd have cut that last part out."

Olivia nodded. Kyle probably thought Martina meant that Olivia should do the job and keep Valencia safe. But if she had to bet, she was certain Martina meant to stay away from him and keep Valencia safe. Because Martina was like that, always looking out for others. "I've got to save her. I'll do whatever I have to. Even steal whatever it is he wants." As long as she didn't have to hurt anyone else, she would easily break the law for Martina's sake.

"That's good, then. Because with him having your friend captive, you're going to have to go along with him until we find her."

"Who's we?"

Skye nodded toward the door. "Come on. I'm going to introduce you to the crew—and your new partner."

CHAPTER THREE

—I should have seen that coming.—

Olivia scanned the wall of screens, amazed at whatever Gage was working on. On one screen was what looked like blueprints for a building. Another showed pictures of a group of men unloading what were definitely automatic weapons from the back of truck. She guessed the images had been captured from a long-range camera. Okay, now she really wondered just what Redemption Harbor Consulting did.

"I don't even know if Kyle Neely is his real name," she said as Gage's fingers typed rapidly on the thick laptop. A type she'd never seen before.

At about six feet tall, he was lean in the way runners were. His bluish-gray eyes seemed to almost glow against the gleam of the laptop screen.

Apparently Gage had been trying to pin the location of Martina's phone. And he had, but it had been moving during the time of the call, and once Kyle had ended it, Gage said he'd tossed it out a window. He knew because he'd been able to capture it in real time via a traffic camera. Which meant Gage had hacked the DMV and was using satellites, and holy crazy, this had to be so illegal. Not that she, of all people, cared. And especially not with Martina's life at stake.

Sighing, Gage pushed away from his desk and stood. "He tossed the phone when he was done with it, and I got an image of the SUV he was in going into the parking garage of a hotel in Miami. The SUV hasn't come out and I never got an image of his face. You're sure you don't have a picture of him somewhere?"

"No. If I did, I'd give it to you. The people I used to run with... None of us did the social media thing. It was too risky." Not like those idiots who stole stuff then posted pictures of it on their private Facebook accounts. She actually had one now that she used to communicate with the moms at Valencia's school. *And,* she realized, she needed to call the school Monday and tell them Valencia would be out of school for the next couple weeks. Hell. She needed to get her head on straight.

Gage nodded. "I understand. I don't think anyone here has a social media account either."

Skye snorted, not looking at either of them as she texted someone. "Mary Grace and Mercer do. She keeps telling me if I want to see every picture of Mia I should join. Like I'm gonna get a Facebook account. Or Twitter." She cackled as she looked up at them, as if the thought was utterly ridiculous. Immediately she sobered. "All right. The plan. Gage is going to do his thing and try to piece together anything he can on Kyle Neely—or whoever he really is. So you're going to come up with a comprehensive list of people you know he's worked with and people you've worked with together. That includes your ex-husband. Gage is going to look into him as well. Gage is magic on the computer, so whatever you give him will be helpful. But you're not going to do it here. I'm taking you and Valencia to Brooks's estate and you're going to get some damn sleep. You look as if a harsh wind would knock you over."

She shook her head. "No. I need to be doing something."

"You *are* going to be doing something. Resting and getting your daughter settled is the smart thing to do right now. Neely is going to reach out to you soon. Maybe in an hour. Maybe a day. Whenever that happens, you can't be foggy. You need a clear head. You need to be sharp. Because if he's going to test your partner, you can be damn sure he's going to test you. Which brings me to another thing. We'll also need a list of all your skills. And we're going to be coming up with the full cover for your previous relationship with Savage."

"Savage?"

"Ah, Zac Savage. Your partner. He's on his way to Brooks's right now, so you'll meet him in a little bit."

Okay, with a name like Savage... Well, she couldn't be choosy right now. And the name Savage was scary. Good. She needed scary on her side. "Okay."

"Since you guys will be working together, and since he's 'into you,' it stands to reason you have a sexual relationship with him. So I'm going to use that for the cover. A man doesn't just drop everything for a woman unless there's something there. So part of your cover will be that you're a couple."

"Okay." She wasn't sure what that entailed but if she had to kiss a man publicly or whatever, she could deal with it. "What are his skills? My ex was good at conning people, which came in handy for getting into places when we needed a distraction."

"We'll go over all of that—at Brooks's place. I promised Valencia she could see some of the horses. And maybe ride one with me?"

Half-smiling, Olivia nodded. "That's totally fine. It's going to be tough telling her no for anything today anyway. I'm ready." She just hoped that Skye was as good as she seemed. Martina's life depended on it.

* * *

Feeling refreshed and a little better after a shower, Olivia stepped out of the bathroom into the huge guest room decorated in country chic to find Valencia on the bed. Lying on her stomach, she was playing a game on her tablet. When she saw Olivia, she pushed it to the side and jumped off the bed. Valencia wore jeans and a bright pink sweater with little daisies all over it.

The second she was on the floor, she tugged on the cowboy boots she'd begged Olivia to buy last time they'd come to visit Skye in Redemption Harbor. They'd also visited this very ranch. She didn't know Brooks well, but he'd been incredibly accommodating then, just as he was now. She was grateful to be able to keep her daughter safe here.

"How long do we get to stay here?" Valencia asked, choosing not to sign. She often switched back and forth with signing and using her voice.

"Well, that's something I wanted to talk to you about." Olivia bent down and picked her up before sitting on the bed. "We're going to be here this upcoming week and maybe the week after. You're going to miss a week of school, but the week after is Thanksgiving so you won't be missing anything." She just prayed they got Martina back a lot sooner and this whole mess could be taken care of before then.

Valencia's bottom lip quivered. "I'll miss the play. I'm one of the turkeys."

Guilt slid right between two of her ribs, sharp and unforgiving. "I know. And I'm so sorry, honey." Her parents had only attended the bare minimum of school events at the exclusive private school Olivia had attended. She'd sworn she'd make it to every school or extracurricular activity for Valencia. "But maybe you'll get to see a real turkey while we're here." It was the only thing she could think of to ease her daughter's disappointment.

Valencia's eyes widened. "Mr. Brooks said that he knew where a bunch of them were. And Skye said I could ride a horse if I sit with her?"

"You can definitely ride a horse. Come on, I'll pull your hair up. Ponytail or braids?"

"Braids." As they headed to the bathroom, Valencia pulled her sound processors off her ears so the coil and cords wouldn't get tangled in the brush.

Working quickly, she fixed Valencia's thick, jet-black hair into place. When she met her daughter's dark eyes in the mirror, she smiled. Olivia might have made some mistakes in the past—big ones—but she'd still gotten this wonderful, sweet girl. Right now it was like looking at a mini version of herself. *You've got one chance to raise this girl right,* she reminded herself. One chance. And she couldn't screw it up. Once Olivia was done, Valencia slid her processors back on and turned her head back and forth as she looked at her braids in the mirror.

Apparently deciding she looked good enough, she spun to face Olivia again and gave her one of those blinding smiles she loved. "Time to see the horses."

"I'm probably going to have to do a little work here at the house while you check out the animals." And she definitely couldn't go into details about her "work."

"No problem, Mommy. I'll be careful." She sounded so grown-up in that moment, something that didn't surprise Olivia.

It didn't take long to find someone in the house. Colt was in the kitchen, pulling a water bottle from the refrigerator. "Hey, guys. I was going to come find you soon," he said, looking at Valencia, who gave him a shy smile.

"Are the horses ready?" she asked, glancing toward the sliding glass doors that overlooked the lanai and Olympic-sized pool as if she could see the stables from here.

"Yep. As long as it's okay with you," he added, looking at Olivia now. "Skye's in the office on the second floor. I can tell you how to get there. She wanted to go over a few things with you."

"Is she still coming with us?" Valencia asked hopefully.

"As soon as she's done talking to your mommy, she'll be down by the stables."

"Okay. See you later, Mommy." After a quick kiss, her daughter raced to the back door, hopping up and down as she waited for Colt to give Olivia quick directions to the office.

Usually Valencia wasn't so open or trusting with everyone—with most people she was shy. But every one of Skye's friends had been incredibly welcoming to them the last couple times they'd visited Redemption Harbor. And the fact that they were all learning ASL because of Valencia... It was no wonder she adored everyone and felt safe enough here to be separated from Olivia. Which helped ease some of her guilt.

It didn't take too long to make her way to the second floor, even though the place was huge. An "estate" was definitely the right term for this ranch. She wasn't even sure how many rooms the house had, but everywhere she looked was real wood, stone and a whole lot of natural light.

Her flats were silent on the wood floor as she turned left down another hallway. When she heard Skye's voice, she knew she was in the right place. As she neared the third door on the left as Colt instructed, she heard a male voice.

One she didn't recognize. Deeper, kinda rumbly. "I'm just saying, what kind of mother drags her kid into something like this? That's some stellar parenting," he muttered. "At least the kid is safe here."

Rage blossomed inside her chest, making her face go warm and her hands ball into fists at her sides. After driving all night, she was beyond exhausted and running on caffeine. Add in that she was terrified about Martina and keeping her daughter safe and she was about to snap. And some guy wanted to question her maternal skills?

Jaw clenched tight, she pushed on the already halfway open door. And came face to face with…The Hulk. Dark hair, green eyes, and huge.

Definitely one of Skye's crew, since Skye was standing right next to him and he'd been discussing *her*. Well, Olivia didn't care who he was. He had no right to judge her or talk about her as if he knew her. She really wished she'd worn heels or something to give her height and confidence. Even though it would have been ridiculous to do so on a ranch. Instead she was in jeans, a frilly feminine top and ballet flats. Meanwhile, this jerk was like a big, hulking…caveman. If he wasn't such a jerk he might be attractive in a dangerous, bad boy type of way.

"Are you talking about me, you ass…face?" Gah. Normally she tried not to curse if Valencia was around so that had come out *awesome*. Internally wincing at her pathetic trash talk, she barreled on, unable to rein in her big mouth. "I didn't drag my daughter into this intentionally. I made some really stupid choices when I was young and impressionable. Do I regret them? Of course. But I can't take them back. And I might be a lot of things, but a bad mother isn't one." She should know, because she'd had one. "I just had to tell my kid that she's going to miss her Thanksgiving play, something she's been looking forward to for weeks. And it breaks my heart. The woman who raised me, my daughter's 'Nana,' is being held captive by a psycho, and you want to talk about my parenting? Whoever you are, keep your thoughts to yourself. I already feel bad enough right now!" Heart pounding, she stared at the hard face of this unknown man. Normally she would never have gone off on anyone, and definitely not someone who must be friends with Skye. No, Olivia did *not* like confrontations. But she was exhausted, beyond stressed, and walking a tightrope right now.

He blinked once, staring down at her before he cleared his throat, and had the decency to look apologetic. "I'm sorry. You're right." His voice did that deep rumbly thing again.

Skye cleared her throat as well, drawing Olivia's attention to her. "Olivia…meet your partner, Zac Savage."

Olivia sighed. Awesome. *Of course* this guy was her partner. Because why wouldn't he be?

CHAPTER FOUR

—She's not for you. Remember that.—

Zac didn't have many regrets in life. A few, but he'd made it a rule to stop having them. Regrets and guilt were useless.

But right now he regretted that he'd opened his big mouth about a woman he didn't know. He had his own baggage where mothers were concerned. He was self-aware enough to realize that. And he'd made a snap judgment when Skye had pulled him in for this job and outlined what was going on. The kid inside him who still resented a mother who'd never given a shit about him had reacted, rather than the man.

Now, staring into the dark eyes and stunning face of a clearly agitated woman—who looked a little like she wanted to throat punch him—yeah, he regretted that this was her first impression of him. Everyone else who worked for Redemption Harbor Consulting, plus Mary Grace and Mercer, who didn't, had all met Olivia Carter. But he'd been away on jobs when she'd visited with her daughter.

Looking away from him toward Skye, Olivia winced as Skye announced he was her partner. "Oh... ah..."

He cleared his throat once, eager to smooth things over. "Skye tells me you've worked jobs with this Neely before. It's been six years since you've seen him. Correct?" Might as well move right past the awkwardness and jump into business. There was no time to waste.

She nodded, and some of the tension in her shoulders seemed to ease. "More like seven, but yes."

"Okay, we'll need to go over the type of jobs you did with him, your role, what he's like to work with and what type of crew he normally uses. Once we've established that, we're going to come up with a cover for our relationship." Standard procedure for building a background. Luckily they could work from scratch and come up with any history they wanted. All Skye had told him so far was that this Kyle Neely thought Olivia was bringing in a male partner, that her ex-husband was a dick, her deceased mom was Korean, her dad was alive, and she was a single mother. Skye *hadn't* told him how stunning she was.

Skye cleared her throat, and when he looked at her, he knew he wasn't going to like what she had to say. Because she looked nervous as she played with a strand of her auburn hair. He'd never seen her do that.

"What did you do?" he asked, suspicion in his voice.

"Nothing big. But we've already established with Neely that you and Olivia have a history. That you're uh, sort of obsessed with her. That you'll do anything for her."

His gaze narrowed. "What the hell?"

Skye lifted a shoulder, not looking the least bit apologetic. "It'll work. Who's the pro at this kind of thing? Me. I told Olivia what to say and Neely is on the hook. He would only believe that a man who was into her would drop everything when she came running. You're a guy, so you know I'm right. So I started building your cover on the fly."

He shifted on his feet and looked over at Olivia. With long, jet-black hair and long, thick lashes, delicate features, sharp cheekbones and a tight body... He glanced away. Pretending to be attracted to her wouldn't be an issue. And he wouldn't be pretending. This woman was walking sex appeal. "All right, so we're...together?"

"For the duration of this job, yes. Olivia made it sound like you'd do anything for her. So once we've established the parameters of your past relationship—the rest of which you two can figure out—you'll just sell it to him. I know undercover stuff isn't normally your thing, but I think you're the best person for this job. I could ask Leighton, but..."

Zac simply nodded. Leighton had been working jobs with them since they'd started their consulting firm, but this was the type of job where he'd have to be on his game 24/7. He didn't think Leighton was up to it. And...Zac didn't like the thought of anyone else being this woman's partner. He wasn't going to analyze why he cared one way or another either. "I got this."

Skye turned to Olivia now, who was a lot quieter than the raging woman who'd stormed in here looking sexier than any woman he'd ever met. "Gage and I are going to start going over the list of data you gave us, see if we can make a timeline of Neely's past movements, where he might be hiding Martina. If we figure that out, all this planning will be a moot point. But it's better to be prepared and act as if you're going to pull a job with him."

"Do you think he has her at that hotel?" She moved slightly and winced, as if she was in pain. When she did, he realized that she had makeup covering what definitely looked to be a bruise on her eye. Her skin tone was a pale peachy color and some of her coverup had been rubbed off.

All his protective instincts went into overdrive. What the hell?

Skye shook her head, her ponytail shifting with the movement. "No. It would be stupid on his part. But I've already sent Leighton down there to see what he can dig up. Gage didn't find anyone by the name of Kyle Neely on the guest list, but that's not a surprise."

"Wow...you work fast. Thank you."

"Who hit you?" Zac blurted.

Both women turned to him and Olivia gently touched the side of her eye. "Thought I covered it up pretty well."

"You did," Skye said. "And it was that asshole Neely. Hit her *and* kicked her in the ribs when she was on the ground." There was a familiar menacing edge to Skye's voice. Skye had a mile-wide protective streak in general, but if someone had hurt one of her friends? Yeah, she'd be feeling lethal. He could relate right about now. He had issues with bad parents—and he knew his snap judgment of Olivia had been his own bullshit—but when it came to women he tended to feel protective. "I'm going to relish bringing this guy down."

Zac had never had a problem with control. Not since he was a kid. He'd learned patience and control were valuable tools in his arsenal. Especially living with an unstable, selfish mother. But knowing that a man had struck a defenseless woman, then *kicked* her when she was down? He saw red for a moment. And whatever was on his face made Olivia take a step back. Which just made him feel like a bigger jackass. "Me too," he said simply. And he was going to make sure he got in a few shots with this Neely when the time came. "Do you need anything for the pain?"

Olivia looked surprised by the question and started to shake her head, but then nodded. "Actually, that would be nice."

"All right. You two start getting to know each other and building your past," Skye said. "I'll be with Gage if anyone needs me. Once he's got a handle on things I'm headed to the stables. Are you okay with Valencia being with Colt and Brooks without me?"

"Yeah," Olivia murmured, a smile tugging at her lips. "She loves her Uncle Colt. I'm not worried. But thank you for asking."

"Okay, then. I've got my cell on me. Oh, if Neely calls or texts you, Gage is monitoring your phone. So any calls that come through, he'll be tracing."

"Good."

As Skye left, Zac started rustling around in the drawers of the oversized mahogany desk. Brooks used this as his personal office, though since starting Redemption Harbor Consulting, they'd all been using it on occasion. Brooks didn't seem to mind the invasion of his house. Zac smiled when he found a bottle of Advil. He looked up to see Olivia watching him cautiously.

"Look, I'm sorry about what I said. It was a shitty thing. I made an asshole comment without even knowing you. It had nothing to do with you." He sure as hell wasn't going to tell her about his past, but he felt he owed her another apology. And if they were going to pose as partners—lovers—there couldn't be tension between them. Not that kind of tension, anyway.

"It's..." She pushed out a breath and raked her fingers through her still damp hair. Still wet, it almost looked blue-black it was so dark. She must have just taken a shower.

Which made him think of her standing under the hard, streaming jets, water rolling over her smooth, soft skin—*Nope.* He needed to get his head in the game. It had been a while since he'd been with a woman. That was the only reason for this reaction he was having to her.

"I'm sorry for yelling at you like that. I probably could have handled it better."

"Nah, I deserved it." That earned him a small smile. "Come on, let's go grab some water so you can take your Advil. And we can start coming up with our cover."

Nodding, she fell in step with him. She was about an inch taller than Skye, but she was still a hell of a lot smaller than him. Not exactly petite, but slender and beautiful. She looked like the kind of woman a man wanted to protect, keep safe. Something told him it was all an illusion, however. Especially after she'd just reamed him out. Olivia might look delicate, but he didn't think she was.

"I'm sorry about your friend," he said as they entered the kitchen. "But Gage is the man you want behind you. If anyone can find her, it's him."

"He already managed to track Kyle down to the hotel he's at."

Savage snorted. "There's a reason he's been headhunted by the NSA." Among other agencies.

"Seriously?"

"Yep. Private paid better." Though Savage knew that wasn't the only reason Gage had declined to work for the government. "So, our history?"

"Ah...I'm open to anything that works. The couple jobs I did with Neely, my ex-husband was involved too, so it's not abnormal for me to have a partner." A brief look of distaste crossed her face as she mentioned her ex.

"Any chance your ex is involved in this? Maybe as a way to separate you from your daughter or something?" They needed to cover all bases and possibilities. Zac didn't like leaving anything open to chance.

She blinked, looking truly confused, before she snorted. "I have no clue where my ex is, but he's not involved in this. Or I seriously doubt it. He wants nothing to do with my daughter."

Zac noted the way she said "my daughter," not "our." Interesting. He handed her a water bottle from the refrigerator. "Okay. Tell me more about Neely." Zac had skimmed the information Skye had given him, but he wanted to be on the same page as Olivia. The more they talked, got to know one another, the better.

She took the Advil with the water then set it on the granite countertop of the center island. Leaning against it, she shoved her hands in her pockets. "Kyle does higher-end robberies. Art, jewelry, stuff like that. Like I told Skye, he only works with crews he knows. He's really paranoid too, always keeps things compartmentalized until right before the job. So, for example, for the first job we did, I knew that I'd need to break into a specific type of safe, but I didn't know the actual location until twenty-four hours before. He kept the whole team contained and we had to go dark. No phones or outside communication during that time period."

"Smart," Zac murmured.

"Yeah. So...what exactly is your experience in this type of thing? You were in the military, right?"

He nodded. "I was in the Marine Corps. Force Recon. Then I did a lot of contract work after. I'm good at being invisible, at getting into places I don't belong." That being an understatement. He didn't blame her for asking though.

"Can you give me an example?"

He watched her for a long moment then decided to give her information that wasn't exactly classified because it wasn't on any books. And screw it, he didn't work for the government anymore anyway. Besides, he wouldn't give specifics. "I've stolen sensitive information from a consulate on US soil in the middle of the day." And that wasn't the toughest job he'd ever pulled either. "With no one the wiser." Which had been the whole point of that job. If he'd stolen the intel and someone had discovered it, the intel would have become useless.

Her eyes widened. "That's...seriously dangerous."

Zac lifted a shoulder.

"Okay, then. You're clearly ready for whatever Kyle throws at you. Probably a hell of a lot better than me."

"Maybe. I read some of the information you gave Skye. Rappelling off buildings and breaking into high-end corporate security systems is some serious shit. And now you work freelance for a boutique security company?" One that infiltrated other companies upon request to test security.

She nodded once, her expression wry. "Figured I might as well make money the legal way doing something I'm good at. And I don't have to jump off buildings anymore to escape."

Zac leaned against the counter, closely watching her. Hell, it was hard to take his gaze off her anyway. "We need to figure out how long we've known each other."

She nodded and he could practically see the wheels turning in her head. "I've been separated from my ex since six months after Valencia was born. To say you and I met not long after that would work, especially if Kyle reached out to my ex. I kinda doubt he did, but just to cover our bases."

"Why'd you and your ex break up? And what's his name?" Zac already didn't like the guy. Didn't have to know him.

She jolted a little at the question, the reaction subtle. Then she narrowed her gaze at him. "Why?"

"If we're together, it stands to reason I'd know personal information about you."

Her shoulders relaxed and she let out a tired laugh. "Oh, right. His name is Heath Price and...if I'm being brutally honest, he left because Valencia is Deaf. He decided we weren't what he wanted." There was no bitterness in her voice.

Oh yeah, definitely didn't like this guy. There were things he wanted to say—and do. Namely hunt down her ex and beat the shit out of him. But he wouldn't, only because he wasn't a barbarian and they had more important things to focus on. What kind of man abandoned his child? He felt like an even bigger asshole for the snap judgment he'd made now that he knew Valencia was a single mom who'd left her old life behind. "Okay, so on to us. Why did you break up with me?"

"Why will it be me who did the breaking up?"

Zac stepped a fraction closer, inhaled the subtle vanilla undertones of her perfume. "Because if I'm obsessed with you and dropping everything for you, there's no way I'd have been the one to leave. Besides, it's pretty clear no sane man would leave you. And you are definitely out of my league."

Pink tinged her cheeks as his words set in. She swallowed loudly enough for him to hear. "Thank you, I think."

"It's definitely a compliment," he murmured, his gaze falling to her lips. When had he gotten even closer to her? All he could do was focus on Olivia, the nervous way she cleared her throat, then bit her full bottom lip. For such a slender woman she had curves in all the right places.

"Maybe things got too intense for us, so I ended things?" Her words came out raspy, a little unsteady.

Then he remembered he'd asked a question. He cleared his throat and met her gaze. "That works." He took another step closer. "But I didn't want to let go. Never got over you. So when you came to see me, I couldn't say no." Before he realized he'd moved, he cupped her cheek with his hand. Hated how callused his fingers were against her soft skin, but he also couldn't pull away.

She didn't pull away either. Just stared up at him with a little bit of shock and a lot of...curiosity. Maybe some lust too.

He couldn't tell and didn't want to read into anything. Still, he couldn't seem to drop his hand.

Her breathing grew shallower as she stared at him and when she nervously licked her lips, he groaned. Because apparently he had no self-control anymore. What the ever loving fuck was wrong with him? He wasn't thinking with his head, that was the damn problem. Women were trouble and the whole happy-ever-after thing Mary Grace and Mercer, and Skye and Colt had? Not for him. And Olivia wasn't the type of woman to have a fling with. Even knowing that, he couldn't pull his hand back, couldn't force himself to step away.

Until Gage stepped into the room—and loudly cleared his throat.

Dropping his hand even as Olivia moved back from him, putting a solid foot of distance between them in a second, he turned to find Gage in the doorway.

"Neely just texted you," Gage said, all business.

"What?" Olivia patted her front pocket and pulled out her cell. A look of self-recrimination crossed her delicate features as she swiped her fingers across the screen. "He wants to meet me tomorrow."

"It's at the same hotel I tracked him to in Miami," Gage said, obviously having read the text with whatever program he used to hack shit. "So it looks as if you two are definitely going to have to meet him. I'm still running the information I have on Neely and I think it's his real name. But you were right, his digital footprint is very small. I've got a few threads I'm pulling at to locate potential places Martina might be."

"When do we need to leave?" she asked.

Zac noticed she seemed to be avoiding his gaze completely as she focused solely on Gage.

"I'll leave that up to Savage. Meeting's at ten a.m."

Olivia looked at Zac, her eyebrows raised. They should leave right then, get settled in Miami. If they were driving they would have to leave immediately since it would take eight hours at least with traffic. But since they'd be flying... "Soon. But get your stuff together."

"I've got to tell Valencia that I'm leaving. I need time to explain things to her. And I want to get her settled in." She definitely wasn't asking, her expression fierce.

He'd definitely judged her wrong. It was clear she cared about her daughter and that this whole thing was killing her. Well he was going to make sure she came out of this okay and that they got her friend back. And he was going to seriously hurt the man who'd put her in this situation in the first place. "Yeah. Go get your girl. We'll leave once she's asleep tonight."

It would mean they'd arrive, have time to get a few hours of shuteye at whatever safe house they ended up at, then head to the hotel.

After the back door shut behind her, he turned to Gage—to find his friend watching him with far too much curiosity. "What?"

Gage shook his head. "Nothing. Nothing at all, man."

"I need to get my gear together," Zac muttered.

"I figured. I'm already getting my gear ready for you guys. Skye's going to stay here for the kid, but Brooks, Leighton and I will be your backup. I'm already getting a safe house prepped for us."

"The job might not even be in Miami."

"I know. But I'm getting it ready regardless. And Brooks's plane is gassed up and ready to go. Your girl will have time with her daughter."

She's not my girl. "Sounds good."

But part of him wanted her to be.

CHAPTER FIVE

—Parenthood is fucking hard.—

How long will you be gone? Valencia's boot-clad feet swung back and forth as she looked at Olivia, her expression serious. A bright moon hung high in the sky, shimmering on the huge pool a few feet away.

I don't know. She couldn't lie, even if she wanted to. Olivia might not always be able to tell the full truth, but she wasn't going to lie to her daughter. Not unless absolutely necessary. *If this wasn't important, I wouldn't be leaving.* She'd never left her daughter anywhere before, other than Martina's house for sleepovers. This was going to be hard for both of them.

A long sigh. *I know.*

Aunt Skye and Uncle Colt will be here. And Mary Grace said she'd be over all the time with the baby. That earned her a small smile.

Mia's so cute... Why are you leaving? Turned in her seat on the oversized, cushioned bench, all Valencia's focus was on Olivia.

I...can't tell you everything.

Grown-up stuff?

Yes. It's important though. That's what I can tell you. And, I'll be able to Skype with you while I'm gone. And...I bet Skye will let you have ice cream for breakfast every morning. Definitely not her most shining parenting moment, but who cared? Olivia was leaving her daughter at a new place without her. If Valencia wanted freaking ice cream every morning, she was going to get it.

Valencia's eyes widened. *It must be really important...and I won't eat ice cream for breakfast. Not every day anyway.*

Laughing, she pulled her daughter into her lap. "I got so lucky with you, kiddo," she said, switching to using her voice.

"I know."

Olivia laughed even harder as she kissed the top of Valencia's head. As she pulled back, she blinked as Zac Savage—a man she thought of simply as Savage because of his fierce demeanor—appeared as if out of thin air.

He nodded politely at the two of them, the brightly lit Olympic-sized pool and fountain his backdrop. *I wanted to let you both know that dinner is almost ready.* He used ASL, taking Olivia off guard. Skye had taken to it like she seemed to with everything—quickly and expertly. ASL was a completely different language so mastering it quickly was rare. The others were learning, but neither Olivia nor her daughter had met Savage until today.

"Hey! You know ASL!" Valencia jumped off her lap and looked up at Savage. *I'm Valencia,* she said, signing.

He crouched down so they were at eye level—earning some points—and nodded. *I'm Zac. I learned ASL when I was a teenager. And I know ASL because my brother was Deaf.*

Was? Valencia asked, her head tilting slightly to the side, her braids sliding with the movement.

He died. Two simple words said with a perfectly neutral expression, but there was a hint of buried pain there.

That's sad, Valencia said even as Olivia murmured the same. Reaching out, her daughter, with her big, soft heart, gently patted his shoulder.

Looking uncomfortable, he cleared his throat. *Would you prefer I sign, or do you prefer that I use my voice instead?*

Okay, more points for asking her daughter. He might have been a jerk earlier, but he was treating Valencia well. Maybe he wasn't so bad.

Valencia looked at Olivia quickly, then back at Savage and dropped her hands. "I like to use both. My speech therapist says I need to practice both talking out loud and ASL." She sounded like such a little grown-up.

A low, rumbling sound came from him and it took a moment for Olivia to realize he was laughing. He looked softer, more approachable when he relaxed like that. His entire expression changed, the way his lips curved up and his eyes creased, he was…handsome. "That seems sensible."

"I know. My mommy says that I'm almost always sensible. I have an old soul."

Olivia started to smile at her daughter's words, when Savage looked over at her. He pinned her with his green eyes and for the briefest moment there was a raw heat simmering right beneath the surface.

It was so quick, that little flash, then it was gone, replaced by pure neutrality. Maybe she'd imagined it. But she didn't think so. Not after that unexpected spark between them in the kitchen earlier. She still felt guilty about that. As she'd been staring into his eyes everything else had ceased to exist for those few moments. Martina, everything. She was ashamed she'd been thinking… Well, whatever she'd been thinking and feeling while a woman she loved was being held hostage.

"After dinner we need to talk," he said to her, his voice low.

For some reason his words sounded ominous, but that was just her overworked brain. He probably wanted to talk about the game plan. They'd have to leave soon, by car she guessed. It would take all night and then some to get to Miami. She wouldn't be fresh or relaxed for the meeting but there was no way around it. She needed another hour with her daughter and to go over some legal stuff with Skye. Ugh. She wasn't looking forward to that. But it was one more thing to get out of the way before going to Miami. She desperately wanted to save Martina but if the worst happened and Olivia didn't make it back, she needed to know that Valencia would be taken care of.

* * *

With dinner over and Valencia with Mary Grace and the baby in Brooks's giant movie room—yes, there was a freaking movie theater-style room in this place—Olivia knew it was time to get the thing she was dreading over with. "Skye, I need to talk to you alone. You and Colt both," she said over the now empty dinner table.

Mercer, Gage and Brooks were talking around the island, all drinking beers, but moved as soon as Skye said, "Everyone out. And tell my sexy husband to get his ass in here."

"You realize this is my house." Brooks's voice was dry, just a hint of humor in the quiet cowboy's words.

"I do realize that." Skye smiled sweetly, making him laugh.

"All right, I'll go hunt down your man. I think he's with Savage. You need him too?"

Hearing Savage's name had heat rushing to Olivia's cheeks and she inwardly cursed her reaction as she told Brooks no. She needed to get this over with. So what if he had that whole sexy, bad boy vibe going on? He wasn't her type and she was simply working with him to save her friend. That was it.

"Gage sent a text from your phone telling Neely that you wouldn't do anything for him until you've spoken to Martina personally—via Skype or some other chat method," Skye said once they were alone.

"Good." Getting to see Martina through a live feed would at least let her gauge if she'd been hurt. Neely had a bad reputation for a reason. Right now she was forcing herself to compartmentalize and not focus on what could be happening to Martina.

Colt strode into the kitchen, still wearing jeans and the same dusty shirt from earlier. "Savage is geared up and ready to go. The plane is ready too."

At dinner Skye had mentioned the plane, which made Olivia feel a little better about their travel time. Apparently Brooks had a private plane. Or his father did. Whoever it belonged to, a private plane was no joke. "That's great... Listen, this has nothing to do with what we're walking into. Not directly, anyway. Would you mind sitting?" She stood even as she asked it. She felt a slight twinge of pain in her ribs, but ignored it. What she had to say was huge and she could barely sit still. Because if they said no, she wasn't sure what she'd do.

Colt nodded, his movements economical as he slid onto the bench seat of the long, farmhouse-style table, next to his wife. Tall and muscular, but not bulked down with muscle, he seemed just as strong and capable as everyone else who worked for them. His green eyes turned her way, giving her all his focus.

Shoving her hands into her pockets, Olivia decided to just go for blunt. They had limited time and there was only one way to say this anyway. "If something happens to me, I need to know that Valencia will be okay. I have a life insurance policy that will take care of her, but I won't risk her going into a shitty system—or with any of my family. Martina is listed as Valencia's guardian in my will, but if something happens to me, it's likely Martina will be gone too, and..." She cleared her throat. God, thinking about this sucked, but she had to do it. "Anyway, I know this is beyond huge, but I want to ask you and Colt to take care of her if I die. I trust you and I know you'd make sure she was cared for and happy." She'd known Skye since college, and other than the women she knew through Valencia's school and her next door neighbors, Skye was one of her only true friends.

Both of them stared at her, their expressions unreadable. They were like statues for an impossibly long moment. Oh hell, maybe she shouldn't have—

"We'll do it," Colt said even as Skye nodded.

Maybe the two of them had a psychic link, because it was clear Skye was in perfect agreement. "You're going to come out of this fine, but yes, we'll be her guardians if it comes to it."

Olivia sucked in a breath as the invisible band around her chest loosened. At least now going into this mess she could be assured that Valencia would have people to take care of her. Not that she wanted to die. Hell no. She wanted to see her little girl grow up, to become the incredible woman Olivia knew she'd one day be. But this eased something inside her.

"Sorry," she muttered, swiping at her cheeks when a few tears leaked out. "Thank you, guys, more than you'll ever know. Like I said, my will has Martina listed as Valencia's guardian but I'm guessing Gage can work some magic and tweak it to add you guys? Or just create a whole new one?" She'd grabbed all her important papers when she'd left her house. It seemed a lifetime ago instead of less than twenty-four hours. "I can sign something and he can use my signature later if necessary."

Skye snorted and stood. "Yeah, he'll take care of it. We're not going to need it though. Because we've got your back and we're going to find Martina—and Savage is going to be with you the entire time."

"Thank you. For everything." A simple thank you seemed pathetic to describe how grateful she was.

"No thanks needed. This is what we do—and you're family now." Skye wrapped an arm around her shoulders and that simple act made Olivia feel as if she might actually be able to do what needed to be done.

* * *

Savage stood still in the hallway, not feeling an ounce of guilt at eavesdropping on Olivia's conversation with Skye and Colt. He hadn't been intending to eavesdrop, but it had happened. Hearing Olivia planning for her death made him respect her even more. She was right—she'd made some stupid choices when she'd been younger, but who hadn't? Now she was looking out for her daughter in case she died.

Which wasn't going to happen. Not on his watch.

Making enough noise that he'd be overheard, he then stepped into the kitchen to find Olivia swiping at her cheeks. She quickly looked away from him and cleared her throat. Her profile was elegant—everything about her was elegant. And sexy as fuck.

Her long, inky hair fell down her back and around her shoulders and all he could think about was threading his fingers through the thick waves. Which was stupid. They were going to be working a job together. He'd be playing a role. Nothing more. And he didn't do more than one-night stands.

"Before we head out, I need a few minutes alone with Olivia." He kept his voice steady, neutral, even though being in her presence unsettled him. Especially considering what he needed to say to her.

"We'll be with Gage. Come find us," Colt said, clapping him on the shoulder as he left with Skye.

"It's time to go?" Olivia wrapped her arms around herself, looking a little lost and a lot sexy.

He replayed in his head the steady way she'd asked Skye and Colt to take care of her daughter if she didn't come back. This had to be killing her but she was holding up like a champ. God, this woman could easily get under his skin. "Almost. Look, we're going to be posing as lovers for Neely, so we're going to have to act like it." Which wasn't going to be an issue for him. It was easy to pretend he was into her.

She nodded. "I know."

Did she? "If I touch your lower back or put my arm around your shoulders, you can't jump. You have to act like you're comfortable with my touch—as if you're used to it. As if you've seen every inch of me naked."

"Oh...oh, right." He could see the moment when she realized where he was going.

"We'll need to kiss before we meet with Neely so we get a feel for each other. Because of the role I'm playing, I'm possessive and obsessed with you. I'm going to at least have my arm around you in Neely's presence. Or a hand on you. So we can kiss now, or on the plane. Or when we land. But we need to do it soon. Because our first kiss can't be in front of him and we have to be prepared for anything." He might not have done much undercover work—he was almost always in the shadows—but he'd done enough contract jobs and worked with enough spooks to understand how things worked. For this job, they had to take their roles seriously. There was no room for error. They would become the people they were supposed to be to get the job done.

"Now's...fine." Though her body language said differently. Her shoulders were stiff and stress lines bracketed her mouth.

Which, okay, made him feel like shit. He wanted her, yeah, but he didn't want her this way. "We can wait."

"No, I want to get this over with."

His lips kicked up. "You're really good for my ego."

Her eyes widened slightly as she realized what she'd said. "I just meant—"

"It's okay." He took a step forward, closing the distance between them, and the heat he'd seen in her dark eyes earlier that afternoon was back. It was subtle, but there nonetheless. Slowly, giving her time to back out of this, he reached out and placed one of his hands on her hip. He wanted her to get used to his touch. He'd have to start slow, work up to their kiss. Which was what he would have done even if they weren't playing a role. He wouldn't just pounce. No, there was no fun in that.

She shifted into his hold as if it was the most natural thing in the world. Okay, maybe this would work after all.

"Something else you need to know about me," he murmured, bringing his other hand up slowly to cup her cheek. Her skin was smooth, soft. Her eyes went heavy-lidded and he bit back a groan. Leaning down, he ran his nose along her ear as she braced her hands against his chest. That subtle vanilla scent teased him. When her fingers curled into his shirt and she pulled him closer, his brain threatened to short circuit. "I like to be in control. Always. So when we're in front of Neely, I'll be taking charge. I need you to be okay with that." He nipped her ear gently, and when she shuddered he couldn't stop his physical reaction to her.

Hell, he couldn't stop that regardless. Just touching her like this was making all of his possessive instincts flare up. When they were in Miami, he *wouldn't* be acting around her.

"Okay," she whispered.

He skimmed his nose along her cheek until his mouth skated over hers. Their lips barely touched, but the way she jolted told him she was as affected as he was. Her fingers dug into his shirt even harder as he covered her mouth with his.

And when she let out a soft moan, he nearly lost it. He slid his hand from her hip to her back and pulled her flush against him. She had to feel his erection—he couldn't hide it. Instead of pulling back, she arched harder into him and slid her hands up his chest and around the back of his neck.

He teased his tongue against hers, just little strokes as they learned each other's taste, touch. Her taste was perfection. And the way she fit snugly up against him—it was as if she'd been made for him. When he slid his hand up the back of her shirt, touching her bare skin, she moaned again. And his cock kicked against his pants. Well too damn bad, because this was definitely stopping at kissing.

Unfortunately.

She arched into him again and he grabbed her hips, hoisting her up onto the nearest counter. The move was swift and unplanned. Tasting her, touching her could easily become an addiction. One he didn't have time for. One he didn't want, period. This would be good for the job though. That was what he told himself anyway.

"Oh shit." The sound of Brooks's voice made him pull back.

Olivia looked at Brooks with a dazed expression—which quickly morphed into one of horror as she hastily slid off the counter.

Just great.

Without looking at him, she adjusted her shirt and, cheeks crimson, muttered something about finding her daughter before she practically raced from the room.

Her reaction shouldn't bother him, but hell. "What do you want?" he growled at Brooks.

His best friend just grinned at him. A shit-eating grin that made Zac want to punch him. "Just checking on you guys. Gage and I are ready to roll out when you are."

Damn, his blood was still racing, Olivia's taste on his tongue. "I'm ready." He and his gear were packed and ready to go.

"I took Olivia's bags down to the SUV." Brooks's smile was still fully in place as he watched him.

For some reason he found himself annoyed that Brooks had gotten her stuff. And he sure as hell wasn't going to analyze why. He wasn't her boyfriend or lover. Still, he should have been the one to do that. "You want a cookie?" he muttered.

Brooks just laughed. "Another one bites the dust."

"Shut the hell up," he muttered. He and Brooks were tight. More so than he was with any of the others. They'd been best friends since Zac moved to Redemption Harbor at the age of twelve.

But his friend was wrong.

Zac wasn't going to correct him, however. "We were just preparing for the job. That's it."

"Whatever you've gotta tell yourself, man."

Zac didn't answer him.

This was just a job. So what if he was attracted to Olivia? Nothing would ever come of it. He'd only ever done one-night stands—though not for a long time. Well, that wasn't changing for Olivia. It wasn't changing for any woman. The house, dog, kid, and white picket fence bullshit wasn't in his future.

That was for other people.

CHAPTER SIX

—Sometimes those little moments aren't little at all.—

Mercer hated it when his wife Mary Grace was unhappy—so thankfully she was just fine right now. But he also hated it when any of the women in his life were sad.

So looking at the glum expression of six-year-old Valencia Carter—a little girl who'd stolen the hearts of all of them—who was staring at the cartoon playing on the movie screen as if she couldn't care less, he wanted to "fix things." Something Mary Grace told him he shouldn't do. "Women just want someone to listen to them, not fix everything" was something he'd heard more than once.

Well, apparently he hadn't learned, because he *had* to do something. And besides, this situation was different. "I'm opening one of my restaurants tomorrow morning and I need help," he said, causing three sets of eyes to look at him: Mary Grace, Skye and Valencia—who was desperately missing her mother who'd left about an hour ago. "You think you'd be up to helping me?" he asked Valencia. He hadn't learned ASL fully yet, but he was trying.

Her dark eyes widened. "Me?"

"Yeah, you. You can help me make some of the dough—and you can make your own pizza. Any way you like it. If it's up to muster, I might even consider adding a new pizza to the menu—and letting you name it."

"For real?"

"Yep. And, if we ask nicely I bet Mary Grace and Mia will come too." At this point he would give her anything to make her smile again.

Mary Grace nodded as she shifted their sleeping daughter in her arms. Since having Mia she'd taken time off from work, which meant she and their daughter were at one of the restaurants all the time. He loved every minute of it. "We love hanging out at the restaurants on Sundays, so we'll be there if you are, Valencia."

Valencia tapped her chin as if seriously contemplating it. "Can I play the new arcade game?"

"Anything you want." He'd just installed an arcade machine with sixty old-school games pre-loaded. Or *retro games* they were now called, as his wife had informed him. The thing was a hit too. With kids and their parents alike. He was going to have another one installed in his other restaurant in the next couple weeks.

"Okay, sounds like fun." Valencia grinned at him, her smile so open. Nothing like the shy girl they'd met months ago. Ever since she'd started coming to Redemption Harbor with her mother, everyone had started to think of Valencia and Olivia as family. And right now their job was to keep Valencia happy and her thoughts off her mom's absence.

"You want to hold Mia for a few minutes?" Mary Grace asked, shifting slightly.

Skye immediately tensed, going into what he thought of as her super-overprotective mode. She was like that with pretty much anyone she considered family or in need of protection. And since the woman had rescued his wife from a cartel kidnapping over seven months ago when everyone else had thought she was dead, he didn't care how protective she was—even if it drove Mary Grace nuts.

Mary Grace snorted as she set their daughter oh so gently in Valencia's small arms. "Skye, you want to wrap them both in bubble wrap? Or cotton?" she asked as she sat back.

"I would if you'd let me," Skye muttered. "And as soon as she's old enough, Mia's getting self-defense training. Green Berets will have nothing on her by the time she's eighteen."

"Sweet baby pandas," Mary Grace muttered right back. "You've *got* to ease up. You're gonna give yourself an aneurysm."

"Not happening anytime soon. And if you think I'm kidding about that training..." Grinning, Skye just shrugged.

Mercer figured she was completely serious—and he was more than okay with it.

Valencia giggled as the two women bantered back and forth, the movie playing more like background noise than anything else. "She's so small," she whispered, looking at Mia's perfect face.

God, he still couldn't believe he was a father. That he had his wife back and they had a family now. Hell, their family was bigger than just the three of them. It encompassed everyone in this house and everyone on the plane down to Miami at the moment. He just hoped Olivia didn't fall for Savage. He loved the man like a brother, but Savage didn't want the family thing. Or more likely, thought he didn't deserve it—at least that was what Mary Grace had suggested once. And his wife was intuitive when it came to people.

Mercer stretched out an arm along the back of the couch, wrapping it around his wife and pulling her close. When their baby had first been born he'd been a little crazy, not wanting anyone to hold her. And okay, he was still crazy when it came to his girl, but he'd eased up a bit. Barely.

It didn't matter that he knew his wife was capable, a survivor; he was probably always going to be overprotective of her and their daughter. And everyone in his life.

* * *

Stretched out in the plush, cream-colored leather seat of Brooks's Gulfstream—that his dad had won in some kind of bet with another billionaire—Zac scanned the next page on his tablet as he went over the details he and Olivia had come up with for their cover. He was staying mostly true to who he was and his skills. It only made sense. It was a hell of a lot easier to remember a cover if there was truth in it.

His name was simply Savage—which would be easy for Olivia to remember. He wasn't going to hand out his information to Neely because that would be even more suspicious. He was here for one reason: because of Olivia and his "obsession" with her. That didn't mean he'd just roll over for Neely. No, he'd make the guy work for any information he got on him. It would all be fake, thanks to the backstory Gage had already started building. But Neely would believe it more if he had to work for it.

Zac rolled his shoulders once as he scrolled to another page. The history he and Olivia had built was simple. They'd met after her ex-husband split, had gotten hot and heavy, then she'd ended things when he wanted to get serious. Then they'd filled in the innocuous details like exactly where they'd met, how long they'd been together, how they took their coffee. Enough things that made it clear they had a past and were intimate. It would work. It had to. He'd never failed a mission and didn't plan to start now. He just had to remind himself that she was a mission. Nothing more. Certainly not a woman who made him think of a different future than the one he knew he deserved.

Thankfully Gage was building a file on Neely, and Leighton was already on the ground in Miami with eyes on the hotel Neely was at. There was little chance Martina was there—keeping a kidnap victim at a hotel was beyond stupid. Not with maids and other staff about at all hours of the day and night. But if the job was in Miami, Zac was hoping her friend was too. Because once they rescued her, they were gone. He'd personally take care of this Neely asshole to keep Olivia safe. But not until her friend was free.

Against his will, he looked to his right where Olivia was dozing next to him. Instead of putting distance between them when they'd boarded the plane he'd chosen a seat right next to her—and ignored Brooks's grin when he'd passed by them. Zac just wanted to get used to being around her. For the job.

Wearing a light sweater, Olivia had it pulled tight around her. Her smooth leather seat was leaned back and she should be comfortable. Her expression was tense, however, so even in sleep he knew she wasn't truly resting. Her long, thick eyelashes flickered as she shifted again.

Frowning, he glanced behind him and saw Brooks sleeping in one of the single recliner seats—of course, that man could sleep anywhere. And Gage was tapping away on his laptop at one of the polished built-in tables. Like usual. Thank God for his skills too. Zac had worked with some of the best government analysts and he'd never found anyone like Gage. The man had some scary abilities—and he was proficient in martial arts. If he wanted to destroy someone's world, he could do it physically or via a computer.

When he shifted back in his seat he found Olivia watching him. "Hey." He kept his voice low.

"Hey," she murmured, moving her seat up as she rubbed her eyes. "Didn't mean to fall asleep."

"You need it. And you'll have time to rest before meeting with Neely." They'd secured a hotel under a cover ID, but eventually they'd let Neely figure out where they were staying.

Because Gage would have the hotel room under his own security. From there they'd be able to follow anyone who tried to check out the room. Maybe they'd get lucky and track someone back to Martina.

"How long was I out?" Olivia stretched, slightly arching her back, and all he could think of was the way she'd arched against him during that kiss.

A kiss that he was still replaying in his head—and he wanted more of it. "Just an hour."

"God, I felt so bad leaving." There was a lot of self-recrimination in her voice.

He frowned, not liking it. "You're doing what needs to be done." For her friend and her daughter. Despite his stupid original snap judgment, it was clear she was a damn good mother.

She snorted. "Yeah. Too bad I feel like the shittiest mom in the world." Her jaw clenched tight as she reached for the tablet Gage had given her earlier.

"Look, I know what I said before, but I was wrong. And trust me, I *had* the shittiest mom in the world. You're not it." Not even close.

She looked at him in surprise and set the tablet in her lap.

He hadn't meant to tell her anything personal, but if they were going undercover together, trust was a big part of playing the right role. Because at some point, it couldn't even be a role anymore. They *had* to trust each other for this to work.

Olivia cleared her throat, looked as if she might ask about it, but he saw the moment she changed her mind. "So...how do you know Colt?"

A change of topic was probably better. "We grew up together. Also worked together when he was with his former employer." Savage wasn't going to spell out who Colt had worked for but he was pretty certain Olivia knew anyway—or at least guessed. And he definitely wasn't going to tell her what he had done. For more than one reason. Mainly he didn't want to see any judgment in her eyes. "I piggybacked on a few missions with Skye as well."

Olivia raised her eyebrows. "What was your profession before you started working for a consulting firm?"

"I can't tell you."

"Can't or won't?"

"Both." He would be honest with her about everything except that.

"Okay... Then tell me something real about yourself. Tell me about your mom. If we're going to do this job together and fake our attraction..." She cleared her throat, her cheeks turning a delicious shade of pink, making him want to lean over and nibble on her bottom lip.

"We won't be faking the attraction." A true statement if there ever was one.

She met his gaze then. "No, we won't."

He blinked once, not expecting the admission. "I want to taste you again," he murmured, low enough for her ears only. He shouldn't be doing this, shouldn't play with fire, but it was hard to care about getting burned where she was concerned. He wanted her like he'd never wanted any woman.

Her cheeks flushed even darker but she held his gaze. "We shouldn't do that. Not unless it's for the job."

"I know." Didn't stop him from wanting her.

"Are you going to tell me something about yourself or not?" The words came out all breathy, from nerves, he guessed.

Zac should say no. "Tell me something about yourself first. Something not in your file."

"I...okay." She let out a little breath. "Making the decision to go forward with cochlear implants for Valencia was hard. The hardest decision I've ever made. For a lot of reasons. None of which I'll get into now. But after her surgery I knew it was right for her. It's not for everyone but it is for my sweet girl. Anyway, when she was about three and a half we were at a birthday party for one of the girls from her preschool. It was at a park, and about an hour into it, it started raining. All the other kids thought it was fun and decided to play in the rain. We didn't have Valencia's waterproof covers for her processors so she had to stay under one of the shelters with me and most of the parents who didn't relish getting soaked."

She took a deep breath and the agony he saw on Olivia's face made him want to reach out and comfort her somehow. He didn't have any experience with that but he'd give it a shot.

"She kept asking why she couldn't play with her friends. She asked me if all of her friends had taken off their processors to play in the rain. I explained that her friends at the party didn't have processors. And it was like a light bulb went off, and in that moment she realized she was *different* from her friends. I could see it in her expression. At the time, she was in a mainstream preschool because there weren't any schools for the Deaf and Hard of Hearing where we lived. She just started sobbing against my neck, wanting to go home."

She cleared her throat and took a moment.

"It was like shards of glass tearing me up inside—and I knew it was worse for her. I just wanted to take away all her pain. I realized that there's only so much I'll be able to do to protect her from the outside world—though I'm always going to try hard to. It was also a sharp reminder of sorts why I was never going to introduce her to my parents. My mom was still alive at the time and I'd started feeling… I don't know what I was thinking. But I knew that my parents would only cause her pain, if only from their indifference. And now I'm rambling," she said, her voice cracking as she blinked away wetness.

His own throat was tight as he listened to her story. The thought of that bright little girl dealing with all those emotions, all that sadness so young—fuck. Childhoods were supposed to be happy, carefree. Not that he knew from personal experience, but it was the way things should be.

"Anyway, after that summer I moved to a new city with more opportunities for her, including a school that has built-in curriculum for the Deaf. Which is incredibly rare." Frustration filled her voice. "So now you know something real about me, one of the worst memories I have, and why I moved a couple years ago."

"I'm sorry Valencia experienced that." He reached out, placed his hand gently over hers.

She seemed startled by his touch, but turned her palm over and gripped him back. "I probably shouldn't have dropped that story on you."

"I'm glad you did." He wasn't even sure why.

"It happened three years ago and it still carves me up when I think about it. Having kids changes everything," she murmured, more to herself than him.

He simply nodded. "I imagine it does."

The plane suddenly dipped and her hand tightened on his a fraction before she let go.

"You okay?" he asked, missing the feel of her soft hand in his.

"Yeah, it's just turbulence." She lifted a shoulder. "And now you have to tell me something. You said you learned ASL because of your brother but that he died—but you're really proficient."

"Before starting our consulting company I occasionally worked with a man who's Deaf. So I kept fresh with ASL with online programs and sometimes classes at a local center whenever I could swing it. It...makes me feel connected to my brother even if he's gone." Something he'd never told anyone.

"Do you mind talking about your brother?"

Glancing over his shoulder again he saw that yep, Brooks was still dozing, his Stetson placed over his face, his arms crossed over his chest in the reclined chair. Gage looked up, caught his eye before turning back to his computer. Since he had his headphones plugged in it was doubtful he'd overhear anything. Not that his friends didn't know pretty much everything about him.

When he looked back, Olivia was watching him. There definitely wasn't a way he could back out of this now. Not when she'd been so honest with him. And she'd given him something real. He owed her the same.

"My brother died of leukemia." It was like David had never been given a break. "We, uh, we had a shitty mother." He wasn't going to get into all those details. Not now; likely not ever. "But when I was twelve and David was ten, she dropped us off with our grandma."

He couldn't help but smile when he thought of her. She'd been the sweetest woman to ever walk the earth. It was hard to understand how she'd had such a selfish daughter.

"For a few years things were really good. Anything would have been better than being dragged around the country by my mother."

"You moved around a lot with her?"

"Yep. Usually in the middle of the night she'd make us pack up so we could sneak out—because she was behind on the rent or had met a new man and was following him somewhere. Her one rule had been 'If it doesn't fit in your suitcase, it doesn't come with us.'"

"That's..." She cleared her throat.

"Shitty? Yeah, I know." But it was what it was. No sense in dwelling on it. "Finally though, she left us with our grandma, which was the best thing she ever did for us. My grandma got my brother a tutor so he could catch up with school, and managed to get a grant to enroll him in a private school for the Deaf. It was three hours away so he stayed there during the week and we picked him up every Friday evening. I hated being separated from him." Something Zac had never really told anyone. "It had always been the two of us sticking together before that." He was the oldest and had always been protective of David. "But it was good for him. So good. He started truly thriving, made real friends, wasn't so frustrated all the time. But then he got cancer and it was pervasive."

He nearly jumped when she reached over and took his hand, her dark eyes full of compassion. It was still so hard to talk about.

"He died before his sixteenth birthday." And that was all he was going to say about that. Zac couldn't force any more words out. Just as he couldn't force himself to pull away from her.

"I'm so sorry," she said quietly.

Zac knew when people were just saying the standard *I'm sorry,* and Olivia wasn't. He could hear the emotion in her voice. "Thank you." His brother's death had left a hole in him.

"Is your grandmother still with you?"

He shook his head. "No. Heart attack."

More sympathy flickered in her gaze. "It's good you have such close friends."

"Yeah." He knew how lucky he was to have such a solid core of people he could depend on. While he still talked to some buddies from the Marines, the six people he'd grown up with were family in all the ways that mattered. Well, seven now since Skye had joined their group and she was like the badass sister he'd never had. He'd do absolutely anything for them—and getting their new business venture off the ground these last seven months had been unexpectedly therapeutic.

He wanted to ask her more about her life, her family, but knew that would involve Martina Cruz. And he didn't want to upset Olivia more. She was already missing her daughter and no doubt worried about her kidnapped friend. He wasn't going to bring it up.

"You said your ex left because of your daughter? What about you?" When they'd spoken before, her phrasing had been specific. It made him curious. And Zac wanted to know if there was a chance her ex was somehow involved in this.

She slowly pulled her hand back, wrapped her arms around herself. "He didn't want things to end with us." Olivia rolled her eyes even as she continued. "Not sure what the fool wanted or thought would happen. When he rejected our daughter it killed any feelings I had for him. And...I'd been unhappy with him since I found out I was pregnant. I'll admit I was hormonal and maybe a little irrational at times, but I met a few friends through a couple pregnancy classes and it was eye-opening seeing the way their significant others treated them. I finally *saw* how selfish Heath was. And after Valencia was born, I had zero time for a man-child. But...he still wanted things to continue with us." Another eye roll. "I'm just glad he's out of our lives. And before you ask—because I can see you want to—no, I seriously don't think he's involved in this. Not in kidnapping Martina. He might be a selfish baby, but he's not a monster. And getting involved in kidnapping? Much less with Kyle... No, I remember him having a healthy fear of Kyle. I can't see him being part of whatever this is."

"If for some reason he is there, you need to be prepared for it." Even the thought of seeing her ex—a man who'd rejected his own child—made Zac feel punchy.

"I know. If he is, he is. That won't change the parameters of what we have to do."

Zac felt the same way and hoped she really did too. Because they were walking into the unknown and had to depend on each other to make it out of this alive.

CHAPTER SEVEN

—We've got this.—

Olivia looked up at the fifteen-story boutique hotel, Savage by her side. The man was an intimidating presence, something she was grateful for. Sunglasses on to fight the bright Miami morning, she murmured, "Getting the penthouse is definitely Neely's style."

Savage wrapped an arm around her shoulders and a shiver of awareness slid through her veins. Almost enough to make her forget the achiness in her ribs. After that intense kiss they'd shared, thoughts of what he tasted like, felt like against her... Yeah, no need to go there. She couldn't afford to be distracted. And thinking about what she wanted to do to him? Nope.

He didn't respond, just leaned down and kissed the top of her head. She knew they were acting, that this was part of their role as a couple in case anyone was watching. No doubt Neely had someone keeping an eye out for them. Either someone on the ground, or he'd hacked the hotel's security system. Maybe both. It had been a long time since she'd worked with him, but some things didn't change. Even if they were acting, Savage had been right on the plane. She wasn't faking her attraction to him and she knew he wasn't faking his own. The erection she'd felt in that kitchen definitely hadn't been fake.

Which just made all of this even more complicated. Her only goal was to convince Kyle Neely that she'd help him steal whatever it was he wanted while Gage and the others tried to find out where Martina was being kept.

"You got this," Savage murmured as they strode through the revolving glass door.

She sure hoped so. She'd worn her "armor" today, needing every ounce of it she could get for this show they were putting on. And that was what it felt like too. An elaborate show. In skintight black pants that laced up the sides, showing off a lot of skin, a formfitting red T-shirt and a black leather jacket to finish off the edgy look, she looked like she would have years ago. Which, according to Savage, was all part of her illusion.

Neely had blackmailed her into doing this, but he was still going to test her. Both of them. And Savage said she needed to look the part, that some part of Kyle's subconscious would relax if she was the same as she was before. It would give him less to focus on. Supposedly. She was trusting that Savage knew what he was talking about—and still really curious about what he used to do for a living before now.

"If things go south, I'll make sure we get out of here." There was no doubt in his voice.

"I've got your back too." She might not be as trained as him, but she had some moves and had gotten out of tight situations before.

He paused once as they strode across the gleaming lobby floor and she would have tripped but he slid an arm around her waist, holding her tight. She liked the feel of him holding her. "If I tell you to run, you run." His words might as well have been a growl.

Well she certainly wasn't leaving him behind, if that was what he was implying. But she didn't think saying that now would serve any purpose other than to annoy him. "Are you always super bossy?" she murmured.

Palm trees were placed strategically around the bright lobby and natural sunlight streamed in from the dozens of skylights high above them, giving the illusion that the area was bigger than it was. They strode right past the seating area and a trendy-looking open bar with glossy high-top tables mixed with comfortable couches, and made their way to the elevators.

"Yes." Savage's voice was deep and too sexy for her own good. "I expect my partners to do what I say, when I say it."

Okay, that should *not* sound so sexual. Heat pooled between her legs as she mentally translated that into what it would be like in the bedroom, but she ignored it. Sort of. Because it was impossible to completely ignore this man and how her body came alive around him. "I'd say you're going to be very disappointed with me, then," she said as one of the elevators opened up.

She stepped inside with Savage right behind her and when a well-dressed man in a business suit started to get in with them, Savage told him to "Catch another ride" and pretty much bared his teeth at him. Okay, maybe not exactly that, but the look he gave the man was a little feral.

And when he turned all his focus on her as the doors slid shut, her breath caught in her throat. He moved at her like a predator, his steps liquid smooth, and before she realized it her back was up against the glass and bronze wall.

He cupped her cheek with one hand, his other sliding back through her hair as he leaned down until their lips were almost brushing. His green eyes were dilated, his breathing harsh and uneven as they stared at each other.

Her nipples beaded tight against her bra cups, the friction sending another rush of heat between her legs. Some insanity almost compelled her to lean forward and nip his bottom lip.

Almost. What the hell was he doing? And why did she like it so much?

At the sound of the elevator dinging, he stepped back and she sucked in a breath, her equilibrium all out of control. He hadn't even touched her, not really. Their lips hadn't even brushed. But she swore she felt as if he'd branded her. And wondered if that had been his intention.

Whatever it was, she needed to get her game face on.

As they stepped out of the elevator onto the top floor—Kyle definitely must have been watching them somehow or given them access to this level—a man standing guard at the only door on the floor knocked once on it and moved toward them, a scanning wand in hand.

She knew the drill and it was clear Savage did too as he held out his arms and slightly spread his legs. She did the same.

"If you touch her inappropriately, I'll break your arms." Savage's voice was quiet, his tone casual—as if he hadn't just threatened serious violence.

The man with light brown skin paused only once before he scanned her, his moves efficient and professional. When he scanned Savage, Olivia noticed the guy subtly checking Savage's ass out—and had the most absurd urge to laugh that Savage had been worried about her. Nothing about this situation was funny, but when she was nervous, sometimes she laughed inappropriately. She forced it back and cleared her throat.

So much depended on this first meeting going right. Because if Kyle thought something was off or if she and Savage couldn't handle the "audition" she knew was coming, Martina wouldn't be useful to him anymore. She knew he'd killed in the past and wouldn't have a problem doing it again.

As soon as the man finished, the door opened. Kyle gave her a welcoming smile, all elegance, as if he hadn't backhanded and kicked her a couple days ago.

She resisted the urge to touch her covered-up bruise. Stupid jackass.

"Olivia, welcome." He held out a hand so that she and Savage could step inside. When he moved, his jacket shifted and she spotted a pistol tucked into a shoulder holster. He'd likely be the only one carrying a weapon right now too. Hence the body scan. It hadn't just been for listening devices, but weapons as well.

"You're Neely?" Savage subtly stepped in front of her, blocking her almost completely from Kyle as the door shut behind them.

"Yes."

Before she'd moved two steps into the room, Savage moved like, well, a savage, at Kyle's positive response.

He smashed his fist into Kyle's pretty face once—hard. "That's for hurting what's mine." A soft, deadly growl of words.

Completely in line with the role of a man obsessed with her, but still surprising. She noted three other men in the room, and none of them made a move to help Kyle.

Feeling at a loss for what to do, she just stood there, her mind trying to catch up to what had happened. Before she'd blinked Kyle had his gun drawn and was pointing it at Savage as blood streamed out of his nose and down his mouth.

She'd never seen anyone move as fast as Savage as he grabbed Kyle's wrist and took his gun. Just...*took* it. As if it was freaking candy. In a few quick moves, he'd disassembled the thing into three pieces. Instead of tossing them on the ground, however, he tucked them into his own pockets.

Well that was...unexpected. Olivia covered her shock but no one else in the room, least of all Kyle, was hiding theirs. If there had been a "who is the scariest guy in the room contest," Savage would have won, hands down.

For a solid five seconds silence reigned, until Kyle looked past Savage at her and snarled, "What the hell?" Murder was in his gaze.

The other men remained where they were seated, two on a long, plush white leather couch and one by a floor-to-ceiling window overlooking the Atlantic.

"Don't look at her. Look at me." Savage was in a completely different mode than she'd ever seen him. "I'm here because she's here, because you need her skills—and it's pretty clear you need mine as well. You assaulted her two days ago. I'd be a shitty partner if I just let that go. Consider that your payback." The edge to Savage's voice sounded a little like payback wasn't over.

But it was hard to tell. Her nerves were shot as she waited for Kyle to respond. What if he kicked them out? What if he—

"That's fair." Kyle's voice was even as he headed to the minibar, grabbed a towel. "Now who the fuck are you?" he asked as he pressed the white cloth to his face.

"Name's Savage."

"And?"

"And what?"

"What are your skills? Your resume? Who have you worked with?"

"Who I've worked with is none of your business. And my skills are acquisitions and deliveries. Occasionally a cleaner." All words Kyle would understand.

Without actually saying it, Savage had just told him that he retrieved expensive things and delivered them to buyers. And he was also a killer. Cleaner, triggerman—there were a few phrases common in circles like this that meant the same thing. Cleaner was the most common for assassin. And she wasn't sure if he really was or if this was just part of his cover. She'd been too afraid to ask him back at Brooks's ranch when they'd been building his background and their history. But she believed that he could be.

Taking Olivia's hand, Savage tugged her toward the seating area, his movements completely confident.

She felt like they were walking into a tiger's den. Of course, *he* was a tiger himself and secure in his strength. She, on the other hand, felt like a scared rabbit.

He oh so gently guided her down into one of the zebra print high-back chairs and stood next to her like a sentry as he faced Kyle and the others.

"I'm going to need more than that. I need to know you're not a Fed." Kyle held the bloody cloth at his side now.

His nose was swelling—something that made her incredibly happy—but she wasn't sure if it was broken. If it wasn't, that was only because Savage had restrained himself. No doubt he could have killed Kyle with a few moves.

"I don't care what you want."

Panic punched through Olivia, but she decided to trust Savage. He was here to help and had more experience than her in situations like this. The whole Redemption Harbor Consulting team did. She'd gone to Skye for a reason, so she was going to have faith, even if her heartbeat was an erratic drum in her ears and she felt as if she could split apart at the seams. She was definitely not cut out for undercover work.

"You do if you care about Olivia." Kyle wasn't even looking at her anymore. As if she didn't exist at all. All Kyle's focus was on the real predator in the room.

Everyone's was.

She subtly glanced around at the other men, took in what she could glean about them. One black man in his early thirties—maybe late twenties. Head shaved, a little stubble on his face, and dressed like he was part of a biker gang in all black and a leather jacket. Not that she could judge since she was dressed similarly. Both the men on the couch were white. One wore gray slacks, a crisp button-down shirt and a vest—with an actual timepiece hanging out of it. From his Brioni shoes to his buffed and polished fingernails, he was likely the con man of the group. Knowing what she did about the crews Kyle had run in the past, she'd bet on it. The other man was dressed simply in jeans, boots, and a long-sleeved sweater. Everything about him was forgettable. Easy-to-look-at face, but not memorable, clothing style boring, and even though he was sitting, she guessed his height to be about five feet nine. He could be anything—someone who posed as a delivery man to get into somewhere to plant bugs. Or he could be a thief. It was too hard to tell just by looking at him.

"Fine. You get to know more about me and she gets to speak to Martina. From a live feed. Skype or FaceTime, I don't care which. Once she does that, you'll know what you need to about me," Savage said.

Kyle looked as if he wanted to argue, but after a few seconds while Olivia held her breath, he finally nodded. When he looked at her there was more annoyance than anything in his expression. Someone else had taken over control of the situation—something Kyle liked to always have. Even as they spoke he was probably thinking of ways he planned to kill Savage. Unless of course Kyle decided he needed to use him. Kyle might be a killer, but he was also a businessman. If he thought he could use someone, he'd use them until he no longer needed them. And if someone betrayed him, they died.

Something she didn't want to think about right now.

"Come on." He tilted his head at her and when she went to stand, Savage smoothly moved in front of her.

This must have been what he'd meant about taking over, being in control. He probably hadn't told her about his plan to punch Kyle because she'd have argued with him about it. Or she assumed that was why he didn't. Once they were alone she was going to talk to him about that.

He took her hand but kept her behind him as they followed Kyle to the minibar. He reached behind it and pulled out a sleek tablet. After he typed in a few commands, he handed it to her. "Keep it brief."

He didn't move far and neither did Savage as she looked at the screen. The camera was pointed at the same chair and the same blue background she'd seen Martina in before. Kyle was texting someone on his phone and a few moments after that, Martina appeared on the screen.

Wearing different clothes than in the video, she appeared to be in good health, but that didn't mean anything.

"Martina!" She couldn't pretend this didn't matter to her. Hell, what would be the point? Kyle had kidnapped Olivia's lifelong friend for a reason. He knew this was her weakness.

"Mi pequeña." Martina's voice was full of warmth. "How are you? Are you okay?"

Olivia wanted to sob. Martina shouldn't be asking her that. "I'm fine… How are you? Are they treating you okay?" She wasn't sure who "they" were, but at least one person had to be watching her. Whoever Kyle had texted. At that thought she wondered if Gage could do something with the number, maybe track whoever Kyle had been in contact with. She'd have to ask Savage about it as soon as they were alone.

Martina nodded, stress lines around her mouth. "This isn't the ideal situation, but it's not terrible either. I have a bed to sleep on and they let me watch television. I miss you guys."

"We miss you too." Olivia so desperately wanted to tell her that everything would be okay, that she was going to get her out of this mess, but held back. She didn't want Kyle to have even a hint that she was planning something.

"All right, that's enough. You see that she's fine." Kyle went to grab it from her but she shifted.

"I love you, Mama." Her voice cracked on the last word.

"I love you too."

Kyle grabbed the tablet then and turned it off. "Now it's time for you to talk," he said to Savage.

"Fine. Call Victor Morales. He'll vouch for me."

Olivia had no idea who this Morales was, but it was clear Kyle did if his expression was any indication. "Victor Morales? As in, *the* Morales crime family?"

"The one and only." Savage slid an arm around her shoulders, pulled her close to him in a ridiculously possessive way that left no doubt to anyone that he considered her his.

Kyle watched him a long moment, then pulled out his cell phone again. "Stay here," he ordered before disappearing into the attached bedroom.

Sweat trickled down Olivia's spine as they waited for him, but Savage was ice cold. She was glad for his presence. If it wasn't for him, she wouldn't be holding up at all. Being here, knowing her friend was still captive, dealing with a bunch of criminals she didn't know—who were all male. God, it was a relief to have this force of nature by her side.

Five minutes later Kyle was back, a half-smile on his face. He looked as if he'd just won the lottery.

"All right, Savage. It sounds as if you're legit. Morales says you're good too. I'm going to need proof, however." He reached into his pocket, pulled out a piece of paper as he strode toward them. "You're going to crack the safe here." He held out a small business card with the name, address and logo of a local jeweler. Tatiana's Fine Jewelry. "It's a Kaira 2000."

Taking it, Savage lifted a shoulder as he removed his arm from around hers. "All right."

"Right now."

Savage stiffened just as she did. "It's the middle of the day and we haven't cased the place."

"So? Morales says you're a superstar. Superhuman, even. And I know she's good. You two do this now. Or Martina is dead."

CHAPTER EIGHT

—Life is all about how you handle Plan B.—

Zac wanted to slam his fist into Neely's smug face again, but the man was smart. Or smart enough for now. He was playing on Olivia's only weakness. And no way would Zac say no. Not when Martina's life hung in the balance. "Fine, we'll do it." This definitely wasn't ideal but he'd done more with less time and information.

Olivia nodded, no pause at all. No surprise. He knew she'd do anything for her friend—a woman who was clearly more like a mother to her than he'd originally realized. "But we need props. I'm not going into this place showing my face. Otherwise we'll become targets of local law enforcement and that could hurt whatever job you're planning in the future."

Neely's jaw clenched and Zac could feel the annoyance rolling off him. Why would he be annoyed though? Asking for props—aka a disguise—was smart.

The hairs on the back of Zac's neck prickled in awareness. He wasn't sure if it was the whole situation or something about Neely's reaction right now.

"Fine. But you're going dark."

"Excuse me?" Olivia asked.

"No phones for the job. And no personal identifiers."

That was pretty standard but Zac didn't like being without his phone. It was one of the company's untraceable ones anyway. And after this they'd have to toss their phones in case Neely put a tracker in or tried to clone them.

Next to him Olivia shifted slightly but nodded in agreement. She had one of the company's untraceable ones as well. Zac pulled out his, handed it over but kept the pieces of the pistol. He definitely wasn't giving that back—for two reasons. One was self-preservation. And the other…he'd just see what Gage could dig up on this weapon. And Kyle Neely. The man's prints were on it.

"I'll need a wig, fake glasses, expensive-looking earrings and a bracelet—real diamonds, preferably—and a stethoscope," Olivia said. "Do you have the right kind of drill for this?"

Neely nodded.

"I need a fedora and glasses," Zac said, pushing up the sleeves of his button-down shirt. His clothes were already the right look for the kind of couple who would enter the high-end jewelry store, as was the insane hundred thousand dollar watch on his wrist. He'd have to thank Brooks later for making him wear it. The thing had been a gift from Brooks's father and as far as Savage knew, the cowboy had never worn it.

Neely nodded once, then motioned toward the two doors that swung inward to the master suite. "I've got anything you need."

Two racks of clothing, mostly men's, but some women's, were lined up near the windows overlooking the ocean. There were also accessories, including wigs. Wordlessly Olivia went to the wigs and grabbed a sleek platinum blonde bob. As she twisted her hair into a tight bun at the nape of her neck and fixed the wig in place, it was clear she'd done this before.

As she finished up, he picked up a tan wool fedora and square black-rimmed glasses. Not the best disguise but he wanted something to block his face enough. The hat covered up enough of his ears that if he was caught on any CCTVs, it'd be hard to say for certain that it was him. Of course, he hoped Gage would be able to hack into any video feeds surrounding the store and delete any images of him and Olivia.

"You'll be taking one of my crew with you."

Yeah, Zac had thought he might say that. "I'm taking the biker."

Neely's eyes narrowed slightly. "You'll take who I say. And Maxwell will be going with you," he said, motioning to one of the men in the other room. A few moments later the pretty boy with the vintage timepiece stepped into the entryway. Of *course* his name was Maxwell.

"Look, I want the other guy, unless he's completely incapable. I need someone to act as a distraction and he fits the type." Which was mostly true. But Zac had seen the other guy before. He'd met him years ago as part of another government-related job. At the time he'd wondered if the man was actually a Fed, or maybe a spook. But the man's role in that previous job had been minimal so Zac never made enough contact to confirm. He wasn't even sure if the man remembered him. "You want Olivia and me to do this with no prep? Then I need to be in control."

Neely's eyes narrowed a fraction. "You'll be in control for this job only. But you're taking Maxwell. He can create a distraction."

Though it went against his instincts, Zac nodded. He knew when to back off and when to act like a dick. Now he had to be in professional mode and let Neely think he was in charge.

"Maxwell," Neely said, still keeping his gaze trained on Zac.

Zac had needed to come in and basically dominate Neely. It had been a risk, yes, but he'd wanted Neely off guard enough to do something stupid. Like open up a live feed on his laptop to a kidnapped woman. Gage was monitoring the penthouse and any communications that came out of it, so if he'd been able to figure out where Martina's IP address had originated from—or at least narrow down an area—they could extract her. Then he and Olivia could walk away.

Maxwell stepped into the entryway now, nodded once at Zac, then flicked a quick, disinterested glance at Olivia. He played with the chain on his timepiece as Neely told him he'd be going in with the two of them.

"You'll be the distraction," Zac said to him. "It would be better if you changed clothes, looked more…flashy. You won't be connected with what Olivia and I do. All you have to do is be a giant jackass."

The man simply nodded and headed to one of the clothing racks. Okay, so he wasn't the chatty type. When he pulled out a shiny gold and black shirt, black slacks, faux alligator skin boots and a gaudy gold watch, Savage nodded in approval. That would definitely work for the kind of distraction they needed.

"I'll take my gun now," Neely said when the four of them were headed to the front door. Looked as if the other two were staying behind. Which sucked—because one of Zac's crew could have broken in and done recon of the penthouse.

Zac simply snorted. "It's going to be my backup." Complete and utter bullshit, because he wasn't planning to pull a weapon on innocent civilians or local law enforcement, but Neely wouldn't know that. And Neely wasn't ever getting this pistol back.

It was clear that Neely wanted to argue, but the man nodded, barely concealing his rage. Oh yeah, he was definitely plotting how to kill Zac. Well, the feeling was mutual.

In the lobby of the hotel, he kept Olivia close to him, linking his hand with hers so their fingers were intertwined. Despite the tense situation, he enjoyed the feel of her hand in his. It felt as if they were really a couple. Something he'd never been part of before. Never thought he wanted to be part of. That was for other people. Not someone like him with blood on his hands, who knew absolutely nothing about relationships. Not healthy ones anyway.

She seemed to be holding up well, not that he would expect less after reading about some of the jobs she'd pulled. But this was different. Her friend's life was on the line. Yet she was clearly ready to do anything to save Martina. Which just made him like Olivia even more.

Out of the corner of his eye Zac saw Leighton step out from behind one of the pillars, his movements casual. Zac kept his focus on where they were going, not making eye contact with his friend as Leighton brushed past him, placing a small earbud in his hand.

Passing anything, whether information or something else, on an undercover job was dangerous. But sometimes there was no other choice.

As they reached the revolving doors, he let go of Olivia's hand and acted as if he was adjusting his hat. When he did, he slid the earbud in place, knowing it would be deep enough that no one could see it. They'd talked about wearing them when meeting Neely but Olivia hadn't been sure how detailed the search would be. It hadn't been worth the risk.

There was a slight burst of static before Gage said, "I know you can't talk, but Leighton says you've got the earbud. And. . .I see you walking out of the hotel. Good news—I hacked into the feed coming from the penthouse and I've narrowed down where the IP address originated from. Not sure if it has anything to do with Martina, but the three of us are geared up and heading over to the address now. I know you can't respond, but if you can give me a hint where you're going, I'll still be listening."

Zac didn't look around, just took Olivia's hand again as Neely gave a card to the valet. He briefly touched his hat, hoping Gage saw the signal that yes, he'd heard him. Less than a minute later they were sitting in the back seat of a white Escalade with dark tinted windows.

"So give us more about this jewelry store," Zac said to Neely. "Why are we robbing Tatiana's and what does the exit layout look like?" All normal things Zac would want to know. Gage should be able to get enough info from that to look the place up.

"You're robbing them because I say so." Neely's voice was pure frost.

Total bullshit. Zac guessed it had to do with the type of safe. Neely probably wanted to see if Olivia could break into it under pressure—because it was likely the type of safe that held whatever the real job was all about. Or it was close enough to the other type of safe.

"Fine. But we need more before we go in there. How many employees, specific security system and more importantly, *exits.*"

"It's Sunday, so just two employees, a father and daughter. The security system will only be armed on the actual locked cases. Everything else will be shut down. Except the two back exit doors. Those will be armed as well. And of course the safe. There's a keypad for the office door where the safe is. The code is 6-7-9-5-4-3," he said, looking at Olivia in the rearview mirror. "Once you're past the door, all you have to do is bypass the safe. Clean it out. That purse you're carrying will be big enough even with the drill."

Olivia had taken an oversized black Burberry purse as part of her ensemble, so whatever they were stealing was likely jewels and cash. Maybe both. Zac didn't much care what they were stealing, only that they got away clean. And he'd make sure Redemption Harbor Consulting took care of the owners if for some reason their insurance didn't cover their losses.

"What about physical security?" Zac continued, wanting to cover as many important details as possible.

"None on Sundays. Times are tight, especially for high-end extras most people can't afford. There's minimal security during the week and none on Sundays since it's their slowest day."

Hmm. Neely knew enough about the store's security that he would've had to case it for a while. Unless he was lying, but Zac didn't think so. It wouldn't make sense to get Zac and Olivia arrested when he'd gone to a lot of trouble to bring Olivia into this. Which meant Neely had probably been in Miami at least for a few weeks. Whatever their end-game job was, Neely had been planning this whole thing for a while. Zac was glad Gage was listening because he could start looking into the CCTVs near the jeweler and seeing what he could find about Neely's movements. "The Kaira 2000 is state of the art. Not exactly cheap."

Neely nodded. "They got it so they could keep their insurance premiums low. And as far as exits, you two figure it out."

Very interesting that Neely knew all this.

"I'm running info on the store now," Gage said in his ear. "Got the building schematics. Best place to exit is one of the back two doors. The place is right on the water and close to a marina. You'll set off the alarm, but you'll be able to disappear easily enough if the cops aren't called right away."

"If something doesn't look right, we're leaving," Zac said, wanting to make sure that was clear. If this was some sort of setup—which he doubted—they were gone.

Neely didn't respond, but Maxwell, who'd been quiet, grunted in agreement.

"We're at the house that IP originated from," Gage said. "Not sure who's there but we're going to check it out. It's a residential neighborhood, seems quiet, has a few for sale signs, including the two houses on either side. Gonna go dark for however long it takes to recon this place. Need to have an open comm line with the guys."

Zac wanted to give him an affirmative response but couldn't risk it. If by chance Martina was in that house, this whole thing would be over for Olivia. She could go back to her life and her daughter and Martina would be safe. He understood why Gage was going dark too. If he, Brooks and Leighton had to storm the house, they'd have to use earpieces to stay connected if they infiltrated from different points.

He shut that thought off, not worried about his guys. They were all pros. And right now he had to have his head in this. Because they'd just arrived at the jewelry store.

"I'll drop you two off here," Neely said. "Then I'll drop Maxwell off a block away."

"What kind of distraction should I create?" Maxwell asked.

"Try to get the female employee's attention, focus completely on her, bordering on harassment, as you ask her to show you watches or whatever. Tell her you want something to go with your boots. It won't matter if they're short-staffed. Her father will come over to intervene or take over for her. Since you took away our phones," he said to Neely, "you're going to order six pizzas from the nearest place and have them delivered to Tatiana's. Tell them it's for a last-minute employee birthday party and that you'll be paying in cash." Not the most elegant distraction, but any distraction was good at this point. And an annoyed delivery guy was a classic.

Neely nodded once. "I've also got another distraction planned for you."

Okay, that information would have been helpful earlier. "What is it?"

"You'll know it when you see it. You need to crack that safe. That's your main concern."

Even though he hated to, Zac knew he had to depend on Neely now. He also hated that Gage had gone dark. But that was part of the job.

Hell, on jobs he'd taken before joining Redemption Harbor Consulting, he'd been on his own more often than not.

He took Olivia's hand as they slid from the SUV and was glad when she linked her fingers through his. He could sense her stress at the whole situation, but she definitely had her game face on. Again, he found he liked her even more. Yeah, he was attracted to her, but this woman had a steel spine. Hard not to respect that.

It was time to do this.

* * *

"Why'd you keep his gun?" Olivia asked as they casually strolled down the sidewalk. Neely had dropped them off a few shops down and so far they'd passed a bridal shop, a café, and a children's clothing boutique among other places that lined the shopping strip.

"Has my fingerprints on it."

"Oh." Of course. She noticed that Savage had subtly wiped his prints from the burner phone he'd given to Neely. And now he had on gloves. The cool weather was a good excuse to wear them.

"More importantly, it has his," he continued. "We're going to run them and see if Gage gets a hit. Maybe Neely is connected to other crimes under an alias, or has a warrant out for his arrest. Who knows."

"You won't really use the gun here, right?" she asked as they neared the jewelry store, her stomach tied up in knots. There were some lines she would never cross, no matter what.

"No."

She let out a subtle breath of relief. She hadn't thought he would, but didn't want to make any assumptions. While she might be attracted to him, she didn't *know* him. Not really. Even if she did trust him to have her back, there was still a lot they needed to learn about each other.

Her heart rate increased as they reached the glass-paneled front doors of the store. Gold, swirled script with the store's name was on the glass and underneath it proclaimed they were a family-owned shop that offered fine jewelry, watches, wedding pieces and custom designs.

Savage held the door open for her but kept his hand at the small of her back. She was grateful for his solid presence. Doing this in the middle of the day was insane but maybe that would work for them. The store owners wouldn't be expecting something like this in broad daylight. And she was really glad she'd kept up to date with safecracking through her current job. That was the only thing she was confident about—that she could actually open the safe. It just depended on how much time she had.

It took her eyes a moment to adjust to the interior lighting. The place wasn't as big as she'd assumed it would be, but it had a spacious feel. One giant chandelier hung over the middle display case, shining down on what she guessed was the bridal jewelry. That would likely be their best sellers so it made sense to showcase engagement and wedding rings. Two smaller chandeliers were on either side, illuminating other glittery pieces. The green marble floors were polished to perfection.

She took all this in within seconds, wanting to have every detail possible. A well-dressed woman in her thirties stood behind the middle display case, talking quietly to a couple holding hands as they looked at three different rings. An older man was at another display talking to a man in his forties, showing him a watch. The woman gave them a friendly greeting, welcoming them and telling them she'd be with them in a few moments before returning to her customers.

"Door to the back is behind the man," Savage murmured as he directed her to a display with necklaces.

"I see it." What they didn't know, however, was if there was someone in the back. They were depending on information from Kyle, someone she definitely didn't trust. Their goal was simple: get behind that door undetected, find the safe, crack it and empty the contents. Or at least take what they could. She hated everything about this job—that it was in the middle of the day, that they hadn't been able to do any recon and that there were people in the shop. Including the owners. She felt terrible about this, but not bad enough to stop. Not when Martina's life depended on it.

"We've recently started seeing each other and I'm looking to find you something that shows how much I appreciate you," he murmured for her ears only.

She nodded as he pointed at a sparkly eternity necklace. "White gold, about fifteen carats worth of diamonds, good clarity. At least forty grand, probably forty-five," she murmured. "You must appreciate me a lot."

In response he pulled her to him, leaned down so that his mouth was near her wig-covered ear. "I see Maxwell approaching the front door, as well as another couple." As he pulled back, the bell overhead jingled.

She turned to see Maxwell striding inside, attitude rolling off him. She wondered if that was part of his cover or if he was pissed to be part of this whole thing. In his new "costume," he looked so different than the polished, elegant man from just half an hour before. He didn't glance at them, just swaggered over to a display case on the right side of the room, far enough away from them that she couldn't see what he was looking at. The woman who owned the shop greeted him as well, her tone just as polite as before.

"Can I get some help over here?" he demanded, not bothering to look up. His voice was overly loud in the elegant shop, booming over the smooth voice of Frank Sinatra singing over the well-hidden speakers. And there was a nasally quality to it. He was playing his role well.

She murmured something to the original couple before hurrying around to where Maxwell was. The other couple split up, the woman going to look at necklaces while the man went for a rack of watches in a locked glass case.

"This one's nice," Olivia said absently as they slowly made their way down the line of displays, closer and closer to the door they needed to get through. It was cracked open slightly, she realized as they shifted positions.

"I want to see diamonds on you," Savage's voice wasn't loud, but he wasn't murmuring now. They were in full-on role-playing mode for this. She giggled and leaned up to nip at his chin. It felt weird to be so intimate with him in such a forced setting.

But she couldn't deny the attraction that simmered beneath the surface.

Out of the corner of her eye she watched as the male owner rang up the other customer who'd been looking at a watch. And she and Savage were a few steps closer to their destination. Adrenaline surged through her even as she tried to tame it. It had been years since she'd done anything like this. And the jobs she'd pulled had been at night, after hours with no one around except security. And she hadn't been a mom then. God, she felt as if her heart might jump from her chest right now. There was no rush to this, only a sick feeling. Because if they got caught, she'd go to jail and lose her daughter. She swallowed back bile at the thought.

"We got this," Savage said, pulling her closer.

"I know—"

"This is garbage," Maxwell said, his voice rising.

Olivia watched as the father hurriedly finished what he was doing. She and Savage were two steps closer now.

The bell above the front door jingled again and a man carrying a stack of pizza boxes strode in, looking around as if he wasn't sure this was the right place. At least Kyle had come through for them.

Savage tightened his grip on her as they moved farther down. They were steps from the little half door they'd need to get through to be behind the cases.

"I'm here with a delivery for Luis? For a birthday party."

"Young man, I'm Luis, but I guarantee you I did not order any pizzas. This is absolutely ridiculous." The man stepped out from behind the door, nodded once at her and Savage before hurrying past them.

"Well, someone's gonna pay for these pizzas."

"It certainly won't be us. I'll ask you to kindly leave," the owner said.

"Not yet," Savage murmured to her. "The opening will come, but not yet. When it does, don't look back. Stride through those doors like you belong."

"I will." And if anyone saw them, they'd just leave. Sure, they wouldn't get what they'd come for, but Kyle would have to understand. Or she prayed he would. No, she couldn't think about that now. She had to focus on the next step. Then the next. Not about anything else. Or she'd never be able to do this. As the moment hopefully approached, she subtly pulled her gloves from her pocket and slid them on.

"Are you kidding me? Are you saying I'm not worth a more expensive engagement ring?" The female half of the couple who had been here when they'd arrived was looking at her significant other, her hands on her hips.

Either this was Kyle's other distraction, or they'd just had really good luck.

"This isn't what I'm looking for." Maxwell's voice carried again, his back stiff, his posture hostile. "I want something with more bling."

"Almost," Savage murmured.

He was right. The female customer raised her voice again as the man with her raised his palms in a "calm down" gesture. Maxwell was bickering with the shop owner. And the father was still talking to the pizza delivery guy while keeping an eye on his daughter. No one was looking their way.

When a loud boom sounded from outside the store, like a car backfiring, all heads swiveled in that direction. Without waiting for Savage to tell her, she knew this was it.

Heart racing, she pushed the half door open and strode toward the door to the back, reaching it in three long strides. She and Savage were inside the hallway in seconds. If anyone had noticed what they'd done, they'd find out soon enough.

The hallway only stretched out in one direction so she hurried to the right and stopped at the second door on the left, since it was the only one with a keypad. Punching in the code Kyle had given them, she breathed a sigh of relief when the door swung open.

"Are you okay without me?" Savage asked as they stepped in.

"Yeah, I got this." The huge safe was in one corner. No way for something of that magnitude to be hidden.

"I'm going to find the security room and take the feeds."

"Okay." Moving into action she shut and locked the door behind him and hurried toward the safe. Her hands were surprisingly steady as she pulled out the drill and stethoscope. The drill was a last choice but she'd decided to take it with her just in case there were any surprises.

Though she hadn't told Kyle, she'd cracked this type of safe before in her regular job in under five minutes. Now she needed to do it in three. There was only so much time before one of the owners realized they'd never left out the front door. It all just depended on how long the distractions lasted.

She put the stethoscope on and tugged off one glove. She would wipe her prints off when she was done, but she needed a bare hand to do this part. It was difficult to explain to people how she did what she did. It was all about touch and sound. The pattern of clicks was distinctive.

Pressing her bare hand against the cold metal of the door, she listened and felt as she started turning the dial. Very much aware of the invisible clock ticking away, she closed her eyes. When she heard the first click she opened her eyes, made a note of the number. Seconds seemed to tick by forever until she heard and felt the second one. On and on until she heard the fifth and final click.

Now her hand trembled as she twisted the dial with the numbers she had, lining up the interior notches with the contact points until...click. Twisting the thick handle, she pulled open the door.

And froze at the sound of the office door handle twisting open behind her.

CHAPTER NINE

—Kicking ass and breaking shit; what Marines do best.—

Weapon tucked into a hidden holster under his leather jacket, Gage strode up to the front door of the one-story cottage-style house in Coconut Grove. White paint was chipping off the shutters, but the dark blue of the rest of the house looked as if it had been painted recently. The grass was cut and the flowerbeds in front of the small porch were perfectly neat. And there were tons of palm trees and other lush foliage in the front yard, along the side of the house and in the back. Good for privacy—but it was a double-edged sword because it was easier to infiltrate a place like this.

This place could belong to anyone—and according to the search he'd done, it belonged to an eighty-year-old woman who'd been born and raised in Miami. And according to one of her social media profiles, she was visiting her daughter in Omaha for a month. So no one should be here. The grass had been cut recently so she might have a service.

Didn't matter. Since he knew that a communication from the penthouse had gone to this address they had to check it out. If the older woman did answer he would pretend to be lost and ask for directions to a neighboring street with a similar name.

He knocked once and heard the faintest scuffing sound inside. Could be a pet, but he doubted it. Dogs or cats didn't try to be quiet, and if the woman was out of town she wouldn't have left a pet home. He knocked again and called out, "Mrs. Clark?"

There was another scuffling sound and he saw one of the curtains to his left flutter at the window. He glanced at his watch, looking bored in case anyone was watching. He called out her name again. When he got nothing, he took a step back.

"Someone's inside," he murmured to Leighton and Brooks who were on the other end of the comm line.

"I've got eyes on the back door. I can't hear anything from here," Brooks said quietly.

"I'm at the side window, east side of the house. Only one window is completely covered with aluminum foil."

Interesting.

"Mrs. Clark, it's John," he called out again. "I'm here about the vintage car you said you wanted to sell." He looked at his watch again. When he did, the door opened up.

A white man in his early thirties kept the door open, blocking it partially with his body.

Gage stepped forward and smiled. "I'm here about the car—"

"My aunt isn't selling it anymore."

"Oh, well I've been out of town for a month. Last time we talked she was looking to unload it." He took another step closer, held out his hand. "I'm John, by the way. I didn't realize she had a nephew."

"I'm inside," Brooks murmured through the comms.

The man just grunted, but didn't hold out his hand. Gage heard a thud at the same time the man did. When the guy turned, Gage reached for his own weapon and drew his leg back.

He slammed his boot into the door at the same time he pulled his pistol free. The man flew back as the door crashed open. His pistol clattered to the floor so Gage kicked it away even as he aimed his own on the man. "Don't fucking move," he ordered. "Got the guy at the front door," he continued, talking to his guys. God, some days he really missed being in the Marines.

"Got the other in the kitchen. He's restrained," Brooks said.

"And I've got the woman. She's scared but unharmed." Leighton.

Talk about a smooth operation. This was the way things should always go. As if they should be so lucky. "Put your hands above your head then roll over. I'm going to cuff you and if you fight me, you'll regret it."

"I have rights man! I demand to call my—"

Gage kicked the man's knee with his steel-toed boot. "I'm not a cop, dumbass. And you kidnapped a woman. I've got no pity for you. So shut up and do what I say. Now," he added when the man paused.

Less than a minute later Gage and Brooks had the two men sitting on the couch, hands tied behind their backs and their feet bound. He'd already taken their wallets and scanned their fingerprints. Neither had IDs on them but their fingerprints wouldn't lie.

"What is that thing?" The one sitting to the right—the white guy—asked.

The Hispanic man Brooks had taken down hadn't spoken at all.

Both had similar tattoos on their forearms, letting him know they belonged to the same gang or some sort of organization. One clearly not based on race. He took a photograph of the tattoos, planning to run them later.

Gage looked up from the mobile fingerprint scanner and set it down on the dusty armoire by the wall. What the hell did the guy think it was? "It's going to tell me exactly who you two are and all your affiliations if you have police records."

Both men's jaws tightened. Okay, so they were definitely in the system. Good.

Gage glanced at Brooks. "I need you to contact Sierra." Their code name for Savage.

Brooks nodded, gave the two men dark looks and stepped out of the room. Gage waited until he heard his friend shut the back door before turning to the men.

"This is how it's going to go. I'm going to ask questions, you're going to answer me. If you don't or if you lie, everyone in your life will pay. You got a woman you care for? Or a man—they'll pay for your crimes. I'll rip their life apart in a way that hurts. It's clear by now we're not cops or Feds. And we care very little about the law." Not exactly true, but he needed to make sure they were all on the same page. And he needed these men afraid of him. Sure, he could threaten torture, but that didn't always work. Hell, it rarely did. Unless done right. Gage wasn't into that shit—and they didn't have the time.

"You don't scare us." White Guy spoke again, clearly the chatty one of the two.

He lifted a shoulder. "I hacked my first website when I was eleven. It was my school's system. After that it was a game to see what I could get into. Which is why..." He picked up the scanner at the soft beep and half-smiled at the information that popped up on the small screen.

He quickly read off their stats including their names, aliases, significant others, known addresses and known associates. When he was done, both men had paled considerably.

"You two mean nothing to me. I just want information. But if I find out you hurt the woman in the kitchen, however—"

"We didn't!" White Guy again, and the Hispanic guy was nodding along with him.

"Good. If she says the same, then you might get out of this unscathed. What about the woman who owns this place?"

The speaker—Kenneth—spoke quickly. "We never met her or did anything to her. She's out of town for a month. The guy who hired us said it'd be fine to keep the other lady here if we lay low and didn't let any neighbors see us. And the two houses on either side are for sale. Empty. He wanted a place not connected to anyone."

Okay, that was believable given the area. They'd be able to lie low. And Gage had checked the owner's Facebook page an hour ago. It looked as if she was having fun with her daughter in Omaha. "Since you're being honest, it seems like we're off to a good start. Like I said, I don't care about you two morons. I want to know everything about the man you're working for, Kyle Neely. Otherwise, I'm going to bury everyone you love. Age and gender mean nothing to my men." A complete lie, but he needed full honesty and he needed it fast. In his experience most people caved quickly under the threat of torture or pain. There were exceptions of course, especially those tied to hardcore gangs or Spec Ops people, but guys like this? They'd give him what he wanted.

Fifteen minutes later he had everything he needed from them—and a confirmation from Martina Cruz that they hadn't assaulted or otherwise hurt her—so he, Brooks and Leighton marched them to their waiting SUV.

Both men had outstanding warrants so they were going to deliver them to the Miami PD anonymously.

"Make a stop at the nearest dollar store," Gage said to Brooks as he steered out of the neighborhood.

"Why?"

"I want to grab a couple bright red bows. It's going to be an early Christmas for the locals."

From the back seat, for the first time in ages, Leighton laughed, the sound harsh and rusty. "You want to deliver them with a bow."

And if Gage could pull a laugh from his friend—who refused to tell anyone why he was so withdrawn since coming home—hell yeah. Today was a good day. They'd saved a woman and Olivia could go back to her life.

* * *

There was nowhere for Olivia to hide as the office door swung open. She wanted to collapse in relief as Savage stepped in. "It's done. Everything's erased for the last forty-eight hours."

"Good." She turned back to the open door of the safe and quickly wiped off the front of it to get rid of her prints then tugged her glove back on.

Savage was already moving, putting stacks of cash and bagged gems into her purse. It took them thirty seconds working together to clean it out.

Palms damp inside her gloves, her heart an erratic tattoo against her chest, she jumped to her feet when they were done.

"We head out the exit door at the end of the hallway," Savage said.

Shaky and a little clammy, she nodded and moved with him to the office doorway. He cracked it a fraction and she heard murmured voices.

Shit.

"We have to make a break for it," he said low enough for her ears only. "You're going to slip out first and I'll be right behind you. Don't slow down." He took the bulging purse from her and looped it over his shoulder as if it weighed nothing.

Bracing for what they had to do, she stepped out into the hall, only glancing to the right once to see the father and daughter both looking shocked to see her. Without pause she raced the other way, her boots pounding against the thin carpet. Her legs strained and blood rushed in her ears. Not loud enough to cover the "Hey!" from behind them.

The exit door was so close. *Four, three, two—*

She slammed her hands into the metal bar even as the alarm blared. Either from the door opening or the owners setting it off. Didn't much matter. Now the race was on. The cops were being called.

The bright sunlight blinded her for a moment as they raced outside.

"This way." Savage grabbed her hand, tugging her west so they were heading toward the back of the string of shops. "There's a parking garage I think we can get to from here."

She could see the four-story building he was talking about as they ran. Risking a glance behind them, she wasn't surprised that no one was following. The owners wouldn't chase after them—because she and Savage could be armed. But they had a very small window before the police arrived and started a grid search for them.

Despite the cool weather and the breeze from the nearby marina, sweat poured down her spine and pooled between her breasts.

They raced past the backs of various shops and a restaurant, slowing down when they neared the end of the strip.

"We need to walk casually," Savage said as they stepped out onto a sidewalk. "Fast but casual."

"You know how to hot-wire a car?" she asked as they headed north now. The parking garage was so close. One more left at the next four-way stop and they should be there.

A siren blared in the distance, sending her heart rate skyrocketing. Savage didn't seem affected by it at all, his body language smooth and efficient.

"Yes. Left here," he said, though she knew where they were going at this point.

They fell in with the flow of the light foot traffic, weaving around an elderly couple even as a police car raced by the parallel street, blue lights flashing.

Without giving the vehicle a second look, she and Savage picked up their pace as they reached the garage.

"I know how to hot-wire too," she said once they stepped into the concrete stairwell. If they had to split up and look for a vehicle, she had no problem doing that. The faster they got out of here, the better.

As if he read her mind, he said, "We stick together. If they decide to put up roadblocks, we've got about eight minutes before that happens."

She knew the cops didn't always pull out the stops for a robbery, but depending on the crime, it was a very real possibility. What they'd just done was bold too. The diamonds they'd taken had to be worth at least two million. Not to mention the cash.

And she felt like garbage for having it at all.

Savage stopped at the second floor, pushed the metal door open. He glanced around, nodded once then grabbed her hand again.

She linked her fingers through his as they hurried up the nearest ramp. In twenty seconds he'd picked a four-door car at least fifteen years old, and in another sixty seconds they were at the first floor exit. After putting a twenty-dollar bill in the machine, the yellow lever lifted and for the first time in what felt like an eternity, Olivia sucked in a long breath. They were almost home free. For now.

"We should be good," Savage said, making a sharp left. The opposite direction from the jewelry store. "I'm..." He paused, then said, "You're sure?"

"What?" she asked.

"Talking to Brooks," he said, pointing to his ear.

She blinked, but realized he must have some sort of earpiece in. She had no idea how he'd gotten one, however, since they'd decided against using them.

"Martina's alive and okay. They're taking her back to the safe house."

"Wh— You're serious?"

He nodded even though she knew that yes, of course he was. He wouldn't lie about something like that.

Olivia wanted to talk to her, but knew they should get out of here first. "Tell her we'll be there soon."

"She knows." Savage reached out, squeezed her hand once. "You're going to be okay now."

Throat tight, she simply nodded and pulled her wig off. She absently finger combed it as she tried to digest that it was over. This mess was finally *over.* She wasn't sure how they were going to deal with Kyle overall, but at least her daughter and Martina were safe. "Thank you," she rasped out as a police car tore past them, thankfully not pausing.

He just grunted, which wasn't much of a surprise.

She didn't care. Soon she'd see Martina and then they could be reunited with Valencia. Her daughter and her dear friend were safe and sound.

CHAPTER TEN

—Sometimes the best things in life,
you never see coming.—

From the open kitchen of the safe house, Savage watched as Olivia sat on the living room couch with Martina, talking quietly and wiping away tears. Just from this visual it was clear how much the woman meant to her. Martina was a lot younger than he'd thought she'd be, in her mid-forties maybe. Olivia was barely thirty, so if Martina had started nannying for her when she was in her twenties, the age fit.

He told himself to look away from Olivia but it was hard to. Hell, impossible. He wasn't sure what was wrong with him, but something about her compelled him, pulled him to her. And since they'd shared that kiss, he couldn't get it out of his mind. She'd made the sexiest little sounds as she'd arched her body against his. She hadn't been acting or pretending either.

He sure hadn't. No, he'd wanted to take her right up against the nearest flat surface, to bury his face between her legs and see if she tasted as sweet as he imagined. Now the scent of vanilla would always remind him of her.

Which was why it was just as well that this job was over. Or at least her part in it was. He needed some distance from her.

"Are you listening to a thing I'm saying?"

He turned at the sound of Gage's frustrated voice. "What?"

Gage glanced past him at the women, then focused on Zac again. "We're going to have to break into the security place that houses the backup security for the jewelry store."

He nodded once. "I know." They'd already talked about it, so why was Gage bringing that up now?

"She's Skye's friend," Gage said quietly, taking him off guard.

Zac wasn't going to pretend he didn't know who Gage was talking about. "I know."

"And she comes to visit Redemption Harbor a lot."

"Why are you telling me obvious shit?" He might not have met her until a couple days ago but he'd heard of her and her daughter, knew how often they were out at the ranch.

Gage just lifted a shoulder and opened his mouth to say more when his phone buzzed across the granite countertop. He glanced at it once, frowned. "Huh."

"What?"

"Just got a ping that someone emailed Olivia."

Gage had been monitoring all her online accounts and her phone in case Neely reached out to her. After they'd escaped with the money and diamonds, they'd come to the safe house—and he'd made sure they weren't followed.

Next he and the others planned to go after Neely personally and make sure he was locked up forever. If that didn't work, Zac would do what needed to be done. He didn't relish the thought, and that wasn't what their company was about, but he was going to keep Olivia and her daughter safe no matter what.

"Hell," Gage muttered.

All the hairs on Zac's neck stood on end. Before he could ask what, Gage turned the laptop to him. The email was from an unknown sender. He read the text, his stomach tightening.

You think you're so clever. You might have your friend, but I still own you. Job's still on. You work with me, or this ends up in the right hands.

Below the text was a video feed. He clicked on it—and wanted to smash his fist through the screen.

There were various feeds from the jewelry store playing, including shots of him and Olivia. He'd seen where the cameras were and had avoided looking up. Olivia had too. Except in two shots, he realized. When they were leaving the office and as they left the building. That was the crystal clear image of her face. Even with the glasses and wig on, the shot of her was good. "Damn it," he muttered. "I erased those feeds."

"Which means he must have an inside guy at the backup security place. It's the only way he would have this," Gage said.

"He planned this. How the hell did I not see this?" Savage rubbed a hand over the back of his neck. He should have seen this. Or at least thought of it.

"I didn't either."

Out of the corner of his eye Zac saw Olivia stand. When he looked at her, she frowned.

"What is it?" She crossed the living room and was in the kitchen in seconds.

He turned the laptop toward her. "Looks like we're still on the job."

She paled as she watched the video. "How did he get this? I thought..." She looked up at Zac then, confusion and fear in her dark eyes.

Gage responded before Zac could. "He must have an inside guy at the backup place where the security feeds go. We'd planned to get in there and erase all the files tonight."

"I'm sorry," Zac said, his gaze still pinned to hers.

"It's not your fault."

"I should have thought of this. Neely seemed frustrated that we wanted to go in disguise. I should have—"

"Stop. You're not omniscient. And you've gone above and beyond what I ever could have expected when I went to Skye." She closed her eyes for a long moment. "Martina's safe now. Maybe I should just turn myself in and—"

"No," Zac said at the same time Gage did. Good. Glad his friend was on the same page. They were going to fix this for her. She wasn't going to jail and losing her daughter.

"Now that Martina is safe we've got a little breathing room. Because no way is he going to turn this over to anyone before he gets what he needs from you," Zac said.

"What about when the job is over? He'll have no reason to keep that video to himself."

"Maybe. But in the meantime, we'll find dirt on him. If we get blackmail on him, he won't turn on you."

She slowly nodded. "Mutually assured survival. And he won't want to go to jail. No way. Okay." She pushed out a long breath, her expression still pinched. "I want to get Martina out of here and back to Redemption Harbor."

"We'll get her on a flight out tonight—on the private plane," Gage said.

"Where am I going now?" Martina joined them, hands on her hips.

Olivia reached out and gently placed her hands on Martina's shoulders. "It turns out things aren't quite over with Kyle. So you're going to fly out tonight and be with Valencia. She needs you and I need you both safe."

"Who will keep *you* safe?"

"I will," Zac said automatically.

Martina looked at him then, her dark eyes narrowing as she sized him up. Then she nodded once and turned back to

Olivia to pull her into a tight hug. "I don't want to go, but I'll take care of our little one."

"I know you will," Olivia rasped out as she hugged her friend back.

Zac looked away to give them the semblance of privacy but was already thinking of the next step. They had to figure out what this job was before it happened. And if they couldn't, they'd have to go through with it. No matter what, Neely was going down and Olivia was walking away from all this.

"I'm responding to him," Gage said, his fingers flying over the keyboard.

Seconds later they got a response from Neely. *Be at the penthouse tomorrow by nine. Come alone.*

Zac snorted as he read the message. That definitely wasn't happening.

* * *

Zac knocked softly on the door to Olivia's room. When she didn't answer, he opened the door. Which, okay, was rude, but he didn't care. She'd been completely silent on the way back from the private airport where they'd dropped off Martina. When they got back she'd said she was coming upstairs to Skype with Valencia but something about her tone was off.

When he stepped inside he saw a small bag open on the bed, including climbing and rappelling gear next to it. Before he'd moved farther into the room she stepped out of the bathroom, a small toiletry bag in her hand.

She jerked to a halt, her eyes widening as she set the bag down. "What—" She cleared her throat, her cheeks flushing a sexy pink as she glanced at the stuff on the bed. "Um..."

"Planning on going somewhere?" He shut the door behind him and strode into the room until he stood next to the bed.

"He told me to come alone tomorrow." Her voice was small, quiet, and the stress lines bracketing her mouth made him want to punch Neely again.

"Well you're not." He shoved the bag and gear to the side and climbed onto her bed, stretching out with his hands propped behind his head as if he had every right to be there.

"What the hell are you doing?" Hands on her hips, anger suffusing her cheeks now instead of guilt, she looked even sexier. Her dark hair was down around her shoulders and her eyes flashed with fury.

"What's it look like? I'll be your shadow until we leave in the morning. In case you try to do something stupid."

"I... You..." She let out a frustrated growl and stood there for a few long moments before setting the bag and other things on the ground with a sigh.

Then to his surprise she climbed on the king-sized bed and lay next to him. There was a foot of space between them and her head was on the other pillow, but he could reach out and touch her if he wanted. Which he *did* want, but touching her was off-limits. She was part of the job. Nothing more. How many times was he going to tell himself that? Maybe if he said it enough, he'd believe it.

Sighing, she closed her eyes. "I feel like everything in my life is a giant mess."

"Did you really Skype with Valencia earlier?" He wasn't sure if that had been a lie so she could try to sneak out.

"Yeah. She's excited Martina is coming to see her, and I can tell she misses me...but she seems okay. I've just never been separated from her before. She's only ever had sleepovers at Martina's. I don't know, maybe it's harder on me than her," she murmured.

"Kids are resilient, which is good for you and her. And it's barely been a day, even if it feels like longer."

"You're right." Her voice was still soft, a little tired, and she hadn't opened her eyes yet.

He couldn't stop looking at her. "I'm always right."

She snorted, the sound making him smile, especially since she still hadn't opened her eyes. "You really are a bossypants."

He laughed, something strange happening in his chest. "I've never been called that before. Not that politely anyway."

"Well my daughter is a bossypants—or so she's been told by her friends at school. Which, she most definitely is." She laughed lightly and opened her eyes, looking right at him. "My strong-willed, sweet girl has no problem taking charge."

He swallowed hard, feeling out of his depth with this woman. His only plan had been to do this job, keep her safe and go home. *Do the job.* That was almost always his motto. Or it had been before he'd met Olivia. "I'm sure she got that from you," he murmured. Olivia was so close he could just lean over, brush his lips over hers. But he didn't.

Not yet. Maybe never. God, Gage was right. He couldn't do anything with her. She was friends with Skye and he didn't relish hurting a woman anyway. And he didn't think he was capable of more than one-night stands.

"Yeah, maybe. Martina too."

"Tell me about her." Because he wanted to know every facet of Olivia's life. How she'd become who she was. "She's a lot younger than I imagined."

"Yeah, she started watching me when she was about twenty. My mom had gone through a bunch of nannies over the years. Finally when we got to Martina I knew I was never letting her go. I was five at the time and man, I just fell in love with her. There was a realness to her, like she actually wanted to be there with me. After I was too old to need a nanny her position in the house shifted and she pretty much took care of my parents' home when they were out of the country—which was often."

"Your parents trusted her."

"They did. And in her own way, I think my mother liked Martina. She was grateful to her at least for all she did." Her head fell back against the pillow. "Martina always said my mother was a complex woman, but honestly, I think she was just a selfish woman who didn't have time for me. The only good thing she ever did was make Martina a full-time employee which meant she got health care and had stability."

"What about Martina's family?" He tried to order himself to stop asking questions. The more he learned about her, the deeper he fell.

"She had terrible taste in men." Olivia grinned, the action fleeting. "One of the things we have in common. Her ex was a deadbeat and split as soon as Martina's son was born."

"She has a son?"

"Did. He died. Car accident, from a drunk driver."

"Damn."

"Yeah. I don't know how she held up so well. Once when I was much older and about to become a new mom myself, she told me that I was the only reason she held on. Because she still had a daughter." Olivia's voice cracked once. She swallowed hard and continued. "I don't care what anyone says. Blood isn't what makes you family."

"Agreed." Brooks, Colt, Gage—all of them, they were his family now. Skye too, even though he hadn't known her as long.

"So what's the deal with you? I've pretty much spilled my life story to you."

"I told you stuff before."

Her lips quirked up. "Stuff?"

He rolled onto his back, looking at the ceiling. "About my past."

"Hmm." She scooted a little closer so they were almost touching.

He froze for a moment, not even breathing. That move was definitely intentional but he had no idea what it meant.

His heart rate was completely jacked up, something he wasn't used to. Not in the field when he'd been in the Corps, not on the job when he'd done contract work, and not usually with women. Sex had always been take it or leave it. If he'd had a scratch, he'd gotten it itched with a willing partner who understood that he was only interested in sex.

This...whatever this thing was with Olivia felt different. It *was* different. He didn't know if he was ready for that. Or would ever be ready for that. "Fine. What do you want to know?"

"Tell me what you did before working with Skye."

He cleared his throat. "I'm not a good person, Olivia." Something she needed to understand. He didn't want her to think he was in any way a white knight or a good person.

"I don't think there is good or bad or black and white. Not always. People are too complicated for that."

"I've killed people." He tightened his jaw, not able to say more than that. But she needed to know what kind of man he was. She might have made stupid mistakes when she was younger, and maybe some of them weren't mistakes but conscious wrong choices. But she'd changed her life, was a different person now. And she'd certainly never killed anyone. What he'd done—no, he wasn't sure he deserved to even be lying next to her.

She scooted a little closer until her head was resting on his shoulder. "If that's supposed to shock me, it doesn't."

Well she'd sure as hell shocked him. And when she curled up against him, he wasn't sure what the hell was going on. So he wrapped his arm around her and pulled her closer. With his free hand, he reached out and clicked off the lamp on the nightstand and she didn't protest.

He could tell himself that he was staying here because he didn't trust her not to try and leave to meet with Neely. But the truth was he was staying because there was nowhere else he wanted to be.

CHAPTER ELEVEN

—So...that happened.—

Olivia cracked her eyes open and realized that yep, she was curled up against Savage as if she had every right to do so. She wasn't sure what had possessed her earlier—maybe the thought of going to jail if things went south—but when he'd stretched out on her bed as if he belonged there, she'd lost her mind and decided to snuggle up with a tiger. And that was exactly what Savage was. A sexy, muscular predator. Who was surprisingly sweet. She wanted nothing more than to get naked with him.

His chest rose and fell steadily, the solid strength of him comforting. Moonlight streamed in from one of the big windows. A cluster of palm tree branches swayed in a slight wind and she could hear a dog barking in the distance. Everything about this moment was surreal. Being here at all was just too weird.

When she looked up she found Savage watching her, wide awake, his eyes piercing in the dim light. She sucked in a breath, startled. Moonlight played off the hard angles of his strong face. He was so hard to read.

"How long have you been awake?" she whispered, because talking any louder somehow felt wrong.

In response, his gaze dipped to her mouth. That single, blatantly *hungry* look sent a ribbon of heat curling through her.

Even though she knew it was like teasing a wild animal, she reached up and traced her finger over his bottom lip. Because apparently she'd lost her damn mind.

His eyes went heavy-lidded but he didn't pull away. Part of her had hoped he would. Then she wouldn't be making what was most likely a mistake. But thoughts of the two of them, naked, entangled together...she really wanted that.

Instead, he nipped her finger—and heat pooled between her legs. God, this man. This whole situation was insane. And she wanted him completely in a way she'd never experienced with anyone before.

She hadn't been with anyone since before Valencia was born. In fact, she was pretty sure she'd forgotten everything to do with sex. Or...maybe not. She let out another little moan as he slowly bit down on her finger.

"I'm not a good man," he growled, before moving lightning fast and pinning her underneath him.

All the air whooshed from her lungs as she stared up at him, her heart beating out of control. His green eyes looked darker in the muted light of the room, but the hunger in his expression was clear. And she desperately wanted to peel off all his layers of clothing so she could finally see what he was hiding. "Okay."

"I can't offer you what you deserve," he continued, the hard length of his covered erection pressing against her lower abdomen.

She spread her legs wider, simultaneously glad and annoyed she had clothes on too. Why was her mind immediately going to full-blown sex? "I'm not asking for anything. Except maybe an orgasm—or three."

He blinked once at her boldness, then made this sexy, growling sound before slowly lowering his head to hers. He was clearly giving her time to put the brakes on, to stop things. Yeah, not happening. Right now she had no clue what the future held and she wanted to experience all Savage had to offer.

Somehow this dark, sexy man had gotten under her skin. She'd never seen him coming. She'd never even imagined a man like him in her fantasies. Which probably said more about the sad state of her fantasies.

When his mouth brushed against hers, it was like something electric passed between them, wild and out of control. She felt the soft touch of his lips straight to all her nerve endings and wanted more. So much more. They might have kissed before, but this was different.

She was on her back. In a bed. And they weren't doing this for any other reason than they wanted to. And she really, really wanted to be naked soon. More than that, she wanted *him* naked. What she felt under her fingertips—the hardness of his chest and shoulders—she wanted to feel all of that bare. She wanted to wrap her fingers around his hard length, to stroke him until he came.

He groaned into her mouth as she clutched onto his shoulders. Then she wrapped her legs around him, arching into him. She was like a cat in heat, wanting to curl her entire body around him and not let go.

When he pulled back, his mouth leaving hers, she blinked up at him. "You're stopping?" Why did she have to sound all panicked? That was not a woman in control. And she felt like she'd been in control, or attempted to be, the last six years.

Until Savage.

"I'm going to strip you. Then you're going to come against my mouth." Harsh, guttural, set-her-panties-on-fire words.

Her brain short-circuited and all she could manage was a nod as another rush of heat flooded between her legs. Had anyone ever said anything so sexy to her? She was pretty sure *no*.

Her nod was all he needed as he reached for the clasp of her jeans and oh so slowly, intentionally and torturously tugged them down her legs. After changing out of her getup from this morning, she'd also changed out of the sexy panties into plain black cotton bikini briefs. Which she was most definitely regretting. From now on she vowed to only wear sexy lingerie—or nothing at all.

Savage didn't seem to care as he stared up at her from the foot of the bed where he knelt between her spread legs. Watching her closely, he tossed her jeans to the side and climbed back up the few feet, his movements slow, deliberate and setting all her nerve endings on fire.

She wanted him to touch her anywhere, everywhere, right now. It was as if he was moving in slow motion, deliberately trying to make her crazy with need. Or more likely it had just been so long since she'd been naked with a man that she was feeling anxious and needy.

Of course the fact that this was happening with Savage, a man who defined sexiness, was what made all the difference.

"Faster," she whispered before she realized she'd meant to speak.

He paused, his hands poised under the material of her panties. "Now I'm going to go even slower." A dark, sensual promise.

She swallowed hard as he did just that, tugging the material down her legs so damn slowly she could hardly stand it. The only thing that made her feel better was that he was so very clearly affected by her too. His chest rose and fell rapidly, his breathing increasing as her pussy was exposed to him.

He actually paused again, staring, transfixed at the juncture between her thighs before he tossed the scrap of material to the ground.

She'd never had anyone look at her like this. As if she was a safe full of precious gems. She swore her heart skipped a beat. It was as if he wanted to devour her whole.

What a way to go too.

"Shirt off," he growled and it took her a moment to realize that he wanted *her* shirt off.

Okay, how sexy was it that he was talking in incomplete sentences? With trembling hands, she tugged the T-shirt off and went to remove her bra but he took over.

"Oh no, that's my job," he murmured, brushing his lips over hers again as he reached behind her back and unfastened the strap. When she was completely bared to him a shiver racked her body.

She kept in shape and was comfortable with her body for the most part. But she hadn't been naked in front of a man for ages, and Savage wasn't just any man. It was as if he'd been carved from stone. And she hadn't even seen him without his clothes on. She was just going by the outline of all those hard lines and muscles from the way his T-shirt stretched against his broad shoulders and wide chest.

"You're the most beautiful thing I've ever seen." His words sounded savage and hard as his gaze swept over her from head to toe. "Perfection." Taking her completely by surprise, he cupped her mound in the most possessive act. He didn't slide a finger inside her, just held her as he watched her intently. "Tell me if you want to stop."

She shook her head, not trusting her voice. Stop? Um, hell no.

The slow smile he gave her was just a little bit wicked, a lot sexy, and it made her inner walls clench with unfulfilled need. She wished he *had* slipped a finger or two inside her because she felt empty.

He kissed her again, covering her body with his, all while keeping his hand on her mound. As if claiming her. Whatever he was doing, it made her insides all melty.

She wrapped around him, digging her fingers into his back even as she dug her heels into his very sculpted backside. She felt as if she could crawl right out of her skin, especially when he cupped one of her breasts and so very gently rubbed his thumb over her already hard nipple.

Needing to feel more of him too, she grasped the hem of his T-shirt and tugged it over his head. He pulled back and finished the job for her, tossing it away.

Then his mouth was on hers again, teasing and taking as she arched her back. She wanted to get a better view of his bare chest, but touch would have to do for now.

Her inner walls tightened again when her hard nipples brushed against his chest. It was like sensory overload having all this deliciousness against her. Running her fingertips down the hard planes of his chest and abdomen, she kept going until she reached his covered, hard erection.

She wanted to strip him fully too, but it seemed he had other plans when he started kissing a path down her body, stopping to tease her breasts and feather kisses along her stomach. He'd said he could offer her nothing but this didn't feel like nothing.

She moaned, knowing exactly what he had planned. Lifting her hips, she was pretty close to begging by the time he was crouched between her spread thighs.

Instead of jumping right into business, he teased a finger down her folds. "You're so wet. Is this for me?"

She nodded.

"Say it." A soft demand.

Oh, he really was bossy. "It's for you."

"I'm going to make you come now." A dark-edged promise.

She nodded again as pleasure spread through her. *Yes, please.*

"I want to hear my name when you come."

"Yes."

"Say it now."

"Savage."

"*My* name."

"Zac."

Something that looked a lot like possessiveness glinted in his eyes before he dipped his head, nipping at one inner thigh, then the other. Her legs trembled with each nip. This was too much and not enough.

She needed so much more from him and was restraining herself from reaching down and rubbing her clit. It wasn't going to take much to get her off. Her inner walls were clenching and her clit was pulsing and aroused. She couldn't ever remember being so worked up. Sex had always been nice, pleasant.

This was something else entirely.

There was nothing nice about it. She felt raw and vulnerable in front of him and she didn't care. Because she knew he would make this good.

Sliding her fingers through his dark hair, she gripped his head. "My clit," she rasped out. She really, really wanted him to tease her there. And she wasn't above demanding it.

The soft chuckle against her thigh made her moan again. And when he teased a finger against her folds, she froze, waiting for him to push inside her. She'd never wanted anything more than she wanted this.

Finally, he pushed one finger inside her, his thick digit spreading her and filling her. God, if just his finger felt this good... She arched off the bed when he added another. The intrusion was more than welcome.

Then his mouth was on her clit and she couldn't think, could barely breathe as she writhed against his face. Pleasure punched through her, the sweet sensation of his kisses and his strokes inside her making everything short-circuit in her brain.

"Oh, God."

He growled against her pussy and she had a vague understanding of what he wanted her to say.

"Zac." His name, on her lips. Oh yeah, she could definitely give that to him. "Zac," she moaned again. As long as he gave her the orgasm that was rushing to the surface, and didn't pull back, she'd say his name all night long. And she couldn't wait until he was shouting her name. Because she wanted to bring him just as much pleasure.

He added another finger and the climax that had been steadily building slammed through her. Her toes curled as wave after wave of pleasure punched through her, making her lightheaded as she arched up against the bedcover.

"Fuck," he growled against her, not letting up with his teases even when it became too much to handle.

The pleasure-pain ratio was off-balance as he continued stroking his tongue against her clit.

"Too much," she rasped out, her fingers tightening against his head.

He stopped then, looked up at her from between her legs. The sight was so sexy and a little dirty, his mouth inches from her pussy, glistening slightly from her slickness.

Her mouth fell open as she stared at him, unable to look away. She didn't want to either. "That was—"

He curled his fingers still inside her and she yelped, arching off the bed at the unexpected move. Oh so slowly he withdrew his fingers—and then licked them one by one, keeping his gaze locked on hers.

She swallowed hard. He totally just did that. And she realized she was way out of her depth. She'd never been with anyone like him before, was pretty sure there wasn't anyone like him anyway. He just seemed so primal and raw and she really wanted to give him as much pleasure as he'd given her.

"Take your pants off," she whispered.

His eyebrows shot up but he did as she said, getting off the bed and quickly shucking his jeans. For some reason she wasn't surprised to find he went commando.

She was surprised, however, at the sight of his cock. Long and thick, it curved up from the perfection of his body, begging for her attention. She might feel out of her depth right now but she wasn't going to let that stop her.

Getting onto her knees, she moved over as he crawled onto the bed. "On your back." She tried to make the words sound like a command, but instead she did that whole breathy thing again. Because around him, finding her voice was proving to be difficult.

He paused, his knees depressing into the bed as he watched her. Then he reached out, cupped her face. "I like to be in control in the bedroom."

She wasn't sure how to respond but didn't have to because he lay on his back. He was...letting her take control. Which made her feel all the more powerful. A man like Savage—Zac—would never give up control lightly. And okay, he wasn't exactly doing so now. Not truly. But he was at least giving her the illusion of it. Which was pretty amazing in itself.

Shimmying up his body, she straddled his legs as she wrapped her fingers around his hard length.

His jaw tightened as he rolled his hips up into her hold. When he groaned out her name, she really felt powerful.

She stroked him again and again, unable to stop watching as his huge body writhed under her touches, her stroking.

Granted, her experience was limited. But this was definitely the sexiest thing she'd ever experienced. A man this powerful and strong giving up control as she worked his cock had her growing even wetter when she should be sated.

With her free hand she cupped one of her breasts, teasing her already hard nipple.

"Oh yeah." He groaned again, his gaze pinned to what her hands were doing.

"Come for me, Zac." She'd never been a talker during sex but she desperately wanted to give him the pleasure he'd given her.

It was as if her words set something off inside him. Maybe it was the order or the fact that she'd said his name. His hips jerked and he started climaxing in long harsh jerks, his come shooting all over his stomach and her hand.

And the sounds he made had all the muscles in her body pulling taut. There was nothing polite or nice about the way he came.

As he fell back against the bed he reached for her, pulling her down to him—and rubbing his come on her stomach with one hand.

She wasn't sure if there was a response for that, but somehow wasn't surprised by Savage's raw action.

He nuzzled his mouth against her neck and behind her ear as he curled his body around hers. Shivers danced down her spine at the contact. She threw a leg over him even as she slid an arm around his back. She couldn't get enough of this man, and no matter what tomorrow brought she hoped this wasn't something casual for him.

Yeah, she'd said she wasn't asking him for anything, and she wasn't. But he'd awakened feelings inside her she hadn't known existed. She didn't want to walk away from whatever might blossom between them. She hoped he didn't want to either.

CHAPTER TWELVE

—Just another asshole.—

Olivia opened her eyes at the sound of her cell phone alarm going off. She'd set it a couple hours before they had to head out because she wanted to leave nothing to chance. She still had to shower and go over all her gear since Neely had told her to bring it. She'd be bringing extra gear for Zac too, just in case they needed it. It was definitely better to be overprepared when it came to a job like this.

But first, coffee.

She was disappointed that Zac wasn't in bed with her, but she vaguely remembered him waking up and telling her he was going to snag a quick shower not too long ago.

Now in the light of day she had no regrets. Last night—or technically early this morning—had been amazing. They'd dozed for a little while after that first round and then he'd shown her once again how talented he was with his mouth and hands. They hadn't had full-on sex even though she'd been ready. He'd been hesitant and she wasn't going to push.

She eased open the bedroom door and stepped out onto the Persian runner lining the long hallway. She wasn't sure where they'd found this "safe house," as Zac called it, but it was comfortable and lush. Coastal-style art could be found all around the place, mostly by local artists, Brooks had said. And there was a whole lot of natural light streaming in from skylights in the living room, kitchen and in a couple of the bedrooms.

Her feet were silent on the stairs. The scent of rich coffee brewing made her smile as she reached the bottom step. When she heard Zac's voice rumbling she smiled even more as her body flared to life. Just his voice sent little tingles of awareness out to all her nerve endings. Today she had to face an enemy but at least she had him by her side.

Turning at the end of the stairs she moved down the hallway toward the kitchen, passing the brightly colored images depicting South Beach—and froze as she heard her name.

"Olivia's a sweet woman. You can't do what you always do with women." Brooks's voice. She didn't know him well but his subtle drawl was unmistakable.

"I'm not doing anything," Zac said.

"Bullshit. I heard you two last night."

Olivia winced, only feeling a touch of embarrassment. She shrugged it off, however. She was a grown-ass woman. And she and Zac were consenting adults. She had nothing to be embarrassed about. But the tone of Zac's voice was off and it made something heavy settle in her stomach.

"Last night is none of your business."

"Yeah, it is. Because she's a big part of Skye and Colt's life. And so is her daughter. How awkward is it going to be after this job when you—"

"When I what? We're none of your business. She's a grown woman and last night was just fun. For both of us. She's not looking for anything serious. And I'm not looking to get saddled with a ready-made family. So back off and mind your own business."

His words were a slap of ice-cold water in her face. A chill snaked down her spine as she took a step back. She'd told him she wasn't asking him for anything and he hadn't made any promises. But she'd thought that maybe… Well, who the hell cared what she'd thought? It clearly didn't matter.

Coffee forgotten, she backtracked the way she'd come, and once she reached the bedroom she locked the door. It wouldn't stop him if he really wanted in, but he'd respect her privacy. It wasn't as if he was looking for anything anyway.

Apparently she'd needed that reminder. They were meeting Kyle today but she was on her own. Last night had been exactly what it was. Fun.

Now it was over.

As she tried to shake off the chill that invaded her veins she started the shower, cranking it all the way to the hottest setting. It was time to get ready. Then they were finishing whatever the hell they needed to with Kyle—and she just prayed they'd be able to retrieve the blackmail he had on her. If they couldn't... She shoved that thought back into a tight mental box. One step at a time.

She just needed to be ready for today. Unfortunately, she couldn't stop thinking about last night. Which, in hindsight, had been stupid. She had no business being with a man like Savage. He was helping her because she was a job to him. Nothing more. She wasn't going to hang on to any regrets because that served no purpose.

But she'd do well to remember that she was just a job to Savage. That they'd just had "fun," nothing more.

* * *

"Is everything okay?" Zac asked Olivia as they strode down the sidewalk toward the hotel's front entrance.

She'd been distant to him all morning and he hadn't wanted to ask why in front of the others. Technically Gage was listening because both he and Olivia had decided to wear earpieces today. Just in case they needed backup or Neely ordered them to go dark again they wanted to be in contact with their team. If they were scanned again, well, it was a risk they were going to have to take.

"Just ready to meet with Kyle." Cool, clipped words. With her oversized sunglasses on it was impossible to read her.

Despite the cooler weather, two women wearing bikinis and roller skates—with knee-high socks—glided past them on the oversized sidewalk. Damn it, they were almost to the entrance of the hotel and then it was game face on. "I mean about us."

"Why wouldn't I be? Last night was fun. Took the edge off. But…I think it should be a one-time thing. We'll do what we have to in front of Kyle but when we're alone…" She lifted a shoulder, but the movement was awkward, stiff.

What. The. Hell.

Where had the sensual woman from last night gone? The woman who'd opened up to him? The woman who'd moaned his name as he buried his face between her legs. The woman who had him all twisted up inside so much that he'd lied to his best friend.

This morning he'd told Brooks that she meant nothing to him. Because if he admitted the truth, it meant admitting that she'd *more* than gotten to him. That he wanted to see where this thing between them went after this op. That if she was willing, he wanted the chance to get to know her daughter too. To be…in a relationship with Olivia. The thought of that didn't terrify him either.

But this cold shoulder from her? Yeah, that did. He didn't like her pulling away from him, and all of his possessive instincts were flaring to life.

He tightened his jaw as he reached the rotating door and stepped through with Olivia. He'd just have to deal with whatever the hell was going on later. They'd arrived.

In the lobby he slid an arm around her shoulders, pulling her close. She wasn't exactly stiff but she didn't melt into him either.

"You're gonna have to sell it more," he murmured. "Make Neely believe we're still an item."

She leaned into him, wrapping her arm around his waist, but didn't remove her sunglasses as they headed for the elevators. Wearing sunglasses inside wasn't strange in Miami but he hated that he couldn't see her eyes. Especially since he'd seen every inch of her naked last night, had tasted all of her—was now addicted to her.

This was why he didn't do relationships or any of that shit. When you let people in, they just let you down.

He rolled his shoulders as the elevator doors shut, closing them inside alone. "If you need help remembering why we're so good together I can remind you of the way you moaned my name last night. 'Harder, Zac. Faster, Zac,'" he murmured. Okay, maybe he wasn't able to lock all this shit back up in a box.

She jabbed him in the ribs with her elbow. "Shut up, Savage."

Oh, so they were back to Savage now?

He tightened his jaw again. Hell no. Maybe in front of everyone else he was Savage—especially for this job—but when they were alone, it was going to be Zac from this point forward. He refused to go back to the way they were before. Before he'd gotten to know her. Before she'd gotten under his skin.

"You know what I'm picturing right now?" he continued before she could respond. "You, stretched out naked on the bed, your beautiful breasts bared to me, all wet from my mouth."

Her breathing increased slightly as the doors whooshed open on the top floor. "You're a jackass," she whispered.

"I've been called worse." There was no guard at the door today which could mean any number of things.

Zac tensed, going into operator mode, putting everything else into a tight mental box when the door opened and Kyle stepped out.

His lips pursed at Savage but he didn't seem surprised to see him. "I said come alone." His words were dry.

"Where she goes, I go."

Almost absently, Neely nodded. "Get inside and toss your phones into the bowl by the door." Stepping back, he impatiently motioned for the two of them to enter.

Zac kept his body half blocking Olivia's as they entered the room. The same guys from the day before were there, including Maxwell. He nodded once at the guy, who nodded back. There was someone else there—and by the way Olivia stiffened, he didn't think the man was a good addition.

Though he hated to do it, he dropped his phone into the bowl and Olivia did the same. At least Gage was on the comms. If shit went sideways, they had backup. It would just be a matter of overpowering any threat and staying alive long enough for the cavalry to arrive. And in his experience, he was his own damn cavalry.

"Go stand over there with the others." Neely's voice was sharp.

Zac looked at the window where the unknown man stood and at the others sitting on the couch or loveseat. Neely wanted them all in the same area—which meant they'd all be easy targets. Yeah, he did not like this setup at all.

Maybe he was overreacting but Zac didn't care. He slapped Olivia's butt. "Grab me a drink?" If he could get her closer to the bedroom door, it was something. There was another exit door through that bedroom so she had a better shot of escaping than anyone.

Right now there was a tension in the room and he wasn't sure what it stemmed from. Maybe Neely was pissed about losing Martina as leverage. But no, he had leverage on Olivia now. Something else was going on. He could feel it.

Olivia looked as if she wanted to argue with Zac but nodded and strode toward the minibar, the sway of her hips too much of a distraction so he looked away.

"You, stand with the others." Neely nodded, not moving far from the door.

Something was definitely off, but now wasn't the time to push anything. He'd been in enough tense situations that he'd learned to play things out. To be patient.

As soon as he'd crossed the room, Neely withdrew a pistol and pointed it at everyone—except Olivia.

"Turns out we have a Fed in our midst," the man snarled, moving his gun over everyone until he paused on Zac.

CHAPTER THIRTEEN

—Fuck.—

Zac realized the weapon wasn't trained on him, but Alonso. The man looked just as he had yesterday—black jacket, black everything else right down to his boots. Like a biker version of Johnny Cash.

"You're gonna want to move that thing away from me." Alonso's voice was deep if slightly disinterested.

Zac noticed the others in the room shift nervously, but Alonso was calm, his body relaxed. Interesting.

"Not happening." Neely took a step forward, but there was still plenty of distance between him and everyone else. So he could take a shot—however stupid it would be—and not miss Alonso or worry about anyone disarming him.

Out of the corner of his eye, Zac noticed Olivia had moved a step closer to the bedroom. Good. He didn't look at her directly, however, wanting all his focus on the current threat.

"I learned something very interesting," Neely continued. "Someone—from an unknown branch of government—called the local PD yesterday and told them to hold off on looking into the jewelry heist. Now, I can hear what your argument is going to be. It must have been the new guy." He swung his pistol toward Zac, held it there for a long moment.

Zac stared coldly at him. It wasn't the first time someone had held a weapon on him and it likely wouldn't be the last.

"But that fucker has worked with Morales. And if he was a Fed, I'd be in jail right now on kidnapping charges and he wouldn't be here. I know it's not Olivia." He snorted as if the thought was utterly ridiculous. "And everyone else I've worked with before. Except you. You were recommended to me by an acquaintance. Sure, you've got the reputation, and what I've seen so far of your skills is solid. But something is off. I can smell it. And I never ignore my instinct—and you were by yourself for a while yesterday while we were gone."

Zac's heart rate kicked up a notch. Neely was either going to call the whole thing off and bail town and the unknown job—which meant Olivia would be a target any time in the future Neely wanted to blackmail her. Or Neely was about to kill Alonso. And Fed or not, that wasn't happening on Zac's watch. Even if the guy was just a regular criminal, Zac wasn't letting Neely shoot him right here. Some part of him simply couldn't let that happen. He'd killed before. More times than he wanted to think about. But things had changed since he'd started with Redemption Harbor.

"So what's the plan? Kill the Fed here?" Zac snorted, making his derision clear.

Neely jerked slightly, seeming surprised by the interruption. His gaze narrowed.

Zac lifted a shoulder. "If you're going to get rid of him, do it away from the hotel. There are too many cameras here. And if you shoot him, they'll find blood. It doesn't matter how good of a job you do cleaning it up. Not to mention someone will hear the shot—unless you have a suppressor lying around. Either way, this is sloppy. I don't care what you've got on my girl, we're not working with someone sloppy."

Neely's eyes narrowed even more, fully sizing Zac up. "I know," he finally said. "That's why you're going to get rid of him."

Well, he had told Neely he was a cleaner. This was a test. He either got rid of Alonso, thus solidifying his reputation. Or he refused. And Neely would shoot him and probably Olivia, and just back out of the job entirely.

Next to him he sensed Alonso shift slightly, his arm muscles tensing as he prepared for whatever was about to happen.

Fuuuuck.

Zac shook his head and stood. "Look, I'm not—" He struck out with his boot, slamming into Alonso's knee. He just needed to disable the guy, not kill him. From there, he'd figure things out. One step at a time.

Alonso grunted in surprise even as he rolled back and off the couch, landing on his feet like a cat. Okay, so the guy might have some training.

Zac lunged, tackling him around his middle. They crashed over the leather ottoman. Alonso slammed a fist into his ribs even as Zac swung at his jaw. The man was strong and fit.

Pain ricocheted up his arm as he made contact. The man's head jerked back and Zac used that moment to get the upper hand. Striking out again, he pummeled the guy in the stomach before flipping him over.

Alonso grunted, reaching back and grabbing at Zac's face, but he wrapped an arm around Alonso's neck and squeezed tight. Shifting, he tightened his legs around the man's body, holding him as still as possible.

The man grunted, struggling under his hold, his body flailing around. Zac had a hard grip on him and ignored the slaps and hits raining down on anywhere Alonso could reach. He hated doing this, especially in front of Olivia, but there was no choice.

Ignoring the pain of the man's blows, Zac counted, knowing exactly how long he could hold the man before he killed him. It was a fine line, however. And too easy to cross. Too easy to accidentally kill this man.

As the seconds ticked by Zac willed the guy to pass out. He needed him unconscious so he could bind him. Then…he hoped that Neely went for what he wanted to do. Otherwise he was going to have to break cover and attack Neely. Because no way in hell was he actually killing Alonso.

The man eventually went limp but Zac held on for another five seconds. When he was certain Alonso was actually unconscious, he let go, dropping the man to the blue and green rug with a thud. "You have zip ties?"

Neely frowned, but nodded and retrieved a handful of them. Working quickly Zac bound and gagged the man. Then he looked at Neely. "I need my phone." He'd already made it known he had people in town—or had at least hired someone to rescue Martina. It stood to reason he'd have someone he could call.

"I'm going to watch you dial."

He shrugged and made a phone call to one of the team's burner phones. There wasn't a protocol for this type of situation but he trusted his team to know what to do. That was why they all worked so well together. They knew how to think outside the box in all situations.

Leighton—who no doubt had heard everything over the comms—answered on the second ring. "Yeah?"

"It's Savage. I need a cleanup detail. Now." He rattled off the name of the hotel. "Penthouse suite. Use a cleaning cart to haul away the garbage." He paused, as if waiting for a response, then said. "One body." He paused again. "Extract whatever information you can get." Then he hung up and handed his phone back to Neely who tossed it into the bowl after turning it off. "My guy will find out who he works for and dispose of the body. Normally he charges five hundred K," he informed Neely.

"Since you took the whole cut from yesterday, you can pay him." The dark look in Neely's eyes told Zac that now was not the time to play dominance games.

He nodded. "That's fair."

Neely tucked his weapon away and turned to the others. "As soon as this piece of shit is out of here we're relocating. And we're all going together. No outside communication until the job is over."

Which meant that the job was most definitely happening tonight. Or tomorrow morning. It would be very soon, no doubt about it.

Zac finally looked over at Olivia—and found her staring at him as if he was a stranger. The look in her dark eyes was unreadable so he glanced away, not wanting to see judgment or recrimination.

Maybe she'd been right to keep her distance from him after all.

CHAPTER FOURTEEN

—Manners cost you nothing.—

Gage stared at the hooded man bound to the steel chair Leighton had found God knew where. Alonso, last name unknown, was awake, even if he was pretending not to be. They'd put a hood over him so he wouldn't see their faces.

Because holy fuck, this had just turned into a shit show. Maybe not completely, but if this guy was a Fed, he didn't need to know their identities or what they were doing.

Leighton and Brooks looked at him, both with expression as grim as he felt. Leighton had picked Alonso up from the penthouse using a cleaning cart and a stolen uniform from the hotel. Gage had hacked into the security and erased the fifteen minutes Leighton was in the hotel at all, recording it over with a loop. Unless someone looked closely, even their own security wouldn't know about it.

Gage pointed at Leighton, indicating he should stay put to watch the man while he and Brooks headed outside. They'd brought the guy back to the safe house, which for the most part was secure. Similar to the home they'd rescued Martina from, it was surrounded by palm trees and a lot of green overgrowth. Unless the guy had a tracker on him they hadn't found—and Gage had personally scanned him—no one was coming after Alonso.

"We need to make a decision," Brooks said.

Gaged nodded. "The less he sees and hears from us, the better."

"We can't let him go until Savage and Olivia are done."

Gage nodded in agreement. If this man was a Fed, he wouldn't give a shit about protecting Olivia and Savage. And if Neely found out that this man was actually alive, he'd be likely to just kill Savage. So, no, they couldn't let him go. Not yet. "I just don't like the idea of having a captive."

"No shit. The info on him come back yet?"

Gage shook his head. He'd been careful about the programs he'd used to run the man's fingerprints. Just as he'd been careful when he'd run Kyle Neely's. In case their captive was government and his files were flagged, Gage didn't want to alert anyone that he was looking into him. Because he could find out who the man in their kitchen was without anyone knowing it was him who'd dug into it. Easily. Covering his tracks wasn't the problem. Unfortunately he could set off an internal alarm that someone was interested in Alonso.

Not good for anyone right now. He hadn't reached out to any of his contacts either. He'd done this all under the radar, never wanting any of this to come back to Redemption Harbor Consulting. So far they'd done well to stay off the government's radar since starting their business. He planned to keep it that way.

"I'm going to call Skye and Colt," he finally said. They'd put it off long enough. And if they were going to back Savage and Olivia up on whatever was going to go down, they needed more people here, especially if someone had to babysit the man in the kitchen.

Brooks nodded his agreement.

"Skye Arévalo's phone, how may I help you?" a sexy female voice answered, taking Gage by surprise.

"Who the fuck is this!" He winced as soon as the words were out of his mouth. But who the hell was answering Skye's phone?

There was a short pause. "When you learn how to speak with manners you should have learned in kindergarten, feel free to call back. Good day, sir." The line went dead.

He stared at his phone for a long moment.

"What's going on?" Brooks asked.

"I have no idea. Some woman just answered Skye's phone." Then had politely told him off in the sultriest voice he'd ever heard. He called Skye again.

And got the same response. "Skye Arévalo's phone, how may I help you?"

"This is Gage, one of Skye's partners. I apologize for my rudeness. May I please speak to her?"

Brooks gave him a weird look but he ignored the man.

He couldn't be sure, but he swore the woman snickered. "One moment please, I'll connect you."

A moment later Skye came on the line. "Hey, what's up?"

"Why is someone answering your phone?"

"Oh, I had my calls transferred to the office. Trying something new with the new girl."

He'd go back to the new girl bit in a moment. "You set up call transfers yourself?" Skye was good with explosives and weapons but usually wanted to take a golf club to anything technology related that she couldn't fix in two seconds. She had the patience of a toddler in non-life-threatening situations.

"I'm not just a pretty face, my friend. And no, Nova did. Colt and I just hired her as the company's assistant. Which we probably should have run by everyone but holy shit I can't handle all the filing or admin stuff anymore. She's also taking over all of our marketing. With Savage gone I have no one to con into doing it for me. We need someone and there's no telling when we'll all be in the same location at the same time." She sounded a little defensive, as if expecting an argument.

And right now, there was no time for any of that. Not that he cared anyway. He trusted Skye. "We've got an issue. Not sure how big it is but it could turn into something." Gage quickly laid out everything for Skye, knowing she'd relay everything to Colt and together they'd decide whether to come to Miami or not.

As soon as he was done, Skye was silent for a long moment. "I'm going to talk this over with Colt but get ready for us. We'll be there in a few hours."

"All right. So...the new girl? She single?" Because her voice alone was enough to get him hard. Even her name was sexy.

Skye hung up on him.

CHAPTER FIFTEEN

—Out of the frying pan, into the fire.—

Olivia sat next to Savage in the back seat of the SUV, trying to remain calm when she felt anything but that. At least she still had her earpiece and knew that Gage and the others were listening.

For a moment back in that hotel room she'd wondered if Savage had actually planned to kill Alonso—or whoever the man was. The fight between the two of them had been so brutal and unexpected. Just...shocking violence in a plush penthouse suite. One moment Savage had been standing up, as if to tell Kyle no, then he'd attacked like the tiger he was.

Everything had been over before it had started, with Savage quickly subduing the other man. Now she was sitting in between him and her ex-freaking-husband. Seriously.

What. The. Hell.

Kyle was in the front passenger seat with Maxwell driving. The other man, Smith, had left on his own, not saying much other than he'd meet up with them soon.

From what she remembered that was pretty standard for Kyle. Keep everything close to the vest. But not telling her that her ex-husband would be here was just a dick move. No surprise, since Kyle was a massive douche kidnapper/blackmailer/murderer.

Gah.

"It's been a long time," Heath said, breaking the silence.

Next to her Savage stiffened. He'd actually wanted to sit in between them but Kyle had said no. Which was probably because he was worried Savage would attack Heath.

She wouldn't be surprised if he did. Not after what she'd seen. And she wasn't sure how she felt about that.

Olivia just scooted closer to Savage. He might be a jerk too, but the devil you knew and all that. And at the end of the day, she might be hurt by what he'd said to Brooks, but she still trusted him to have her back. And she couldn't say he'd lied to her. He'd been honest about what he had to offer: nothing. She decided not to respond to Heath because why bother?

"How's Valencia?" he asked a few minutes later.

"The daughter you abandoned? She's fantastic." Okay, so much for keeping her mouth shut. It was taking all her restraint not to lash out at him. If anyone deserved a good throat punch, it was Heath.

Savage put his arm around her, and screw it—she leaned into him. Not because she was acting either. She missed her daughter, was terrified she might not make it home, and now she was stuck in a vehicle with her ex-husband and a monster who just might kill them all given the chance. Her life had gone from PTA meetings to this.

Her ex started to say something else but Savage let out the scariest growl she'd ever heard. Like the tiger he was. "Don't talk to her unless it's related to the job." A soft, deadly order with an unspoken *or else.* And after what had happened in the penthouse the *or else* was pretty clear.

Heath was silent, turning to look out his window and basically sulking like the man-child he was. Which felt familiar, so some things definitely hadn't changed.

She certainly had. She'd actually wondered how she'd feel if she ever saw him again. Maybe a bittersweet sensation or sadness? Instead...there was nothing there. Well, other than annoyance, and a sadness for him that he'd missed out on knowing his own daughter. Closing her eyes, she turned her face into Savage's chest, sliding her arm around him as she did.

The drive took about thirty minutes until they were very much outside Miami city limits and near the Everglades.

Under a clear blue sky, Maxwell turned from the two-lane bumpy back road they were on, onto a dusty unpaved road. A warehouse was about half a mile away in the distance but she couldn't see anything else all around it. Just an expansive grass field—that actually looked like it had been mowed recently. Far, far behind the warehouse was a tree line of palm trees and then a body of water. Probably a swamp or some kind of retention pond.

Well this definitely couldn't be where they were stealing from so it must be the base of operations before the actual heist.

Tense, sweat dripping down her spine despite the cool interior, she tried to mentally prepare for whatever was about to come. Because after the job, she was disposable to Kyle.

Unless they could get some dirt on him or get the upper hand... She shook off the thought. One step at a time right now. And it wasn't like she was alone. She had Savage with her.

Despite everything, the thought was comforting.

* * *

Savage kept Olivia close to him as they strode into the wide-open warehouse. Whatever this place was used for, it would be impossible to engage in a sneak attack. Not with the flatlands surrounding it. Neely had picked it well if he had security in mind.

He wanted to tell Gage where they were but there hadn't been an opportunity and no one had been chatty in the SUV. When he'd first met Neely he'd needed to show him what type of man he was. Now, he needed to blend better, to not stand out.

He was pretty certain he had Neely's trust—at least to an extent. But he still needed to fade more into the background so that Neely almost forgot he was there.

Two conference-size tables had been pushed together and a 3-D model of what he guessed was downtown Miami had been set up on one table. One building was a different color than the other plain gray, scaled buildings. It was a pale blue. Next to the first table was an oversized version of the blue building, but it was missing one exterior wall, showcasing all the floors inside from the lobby to the top one. More than a decent scale. This was high-quality professional grade.

Neely strode straight to the scale model and pointed at the blue building. "This is what we're hitting. The Prisock building."

Savage wasn't familiar enough with Miami to have heard of it, but Olivia had told him that Neely had always stolen antiquities, artifacts and jewelry.

Neely nodded once at Maxwell. "Maxwell is our inside man. He's on the security team. Olivia will be posing as an IT employee who needs to work late. She's going to drive us into the parking garage here around ten." He pointed to that section of the model. "As a woman she's less threatening, and Maxwell will be the one who lets her in—so no one else sees her face." He looked at Olivia directly. "The credentials we have for you are real—taken from another employee and mirrored."

He looked out at everyone now, scanning faces.

"We'll all be in the back of the van, concealed behind a fake panel. Once we're inside, we'll have exactly five minutes to make it to the security room. Maxwell will signal a guy in the security room to run a loop. It's very short. Once we make it to the security room, you," he said, looking at Savage, "and I will take over. We'll subdue the guards and turn off the recording."

"Fine. But no killing."

"You didn't seem to have a problem with it earlier." Neely's face scrunched up slightly, the dark bruising under his eyes from Savage's punch making him internally smile.

"And I don't now. But unnecessary deaths are messy and stupid. The kind of shit that gets you the needle if you get caught. In and out clean is the way I do things."

Neely didn't respond, just turned to Heath—an asshole Savage wanted to punch on principle. "As soon as Savage and I subdue the detail in the security room, you'll make your move on the front lobby guard. He's armed but you'll be posing as a tech guy working late. You'll tase him, bind him, and take over downstairs as our extra lookout. I've been watching the place for a month and we shouldn't have any late night visitors, but I want eyes on the lobby just in case."

He continued talking through the plan before turning to Olivia again.

"You'll be on the eleventh floor here," he said, pointing to the scaled building again. "The newest version of the Kaira is in office 1132. You'll have forty-five minutes to crack it, but after seeing what you did with the 2000, it shouldn't take that long. Once you're in, radio me and we empty what's inside and leave the way we came. Smith will be moving around the building as extra security so if there's an issue, radio him first."

"What about the guys in security?" Smith asked.

"We'll leave them behind tied up to be found. And Maxwell will employ another distraction before he exits."

"What's the take?" Savage asked. It was a fair question. And one Neely would expect him to ask.

"A little over eight million apiece."

The room went eerily silent for a long moment. That meant this job was close to fifty million. Which meant Neely had to have more inside people. No way Maxwell was the only man. It also meant this wasn't jewels or antiquities. It had to be something else. Maybe tech related.

"What are we taking?"

Neely shrugged. "Files. All in flash drive form. I don't know what's on the drives either so don't ask. And I don't care. What I do know is we'll be paid enough that we won't have to do another job for decades if we don't want."

So he was working for someone. There was another unknown. Son of a bitch.

"How are we going to get paid?" Zac asked. He had to keep his role going.

"Deposits into untraceable offshore accounts."

After that, Neely pulled Maxwell to the side and started talking to him right about the time Smith showed up. The man immediately joined Neely and Maxwell, murmuring in low tones with them.

"Olivia, can I talk to you for a minute? In private?" Heath looked at Zac once before focusing on Olivia.

Jaw tight, she nodded once. "Fine."

Zac didn't want to let her go, not even for a moment, but with Neely distracted he wanted to communicate with Gage as best he could. "You hear all that?" he murmured as he approached the table.

"Yeah," Gage said into his ear. "I ran the Prisock building. Private company but they've got government contracts. Too many to filter through to figure out what Neely is after. But he's working with someone else, something I know you've already figured out. It'll be whoever's willing to fork over fifty million for whatever's in the safe. And if it's in a safe, I'm guessing that this information isn't available digitally. Which is why it has to be a physical job. Otherwise, whoever hired Neely would just hire a hacker to take what he or they need."

Savage made a quiet, agreeable sound. This was tech related or information. And information worth fifty million? He could only guess what it could be.

"We don't have anything on Neely yet but Colt and Skye are on the way down. Should be here in an hour. And after what I've just heard of his plan—I've got an idea how we're going to get him to hand over the blackmail he has on Olivia without realizing he's giving it to us. And how to make sure he goes down for everything without dragging you or Olivia into it."

As Gage started talking, Savage resisted the urge to smile. This could definitely work. Timing would be critical but it could work.

CHAPTER SIXTEEN

—Actions are everything.—

Olivia watched her ex, wondering how the hell she'd ever fallen for him. She'd been young, feeling lost after graduation, and he'd been absolutely charming. He'd played up on her insecurities, her fears and she'd walked right into it.

They'd met at an off-campus coffee shop and he'd bought her latte and nearly charmed the panties right off her that day. Ugh. She'd been such an idiot. Later, she'd realized his charming act was for everyone. She hadn't been special.

Heath ran a hand over his perfectly styled blond hair. He was tall, fit, with the type of looks that belonged on the big screen. Strong, square jaw, piercing blue eyes, a sort of classic handsomeness. And the real draw to him was his smile—insincere though it was. Like he had a secret and wanted to tell it to you and you alone. "I'm sorry you got dragged into this."

Oh yeah, she just bet he was. She resisted the urge to snort at him. "When did he contact you about this job?"

"A week ago." His answer was too fast, as if he'd been prepared for it. And he did this little thing where he clenched his jaw when he lied. It was his only tell—and she'd never told him that he gave himself away when he lied.

Hmm. "So why didn't he bring you in for the first meeting Savage and I were called in for?"

Heath shrugged. "I don't know." Still lying.

"Did you know he threatened Valencia? And kidnapped Martina?"

"No." Another lie. *That bastard.*

She kept her expression neutral even if she wanted to throat punch him. "So why'd you want to talk to me?" She was stressed out enough about what they had to do. Standing here chatting with her ex wasn't going to help matters.

"I just wanted to get you away from that thug you're with so we could catch up. When did you take up with him?"

She lifted a shoulder and glanced over at Savage—who was eyeing the scaled building setup as if he was memorizing every inch. "We got together after you." A vague answer with no time frame. And she had a feeling that Heath was only asking to corroborate what they'd told Neely. She didn't trust this snake one bit.

"He doesn't seem like your type."

Ugh, she shouldn't indulge him, but... "He's the opposite of you. Which pretty much makes him my type."

He gave her this wounded puppy dog look, which from anyone else might have made her feel bad. But he'd literally rejected their daughter. He could suck it.

"I don't remember you being like—"

"Oh sweet Lord, what do you want, Heath? I don't care what you remember me being like. I'm not that impressionable young woman from back then. And I'm glad. So unless you have something important to say..." She paused as Savage appeared at her side. Wow, he was quiet. And fast—and he looked pissed.

"Get lost," Savage growled, looping an arm around her and pulling her into his arms. He didn't say anything else, just held her close.

And damn it, she was still hurt by him but she hugged him back, burying her face against his chest. It was simply as part of her role. That was all. She could tell herself that and almost believe it.

Heath practically ran away from them, his shoes pounding against the floor as he retreated.

"After this job is over, I want to hunt him down and hurt him."

Startled by his harsh words, she pulled back slightly. "Are you serious?"

"I told you I wasn't a good man." Okay, he definitely wasn't joking.

"He's not worth it."

His jaw clenched once. "What did he want?"

"Nothing. Just to talk." It was so inane, so freaking pitiful she didn't want to waste any more space in her head thinking about him. "He knew about Martina being kidnapped though," she said quietly.

"He admitted that?"

"No." Out of the corner of her eye she could see that Heath was far enough away that he wouldn't overhear. "But I can tell when he's lying. He also knew that Kyle threatened Valencia."

Savage's expression went...savage. Yeah, he really lived up to that moniker. "I'm actually going to take pleasure in hurting him," he deadpanned.

She smacked his chest, hoping he was kidding.

"Why were you so cold to me this morning?" he asked suddenly, a hint of hurt in his eyes.

No. He didn't get to look hurt. She started to drop her arms, to pull back, but he simply tightened his grip. "Now's not the time." No one in the warehouse could hear them, but still.

"It's definitely the time. We're about to go on a job together. I want to know where your head is at."

"It's nothing..." She hated that Gage and likely the others could overhear their conversation right now. Gage was good about not communicating and distracting, but she knew he was always listening. At least that was what he'd told her. Which was beyond embarrassing, considering the dirty things Savage had said to her in the elevator at the hotel. "I heard what you said to Brooks about not wanting a ready-made family or relationship. And you were upfront about not being able to offer me anything." Gah, she inwardly cringed that she was having this conversation with the others on their team listening in. But screw it. "So I have no reason to be hurt but I still was. Okay, I *am* hurt, if I'm being honest. I thought we shared something special but at least I know where I stand." And that was that. She wanted to shove him off and step back, but didn't want to make a scene. Now more than ever they had to appear like a team, a happy freaking couple.

"I lied to Brooks. And I lied to myself. Olivia—"

"No. I don't want to hear it. Trust me, I'm done listening to garbage from men."

His jaw tightened and there were so many emotions in his green eyes as he looked down at her. "After this job I'm not walking away from you."

Something buried deep inside her flared to life but she shoved it away. She kept a smile on her face and her voice low. Her smile was fake but everyone was far enough away they shouldn't be able to tell. "I give zero fucks what you say right now. I heard what you said when you thought I wasn't listening."

"That's fair. But I'm not walking away from us. Last night was incredible and I think we could be good together. No, I know we can."

She nearly scoffed but kept the stupid smile plastered on her face and her voice pitched low. "We live in different states. I have a kid. You don't want a ready-made family." She couldn't keep the hint of anger out of her voice. When she'd heard him say that, it had cut deeper than when her ex had split. Because she cared about Savage in a way that should be impossible for how long they'd known each other. Emotions and logic were two different things. When it came to Savage, logic took a back seat.

"I can live in any city I want. And I lied. I'd be lucky to have you and Valencia in my life. I want anything and everything you have to offer. You don't have to believe me. I'm going to show you that I'm not just another asshole." He paused. "Okay, I *am* an asshole sometimes. Maybe a lot of times. But not to you. Never to you."

"If you're doing this because you think I need to hear this before a job, then—"

He took her by surprise, crushing his mouth to hers for a hard, demanding kiss. She didn't want to like it—love it. She should push him away. But she couldn't. Because of the role she was playing. *Riiiiiigghhtt.* She couldn't even buy her own lie as heat rushed between her legs.

Zac Savage was seriously messing with her head. And her body. Her nipples tightened against her bra cups as she leaned into him, teased her tongue against his. He tasted like coffee and something sweet. She wanted nothing more than to wrap her legs around him and—

At the sound of a throat clearing, she blinked and lifted her head to find Kyle watching them with interest. Freaking perv.

"Sorry to interrupt but I want to go over the safe specs with you," he said to Olivia. "Just want to make sure you're up to the task."

She resisted the urge to snap at him and nodded instead. Pissing off Kyle was the last thing she wanted to do. And she was pretty sure he was just being a dick. He didn't want to go over any specs with her. He'd recruited her—blackmailed her—for a reason.

As she stepped away from Savage she heard Gage's voice in her ear. So he'd definitely overheard their conversation. Great. All embarrassment faded at his next words.

"Colt and Skye have arrived. We've all got your back tonight."

She didn't let herself outwardly react. But Colt and Skye weren't supposed to be in Miami. They were supposed to be with her daughter, making sure she was safe. Did Savage know about this? She wanted to ask him but there was no normal way to back out of going over safe specs with Kyle. Not unless she wanted to draw attention to herself.

As soon as she was able she was questioning Savage. Or Gage himself. She knew Martina was with her daughter but she'd felt a lot better knowing Valencia was being watched by Colt and Skye.

CHAPTER SEVENTEEN

—FUBARed.—

Crammed in the back of the midsize van with three other men wasn't Zac's idea of a good time. And he hated that Olivia was the driver, putting herself right in harm's way as they infiltrated this building. Alone in the front, she was completely unprotected.

They'd barely had a moment to themselves at the warehouse today. Neely had been edgy, wanting to go over every last detail until he was just repeating himself. Zac understood being prepared but Neely had seemed almost nervous. A change from the arrogant man Zac had originally met.

And Olivia's ex had been watching her too closely—with barely disguised lust. Because who could blame the guy? Olivia was perfection. But it wasn't just that.

No, there was something else there. Anger. It was below the surface and Zac had only caught glimpses of it—but it had been there more than once. Angry men could be very dangerous. Especially an ex who felt spurned or some other bullshit.

Zac didn't like that Heath's presence had been sprung on them at the last minute either. His appearance in this whole thing felt wrong. It could be a coincidence that Neely had asked him, since the man had worked with him before. But Olivia had been pretty insistent that Heath had been afraid of Neely too.

He rolled his shoulders once against the cold metal wall of the hollowed-out van. If anyone looked into the cab from the driver's side window they'd just see the doors and a bunch of computer equipment. Neely had hollowed out a small section of the back and input the same back doors over it. They didn't open; they'd been welded in. But unless someone inspected it closely or realized something was off about the measurements of the interior, it was a solid way to sneak into this place.

In fact, Zac had done something similar before but he'd been on the undercarriage of an M939 truck. And it had been a weapons dealer's compound he'd infiltrated.

As the van slowed, everyone went still. Enough time had passed that they should be at the final destination.

Olivia's voice was muffled but she didn't sound stressed. And he only heard one other voice. Should be Maxwell. Good. When he looked over he realized Heath was watching him. Zac stared right back, wanting her ex to see exactly the type of man he was, what he was capable of—and how Zac would enjoy hurting him.

The other man looked away.

A second later the van started moving again. They all slightly swayed back and forth as they headed up a ramp of the parking garage.

A few more minutes later, they stopped moving, the engine shut off, then there was the coded knock on the back door. Olivia's knock.

Neely opened it and they all jumped out. A total of three vehicles were in the parking lot that he could see, but the place appeared nearly deserted. According to Neely, it was supposed to be. Zac immediately tugged a black ski mask on. Even though the video feed was supposed to be on a loop for the next five minutes, he wasn't taking the chance. Especially since Neely had burned him and Olivia before.

Olivia gave Zac a tight smile before she did the same, tugging a mask over her face and hair. He hated the stress he saw there. Hated everything about this situation. If he could have done this without her, he would have. Hell, he'd wanted to call the whole thing off and just pull out with her when a chance opened up.

But she'd said no. And so had Gage. And Skye. Because Olivia would never be free of Neely if they pulled out now. And even if he wanted to simply make Neely disappear, the man had blackmail on Olivia. There was no telling where it was or what would happen to it if Neely went missing.

"Clock is ticking." Neely's voice was clipped, tight, as he put his own mask on. The others did the same. "Savage, you're with me."

Every fiber of him wanted to go with Olivia, to protect her. But they had to stick to the plan. It wouldn't make sense for Neely to kill her. He wouldn't have brought her into this if that was the plan.

Most likely *after* the job he planned to kill them, but Savage's team would be waiting. So he had to let her go.

Olivia gave him a small, reassuring smile before she turned and headed toward one of the east set of stairwells. He and Neely would be taking another set because it was a quicker path to where they needed to be.

As his legs ate up the distance toward the metal door, he replayed that smile in his head. She'd been trying to reassure *him*. He didn't think that had ever happened on an op. From anyone.

This woman had snuck under his armor and she wasn't going anywhere. He didn't want her to. Hell, he just hoped he hadn't screwed up so badly that he didn't have a chance with her. He'd tried to remember every word he'd said to Brooks this morning and it wasn't pretty. No wonder she'd been so cold to him.

"We'll have to move fast, disabling the team in the security room," Neely said as they jogged up the stairs. He'd already been over this a dozen times but Zac just nodded.

When Neely's radio buzzed he lifted it, spoke quickly into it. It was Maxwell telling them their time frame was getting shorter.

Zac increased his pace as they hurried up the stairs. The overall plan was solid but he wanted to know what the hell was in the safe. And who Neely planned to sell the contents to.

As they reached the tenth floor they both slowed and Neely withdrew a pistol. Zac tightened his jaw. He'd known Neely was bringing a weapon on this job but he didn't like it.

In the hallway Zac scanned for any signs of life, saw none. It looked like a typical high-rise building with offices. Each office they passed looked normal enough. Desks, laptops, bookcases and filing cabinets were in most of them. A few doors were closed. And all of them were dark. There were no typical signs of life indicating someone else might be working late. The only lights were from the city beyond. As they passed a conference room, Neely signaled with his hand.

"First door," he murmured.

The last three doors led to the security rooms but the main hub was the second door from where they were. So they were going to enter through the first door and sneak into the main hub and take out the four men inside. At least that was the plan.

Neely stepped back as if to let Zac go first but he shook his head and nodded at the weapon. If Neely wanted to bring a pistol, he could go first. No way was Zac giving this guy his back.

Neely didn't respond, just slid a keycard he'd gotten from who knew where across the black electronic pad. There was a soft snicking sound. Once inside Zac swept his gaze over the small break room.

Neely had been right. The security team had their own break area, separate from the rest of the building. These guys really stayed contained. Smart.

As they stepped inside, a side door opened and he froze as a man holding a Glock 19 at full extension moved into view. The weapon was trained right at Zac.

Neely raised his own weapon—at Zac's head.

Fuck.

"Are the others contained?" Neely's voice was low, the question not aimed at Zac.

"Yes. Everyone's contained and the system is now offline."

What the hell did that mean? Neely had told Zac and the others that they'd have to take over the control room.

The man with the Glock had a faint accent and wasn't bothering to cover his face. Square jaw, five feet ten give or take an inch, dark brown hair, blue eyes. And the accent wasn't pronounced enough for Zac to pinpoint an exact origin. But if he had to guess, Zac was going with Russian.

Without warning Neely smashed Zac in the temple with the butt of his weapon. "Keep this one alive for now in case I need to use him later."

Zac crumpled to the floor, feigning that he was more affected by the blow than he was. His head throbbed as the door shut behind Neely.

Right about now he had a shitload of questions, but unfortunately for him Neely wasn't an evil movie villain willing to give him a monologue. So the only thing he knew: he had to take out this current threat and get to Olivia.

"Get up slowly." The man moved closer.

Zac groaned and pushed onto his knees but held his head.

"Don't make me ask again." He strode across the room, past the small round table and chairs as Zac stood, still bent over at the waist. The man muttered something under his breath but Zac tuned it out when the man was within striking distance.

He popped up, grabbing onto the wrist of the gun-wielding hand, and struck out with his other hand, wrapping it around the man's arm and yanking up. Hard. It was a move he'd done more times than he wanted to remember.

The weapon went off as the man's wrist broke.

Crying out, the man pulled Zac close with his good hand and lifted his knee, jabbing it into his thigh.

Adrenaline pumping through him, he barely felt the blow. Instead of trying to pull away, he jabbed at the man's ribs with his fist.

Thud. Thud. Thud.

Groaning, now the dark-haired man tried to pull away. Zac twisted and slammed his elbow across the man's face. His head snapped back.

The man slammed his foot on Zac's instep. Pain ricocheted through him. Cursing, Zac crushed the man's nose. No holding back. They pummeled each other, back and forth until the man fell onto his back.

Zac went to stomp on his throat. The man rolled to his front and Zac pounced, using the full weight of his body to hold him down.

Even as the man thrashed underneath him, he wrapped his forearm around the guy's neck, and using his other arm as leverage, broke his neck.

Shoving to his feet, he quickly palmed the fallen Glock and tucked it into the back of his pants. Then he checked the dead man for any ID. Found none. But he took the key card hooked to the man's belt.

"Olivia, can you hear me?" They had the upper hand on the others because of their comm system. But she didn't respond.

She'd told him that she'd have to take her earbud out when cracking the safe because she needed to use the stethoscope. Heart pounding, he shoved back the fear that wanted to overtake him.

He'd been trained for situations like this. The government had spent a shit-ton of money making sure he was a killing machine. But nothing could have prepared him for Olivia. For how it would feel to know she was in the same building with a man who would definitely kill her once she'd lost her usefulness.

Screw that.

She'd told him it would take less time than Neely had given her to open the safe and he'd only been here maybe six minutes. Even if it felt like a lifetime. Combined with the five minutes it had taken to get up to this floor, the clock was ticking down. He had to get to her.

Neely must have lied about more.

Stepping over the dead body—and trying to ignore the pain in his foot—he moved toward the door the other man had come out of.

"What's going on, Savage?" Gage's voice came over the comm.

"Neely was working with someone on the inside," he murmured. "And no one came out of the security room while we were fighting to the death. I'm moving in now." He tried the door. Locked. Then he waved the card over the black panel.

Snick.

He pulled the door open—and found four men with their hands tied behind their backs, feet bound and hoods over all their heads. They were still enough as they lay on their sides but all of them were breathing. And he couldn't see any blood or wounds anywhere.

"He's disabled all the security. And..." Zac moved to the security panel and realized that the entire system had been shut down. "System's shut down completely."

"If there's a failsafe in place, someone in the company will receive an alert. At least they should," Gage said. "And with a company this size, there will definitely be a failsafe."

Neely had already lied to them. What if he was wrong about this too and an alert had gone out to local law enforcement?

He moved to the nearest bound man, tapped the guy's leg with his boot. "Did any of you trigger an alarm?"

"No." The man he'd tapped answered.

"You sure about that?" He crouched down and pressed the Glock to the man's temple, then chambered a round. He wouldn't use it. But the security guard wouldn't know that.

A pause. "I have three kids."

"Then tell me what I want to know."

"The system was undergoing a reboot tonight. A security protocol where everything goes offline. Standard. Happens every three months like clockwork. When it comes back on if the security system doesn't link up, an alert goes out to the CEO—and the police."

"How much longer will it be offline?"

"Maybe another hour. Give or take a few minutes."

"Okay. You four are going to remain here while my buddy keeps watch. Do anything stupid and..." He tapped the weapon against the man's head.

Then he left. Either they'd figure out there was no "buddy" watching them or they wouldn't. But they were secured well. It would have to do.

Now he had to find Olivia and get the hell out of there. Screw everything else. She was his only priority.

CHAPTER EIGHTEEN

—I don't want a knight to save me. I want a man who fights by my side.—

Olivia pushed out a long breath as the safe opened. It didn't take remotely as long as it could have. She took the stethoscope out of her ears and stood, pulling the safe completely open.

Heavy duty and basically immovable, the interior was filled with files. Some paper. There were also...passports. With a gloved hand she reached in and pulled one out. Then another. Huh. Same person but different names and countries for the passports. And there were stacks of cash.

On the middle rack was a small velvet bag full of flash drives. A handful of them. She started to pull the radio out that Kyle had given all of them but decided to tell Savage first. As she put her earpiece back in, the sound of the office door opening had her heart flipping over—until she realized it was Heath. He had a black and gray duffel bag hooked over one shoulder.

"What are you doing here?" She kept her voice low then glanced at the radio. Had hers malfunctioned? She'd thought he was supposed to be downstairs manning the lobby security desk.

He stepped into the room. Aaaannd, that was when she saw the gun in his gloved hand. He held it up and pointed it directly at her, his blue eyes ice cold. "You're even better than

I remembered. That only took you half the time I expected." Despite his words, bitterness laced his voice.

"Why are you holding a gun on me?"

"I'm coming," Savage said into her ear. "Keep him talking."

Okay, she could hold on for however long it took him to get to her. She had no choice.

"Step away from the safe." His voice was low, but hard.

For a split second she thought about slamming it shut but didn't want to risk that he would shoot her. She did as he said, sliding sideways toward the panel of floor-to-ceiling windows.

Keeping the gun trained on her—and he held the thing with way too much ease for her comfort—he covered the distance to the open safe in seconds. "You really are gifted," he murmured.

"Why are you doing this?" she asked. "Did Kyle tell you to kill me?" Maybe that had always been the plan. She'd figured Kyle would try to double-cross them. So had Zac. Which was why he and the Redemption Harbor team had a backup plan in place. But this... She hadn't even expected her ex-husband to be here, much less pull a gun on her. For all his faults, he'd never been violent. Just self-involved.

He snorted. "Neely's not in charge. I am. *I* brought *him* into this, not the other way around."

"So you brought me into this, then?" She balled her hands into fists at her side. Heath had done this to her? To their daughter?

He nodded, as if proud. "You never should have kept that blackmail on me."

Ice slid through her veins, sharp and cold. Was that why he'd pulled her into this? But to what end? "I had to and you know it."

"You really think I would have come after you later? The mother of my child."

Her jaw clenched once. He didn't get to call Valencia his. He'd given up all parental rights when he walked away. Instead of telling him exactly what she thought she said, "Were you behind Martina's kidnapping?"

He lifted a shoulder, looking smug even as he reached into the safe and pulled out the bag of flash drives. "It was my idea but Neely took care of that. There was never any connection to me."

"So...you brought Neely into whatever this is?" She motioned to the safe. "To steal a bunch of information. Why involve me?"

He reached in again, pulled out the stacks of cash and started dumping them into the duffel bag. "I needed the best." He looked at the passports, frowned, then shoved them back into the safe. "And I needed blackmail on you. Now I have it. You ever go to the cops with what you have on me, I give them what I have on you."

Damn it. She gritted her teeth, willing the rage building inside her to tamp down. For now. Despite what he said, there was no way he'd come up with all this on his own. Unless he'd changed so drastically in the last six years that he'd become a criminal mastermind, someone else was behind this. "Who are you giving the flash drives to?"

He faltered once before pulling out a stack of paper files and shoving them into the bag. "Why do you assume I am?"

"You have to be selling them to someone or..." *Oh, God.* "You're paying off a debt." That made way more sense than anything else. The Heath she'd known had liked to live large and way out of his means. He'd thought he deserved it. He'd always liked to gamble too.

His jaw tightened and she knew she'd nailed it. After a long moment, he said, "I got in deep with some Russians. In exchange for letting me live—and you and Valencia—I had to take something big for them."

She seriously doubted whoever these guys were had threatened her, especially since Heath had as much as admitted he wanted blackmail on her, but she was silent as he continued.

"So I reached out to Neely and set this job up."

"And getting blackmail on me in the process was a bonus."

"You never should have had that shit on me in the first place," he snarled, looking up from the safe now, all his focus on her.

Out of the corner of her eye she saw the office door easing open and resisted the urge to look in that direction. Sweat dripped down her spine and her palms were beyond damp in her gloves.

"What kind of wife does that?" He stepped toward her then, his duffel and the safe forgotten for the moment.

"So what, you're going to kill me?"

He laughed, all angry and bitter. "Oh, no. But your boyfriend is dead by now." He gave her the most pleased, Cheshire cat grin. She wanted to smack the smug look right off his face. "And as soon as this job is over, Neely is giving me his blackmail on you. You're mine now, bitch. Any job I want you for, you're in. If I want you to suck my dick, you'll do it. You. Are. Mine."

If Savage hadn't been moving up behind Heath right now, panic and nausea would have taken over. God...she didn't even want to think about Savage being hurt. Or worse. "Why would you hurt him?" she asked, ignoring everything else he'd said.

"Blame yourself. You never should have brought someone in for this job. I had it all planned out and you decided to bring some asshole with you. Him dying was a foregone conclusion."

Savage struck fast, wrapping his forearm around Heath's neck even as he grabbed Heath's arm.

Olivia ducked as she heard Heath cry out—at the same time she heard the snap of a bone breaking. She dove for the gun as it tumbled to the carpeted floor but it didn't matter. Savage had Heath on the floor, facedown and unconscious. And...her ex had soiled himself, if the scent tingeing the air was any indication.

"I should kill him." Savage didn't move from over Heath's body, his knee in the middle of her ex's spine. Savage's gaze clashed with hers. The glittering downtown lights of Miami played off his dark expression, making him look deadlier than normal. She could definitely believe he'd done wrong things in his life. And she didn't want to be the cause of any of them.

Right now, she realized he was serious about killing Heath. Stepping toward him, she handed him the gun. "Please don't. He's not worth it. And he has nothing on me. You heard him. Kyle has the blackmail on me."

"*He* brought you into this. You should be home with your daughter right now." Savage tucked the handgun into the back of his pants and ripped a keyboard off the desk. It was old school, with an actual cord. He ripped it free and used it to bind Heath's hands behind his back.

If he was binding him, then Savage must not mean to kill him. But she needed to be sure. "He did drag me into this. But I don't want his blood on your hands. Let's just leave him." She moved toward Savage, placed a hand on his chest. Even if deep down she wouldn't lose any sleep over Heath dying, she still didn't want Savage involved in the man's death. His chest rose and fell erratically under her hand, the beat of his heart steady. "Please leave him be. I care a lot more about you than I do him." True words. So true, and it hurt because she knew Savage wasn't available for the kind of relationship she needed. "Please, Zac." When she said his first name it seemed to snap something to life inside him.

He nodded once and stepped away from Heath's broken, bound body. "We have to get out of here." Picking up the duffel, he glanced in the safe, then slung the duffel over his shoulder and zipped it up. "But we can't go out through the parking garage or the front. Neely tried to have me killed."

"Is he dead?"

"Neely? No. But the guy he wanted to kill me is. Russian accent," he said, moving to the office door, slightly limping.

She wanted to ask him about it but knew they didn't have time. Olivia picked up her bag of tools and gear and hurried after Savage, leaving her ex where he lay. "Heath said he owed some Russians. Not sure who he meant though."

"I'm going to figure it out," Gage said into their ears and she nearly jumped.

"Jeez. I forgot you were there. You caught everything Heath said?" she asked.

"Yep. Now that you've taken what he needs to pay off whoever he owes, I don't think you need to worry about him being a problem anymore."

Her stomach twisted at Gage's words. She might not care for her ex, and okay, he'd been planning to use her, but... She shook off the thoughts of whatever would happen to him. Her only concern was getting out of here with Savage alive. And making sure she didn't end up behind bars for the rest of her life.

"Shut the hell up, Gage," Savage murmured, taking her hand in his. "She doesn't need to hear that. And we need to get to the roof," he said to her.

She nodded as they raced down the hallway. Her heartbeat was an erratic tattoo against her chest, pulsing in her ears so loudly she couldn't hear anything else. Glancing over her shoulder, she saw no one. It still didn't give her any relief.

It took seven solid minutes to get to the roof and when they burst out into the night air, she sucked in a breath. They were almost home free. Almost.

First they had to scale down a thirty-story building.

Savage shut the door behind them and shoved a piece of rebar against the door and handle. It wouldn't hold forever if someone tried to follow them, but it was better than nothing. "Give me your eyes," Savage said to Gage. "What side is the best for you guys?"

"West side of the building. Out of the range of any CCTVs."

Savage looked at Olivia. "Is that best for us?"

She nodded. They might have on masks but she'd just as well avoid any cameras. "East or west works well."

"We'll move in now," Gage said over the comm. "Provide cover if necessary."

"Cover?" Olivia asked as she unzipped her bag and pulled out her climbing harness. She tossed the extra to Savage.

He snagged it in midair. "In case there are men on the ground with weapons."

Oh, right. *Of course.* She was just worried about the threats inside. But there could definitely be more threats outside. "I'm not cut out for this kind of life." No matter what she'd thought at one time.

"You're holding up like a champ." Savage stepped into his harness—which was snug—as she did the same. Hers fit well enough but she adjusted it, tightening it so it was perfect.

It sure didn't feel like she was holding up, but she didn't comment. Instead she focused on setting up her rappel anchor as he did the same. "You've done this before," she said, holding out her rope for his help.

He didn't even question what she needed, making it clear he knew the drill for rappelling or climbing. He took the rope from her and stepped on it to create slack so she could clip herself in.

He paused as he handed her his own rope and she did the same for him. "I've fast-roped out of an Osprey before."

She blinked but didn't stop what she was doing. A clock was ticking down in her mind and it felt as if Neely and his men could barge through the door at any moment. Adrenaline punched through her at lightning speeds but she managed to keep her breathing and voice steady, even if it felt as if she could crawl out of her skin. "That's impressive." And sexy. She could actually see him doing it. Her hands were somehow steady as she created two bights with her rope.

Savage just grunted a non-response, moving as quickly as she.

Her palms might be damp in her gloves, but her fingers were nimble and steady. She could do this. She had to. Normally she liked to quadruple-check everything, but tonight she was going to have to deal with simply double-checking.

"What are you humming?" Gage's voice cut through her concentration.

"What?" she asked, pulling the brake strands up. She might have rappelled off buildings before but this was different. There were actual men with guns in the building who wanted to kill them. And there could be people waiting for them on the ground.

"It's catchy," he continued.

Sweet Lord, he wanted to talk about this? "It's a silly song from a kids' show. And humming calms me." Years ago when she'd done heists she'd almost always been alone during her portion of the job.

"So...you're basically humming your own theme music right before you two jump off the side of a building?"

"Dude, shut the fuck up," Savage snarled as he did the same to his rope.

"I'm googling the song later," Gage said, seemingly unfazed by Savage.

And Olivia felt absurd laughter bubble up as she double-checked that her carabiner was locked. "Gage has issues, doesn't he?" she muttered.

"Like you wouldn't believe." Savage gave a tug on his own—then did the same on hers. "You ready for this?"

She checked his carabiner, pulling hard. "Let's get out of here."

He gave her a small smile. "When we do, I'm taking you on a real date."

Oh no. Now was *not* the time for this. "Savage—"

"It's Zac."

Ignoring his words completely, she perched on the edge of the building next to him, and set her brake strands in a locked-off position. "Are you okay? I saw you limping."

"I'm good." He held his rope like a pro.

Okay, then. That was good enough for her. A soft wind rolled over them, the air crisp, tinged with the salt of the ocean. She breathed in deeply as she bent her legs at a ninety-degree angle. With her other hand, she started feeding the rope through the belay device—when the roof door slammed open.

Pop. Pop. Pop.

Bullets whizzed past her as Savage shouted something, pulling his own gun free. He returned fire. "Go now! I'm right behind you."

She didn't want to leave him but he had the weapon and knew how to use it. As sound exploded all around them she started moving down at a fast clip, using her feet to push off the thick windows. Though she wanted to keep all her focus on her rope she looked back up. She had to know he was okay.

Ten stories above her, Savage started descending fast.

"Faster!" he shouted.

Heart racing, she did as he ordered, going as fast as she could without losing control. Savage zoomed down until he was next to her, moving faster than she'd ever seen anyone rappel. He moved past her but she didn't look, needing to keep all her attention on her own rope.

Ten floors to go. Five. Three.

Almost there. So close to freedom she could almost taste it. Her legs and arms burned with the exertion.

Her rope slackened. She started falling. Oh, God, they'd cut her rope!

She went into a free fall and everything flashed in front of her—

The day Valencia was born, the day she'd learned her daughter was Deaf, her daughter's first steps, Martina holding her and wiping her tears away in high school after her first boyfriend broke up with her, the first time she and Zac kissed.

A scream caught in her throat—until a strong hand grabbed her upper arm midair. Crying out at the abruptness, she grunted as her back slammed into the window. Her arm screamed in pain but she scrambled onto Savage's back.

"I got you. Just hold on." He continued rappelling down at warp speed even though she'd knocked him off-balance and added a hundred-plus pounds to him.

As the grass zoomed up at them, Savage's own rope slackened five feet above the ground. They'd cut his rope too. She hit the grass with an oomph but Savage was on his feet like a cat and pulling her to her own.

Fingers now trembling, she unhooked her carabiner as he did the same. If they hadn't been so fast, if those men had cut their ropes sooner, she and Savage would be dead. Or close to it. An icy clamminess washed over her and she shuddered.

When the side door opened she froze, her hand on her harness. "Can we catch a break?" she muttered as Neely stepped outside, pistol in hand.

Aimed right at them.

Savage raised his own gun, fired—*click*.

CHAPTER NINETEEN

—You really don't want to be my enemy.—

Thirty minutes earlier

Skye stood in front of their captive, hands on her hips. He still had a cover over his head and was definitely awake now. Though he hadn't moved much.

According to the research Gage had done, the man known as Alonso was really named Darius Moore. They weren't sure of anything else—who his team was or if he even had one. But Skye was guessing he did. All they knew was that he was DEA. Undercover. And it wasn't because of Gage's hacking skills they'd found out. It was from a contact he had.

Using ASL, she started talking to Colt. *You ready?*

He nodded.

She turned to the man even though he couldn't see her. They needed to get the hell out of here. Once they left this safe house, they'd never be coming back. They'd already sanitized the place but just in case Moore figured out where he'd been staying, they weren't giving him any clues as to who they were. "We're about to go for a drive," she said quietly.

The man shifted slightly at her voice, probably because it was the first thing anyone had said to him directly.

"And you're not going to give us trouble, Mr. Moore. Yeah, we know who you are. And if you play things right, you're going to get credit for bringing down Kyle Neely and his crew."

The man stiffened slightly but still didn't respond.

"You're outmanned and outgunned. So when one of my boys here releases your restraints, if you attempt to fight him, I will tase you. Then I'll put a sock in your mouth and hogtie you. So you play nice and you'll be treated with respect. Got it?"

"Yeah." His voice was raspy, but he nodded under the hood.

"All right, then." She looked at her "boy" then.

Colt just gave her a half-smile and cut the zip ties securing Moore to the chair. "Hands behind your back," he said as Alonso stood.

The man paused but did as ordered. Colt quickly bound him again. "Now walk forward. We're getting into a van and taking you to the site of Neely's heist."

"Who are you guys?"

Neither of them answered as they led him to the van in the garage. Once he was in the back, Colt hooked him up so he wouldn't get knocked around. She wondered what the DEA wanted with Neely but maybe it had something to do with whoever he was selling...whatever they stole. Didn't much matter at this point.

Colt palmed the keys and Skye held out a hand. "Rock, paper, scissors for who drives?"

Snorting, her husband just tossed her the keys. Once in the vehicle, she slid her earpiece in and Colt did the same.

"We're on the way," Colt said.

"Good. Looks like we might have an issue," Gage said.

She tore out of the driveway, cringing a little as Moore grunted from the back. Colt turned around to watch him, Taser drawn, and she kept an eye on him in the rearview mirror as Gage relayed everything that was going on.

It took too damn long for them to get downtown. Even if she'd wanted to drive like a bat out of hell, getting pulled over by the cops for a violation with a federal agent tied up in the back of the van wasn't something she could talk her way out of.

Instead of parking directly across from the target site, she parked two blocks away. It would give them enough time for what they had planned. Once in Park she and Colt pulled their ski masks on. She'd already put contacts in and she intentionally pulled out some of the blonde hairs of her wig so that they were visible. Then she shoved up one of her sleeves so her temporary tattoo was showing. He would remember a brown-eyed woman with blonde hair and a tribal tat wrapping around her wrist.

Then she climbed into the back as Colt got out of the passenger seat and headed to the back doors.

She ripped the man's head cover off. He blinked, his dark eyes full of rage. That was to be expected. "I know you have questions. Unfortunately for you, you're not going to get any answers." When she reached into her back pocket he tensed. She tossed a burner cell phone onto the metal floor of the van. "This is yours. As soon as you free yourself, you're going to call in backup for the heist that just occurred at the Prisock building. We're currently two blocks away—east of it. And you will single-handedly take credit for bringing down Kyle Neely and his guys. I don't know if he's your real target or not and I don't care. The only thing I care about—you're going to leave out any mention of Savage and the woman with him."

His jaw tightened.

"Did you already report them to your team?" On undercover jobs often the person undercover couldn't communicate for long stretches of time. It was too dangerous.

"The only thing I asked my boss to do was put in a call to the locals not to investigate the jewelry store robbery. No details why though. It was too risky."

She continued, her voice low and controlled. "Good. You'll tell your boss and your team that there were two people originally involved in this job but they backed out of it. You don't have shit on them, including their names. And the woman was white with blonde hair. Average height, average weight, average *everything.* You know nothing about them and you never saw them commit a crime."

"Fine."

"This is how things are going to work. You got it?"

He nodded. "Why are you doing this?"

Instead of answering, she leaned closer and dropped her voice. "You're alive because of Savage. If it wasn't for him, you'd be gator food right now. So if you betray him or mention him *or* the woman in any capacity to your team, you're my enemy. And if you're my enemy..." Grabbing him by the neck, she squeezed tight and slammed him against the wall of the van. "You'll end up losing every shred of evidence in this case. Because we're taking everything of importance from this heist. For now. Unless you play ball."

"How so?" he rasped out.

"You're going to tell your team there was some unknown player on this job who got away with the flash drives—which isn't technically a lie. The only thing Neely will have when you find him is a shitload of cash."

He seemed to be surprised by the flash drives mention but nodded.

"Once I know you can be trusted, you'll get an anonymous tip where to find all the evidence. Neely's 'partner' will be in the wind but that's okay. You'll still be an instant hero."

"How will you know I can be trusted?"

She nodded once at the phone. "When Neely tries to give up the man and woman with his little blackmail video—and I know that he will because he'll do anything to save his own ass—you're going to text me the location of the evidence. Your team will go to get it and nothing will be there. Proving Neely to be a big liar. That there was no one named Savage and no woman involved. So when he tries to give your team the name and information of this woman, you'll be able to give your version of events with no problem." Skye knew Neely would give up Olivia's real name and information but if the DEA couldn't get proof against her—and Moore actually played ball—they'd be okay.

His gaze narrowed. "He's not the only one from that crew who saw the woman and her partner."

Skye nodded. She was already ten steps ahead of him. Maxwell and Smith shouldn't be a problem if things went right. And if Heath tried to narc Olivia out, he would just look like a bitter ex. "I know. Don't you worry about that. There's one phone number in that phone. It's to another burner. Now, you can try to track me with it but you'll fail. Or you could try to set me up and lie to me about where the evidence is. You'll fail."

"You're pretty sure of yourself."

"I am. And I don't think you're stupid. You'll do the right thing. We're both on the same side. We want Neely taken down and for him to pay for his crimes. So you let me know where that evidence is and you get what you need to make Neely go away for a long time. He's a piece of human garbage."

"You could be too, for all I know."

Her lips curved up at his attitude. "True. But if I was, you'd be dead." She scooted to the back of the van and released the door latch.

"You can't untie me?" he snapped.

"Hell no. I give you ten minutes to get out of your restraints. If you can't do it on your own, then you don't deserve to work for the DEA." She slid from the van and kept her mask on. The streets of the business district were ghostly quiet so she wasn't worried about being spotted. And she didn't want to get caught on any CCTVs in case Moore decided to try to figure out who she and Colt were.

Which she figured he would. They might not have the resources the CIA did, but the DEA still had a lot of intel and technology at their fingertips. And they had a big presence in Miami. Even if he didn't betray them, he'd still want to know who she was.

"You plant the listening device on him?" Colt asked as they broke into a jog.

"Yep."

"Think he'll try to betray us?"

"Don't know." If he did, they'd know ahead of time and be able to get in front of it. At least that was the plan.

"This plan is a little insane. We've *got* to have perfect timing with everything."

"I know." It would work. It had to. No matter what, Skye wasn't letting Olivia go to jail. No way was she letting Valencia grow up without her mother.

CHAPTER TWENTY

—I've seen all of you and I'm all in.—

Zac estimated how long it would take him to get to Neely before the man got off a shot. Zac would likely be shot, maybe die, but he'd be able to break Neely's arm, knock him out before he hurt Olivia. Yeah, he could do that.

And have no regrets either.

"Drop the bag on the ground," Neely ordered, keeping his pistol trained on Olivia.

If Zac tried to make a move the man would just shoot Olivia. The woman he was pretty sure he loved.

He dropped the empty Glock and then the duffel bag. "Olivia, I need to tell you something. I love you. It's too soon and I've never said it to another woman. But I don't care. I'm not playing a role either. I *am* obsessed with you." He kept his gaze on Neely even as he spoke. Gage and the others were supposed to be down here but in case shit went sideways, he was letting her know how he felt. He wasn't going to die with anything unsaid. He'd lived most of his life without regrets. He wasn't going to die with any.

"Zac, no," she whispered.

"God, you two are annoying. I'm going to take pleasure in killing you both. Step back and away from the bag." Neely didn't move any closer to them, likely because he knew Savage could disarm him. Apparently he wanted to make sure his loot was in the duffel before he killed them.

Savage held out his arms and pushed Olivia behind him as they started slowly stepping backward. "You're the most incredible woman I've ever met," Zac murmured. "Whatever happens, I want you to know that."

Olivia tried to step out from behind him but he shoved her back, keeping his hands visible and wide open. If he went for the other weapon tucked at his back, Neely would fire.

She sucked in a little breath, likely having finally seen the pistol. Yep. She pulled it slowly out from his waist. From what he'd seen she didn't seem to care for weapons but he hoped she'd be able to use it.

Neely crouched down by the bag, unzipped it. His weapon hand wavered only slightly as he looked inside, distracted for a moment.

That was all Zac needed. Reaching back he grabbed the weapon from Olivia. In two moves he had the pistol up—fired.

Neely pulled the trigger at the same time. The man flew back from the impact of Zac's hit.

Olivia's arms wrapped around him as she tried to tackle Savage to the ground. Already in motion, he dove with her, twisting in midair to fire again. Dirt flew up a few inches from Neely, who was clutching his shoulder, his weapon on the ground.

Zac shoved up as Gage, Brooks and Leighton sprinted along the side of the building dressed in tactical gear from head to toe.

"Stay," he ordered Olivia as he ran at Neely, weapon trained on him. He kicked the pistol out of the way and slammed his boot into Neely's side.

Before he could do any more, Gage tased Neely, full force. "We need him alive," Gage snapped as Neely writhed on the grass in pain.

Zac knew that. Didn't mean he had to like it. They had a plan and had to stick to it. Especially in order to keep Olivia out of jail. Everything hinged on what happened next.

He stripped off his harness and pulled it onto Neely's now unconscious body. The cops were going to have a hell of a time figuring out what had happened and would likely never cross their t's and dot their i's but they'd have a few bad guys in custody.

"Did Skye—"

"Yep. She and Colt took care of the other thing. We're gonna get what we need," Gage said.

Sirens wailed in the distance. He turned to find Olivia right next to him, because of course she wouldn't stay put.

She held her harness and other gear in hand. "Are they coming for us?"

"They're coming for Neely and the others. Let's go." Savage reached into the duffel bag and grabbed the small bag of flash drives but left the cash and files right next to Neely's body.

Olivia looked as if she wanted to say more but nodded and fell in step with them as they raced back along the length of the building toward the main street.

Before they'd made it halfway, a van jumped the curb and came tearing up over the grass, kicking up dirt and taking out bushes as it sped toward them. No doubt in his mind who was driving.

It screeched to a halt and Colt threw the side door open. "We've got about three minutes."

They all jumped in and he didn't give a shit what anyone thought, he pulled Olivia into his lap, wrapping his arms tight around her as Skye jerked the wheel, tearing up more of the pristine lawn as she booked it toward the street.

"What happens now?" Olivia asked quietly. "Kyle will sell me out. He'll try to make a deal and turn over that video footage."

"That's what we're counting on," Gage said.

"What? Why?" she asked.

Zac hadn't been able to relay all of the plan to her earlier and she hadn't been on the same comm channel. So he understood her fear and frustration.

Skye turned down a side street and the sirens grew fainter. Some of the adrenaline surging through Zac abated. But not completely. That wouldn't happen until they had exactly what they needed.

"We've got a listening device on the DEA agent Neely thinks is dead and we've got one on Neely now." Gage looked inordinately pleased with himself as he pulled out a laptop and earphones. "We'll hear everything either one of them says in the near future."

"If he tells them where his evidence is—"

"We'll steal it before they get there." Zac wrapped his arm around her tighter and was pleased when she leaned into his hold and placed her own hands over his. He wasn't under the illusion that it meant anything to her but he'd take what he could get. Because he wasn't giving up on them. This woman was his and he planned to claim her forever.

"Okay." She didn't sound convinced but that was okay. Zac was going to personally retrieve what Neely had stashed.

* * *

Olivia couldn't stop the nervous energy crackling through her as she stood in the small kitchen of the new safe house with Gage. Skye had driven them to a one-story ranch-style house that was under a foreclosure notice. She wasn't sure how they even had power at the house but Gage was clearly a miracle worker. Everyone except Leighton were elsewhere in the house keeping an eye out for cops but she couldn't leave Gage or his laptops. She'd wanted to ask where Leighton had gone but figured it must be important.

Two laptops were set up on the kitchen table as they listened to Agent Darius Moore—aka Alonso—interrogate Kyle.

Everything seemed to be happening so slowly. It had been hours since Kyle and the others had been arrested and then processed. Then they'd had to listen to Agent Moore give a brief report to his boss. And Kyle had to go to the hospital to be checked out and patched up. It turned out he wasn't as injured as they'd thought. His shoulder had been grazed and he'd lost blood, but he was going to be fine.

Unfortunately.

Fortunately, however, and to Olivia's surprise, Agent Moore had lied about her and Savage to his boss, just leaving them out completely. And Maxwell and Smith hadn't said a word about her or Savage's involvement either according to what she'd heard when Agent Moore had been talking to them. Neither had Heath—but he hadn't said a word at all apparently. As in, *nothing*, according to Moore. Not even to ask for a lawyer. He was in the hospital, refusing to speak even to the doctors. Soon he was supposed to be transferred.

Which still didn't make her feel any better. Because soon enough Kyle would narc her out. And what happened then? What if they couldn't get to the evidence in time? Or what if he had it uploaded somewhere? What if—

Skye stepped into the kitchen suddenly and placed something warm in Olivia's hands, making her blink. "What's this?"

"Hot chocolate. Now sit." She pointed at the fold-out card table that one of the guys had brought in from the garage. They'd also found rusted chairs. Things the previous owners hadn't cared to take with them, because this place was otherwise unfurnished.

"Where'd you get this?"

"Savage did a run to a Quick Stop. You look like you're about to have a panic attack so I need you to listen. Smith and Maxwell won't be telling the Feds that you and Savage were part of the heist."

"Just because they haven't yet doesn't mean anything. They could still say something." And she wasn't certain why they hadn't yet. Maybe they had, and it hadn't been to Agent Moore. Unless Moore was in the room with someone, Olivia or the others couldn't hear a word of what was going on. They were completely dependent on the listening device planted on him for knowledge.

"Leighton took care of it."

She blinked. "He hurt them?"

"No."

"Then how?"

"I'm not going to tell you—it gives you plausible deniability."

Olivia didn't think to push Skye for more details as relief flooded her. She was too damn grateful. "Thank you."

"If Heath brings you up, he'll just look like a jealous ex."

Olivia nodded, still uneasy. She might have blackmail on Heath, but Kyle still had blackmail on *her*. There were too many damn balls in the air and she was terrified one of them would fall, causing everything else to come crashing down.

She looked past Skye to the doorway of the kitchen, as if that would make Savage magically appear. He didn't, of course. Which was just as well. That whole "confession" he'd laid out for her had to be utter crap. She'd realized it when he'd pushed her behind his body and she'd seen that gun. He'd just been trying to distract Kyle long enough for her to get the weapon. It had been a good plan too. Even if her heart hurt when she realized nothing he'd said was true. Not that any of that mattered right now. Well, it did matter but it wasn't something she could focus on.

"Thank you." Olivia lifted the Styrofoam cup to her mouth and sat on the uncomfortable metal fold-out chair.

Skye crouched in front of her, the dark contacts and blonde wig making her appear like a different person.

She started to say something just as Gage snapped his fingers at them. "Moore is in with Neely again." He turned up the volume.

"My client should still be in a hospital," a male voice said, definitely his lawyer.

"Your client has been reviewed by the best doctors in Miami and deemed fit to speak to us. And *your client* is in a lot of trouble. He was found with a couple hundred thousand in cash, and classified files."

"Anyone could have planted that."

Agent Moore snorted. "Oh yeah. Did we also stage the heist itself, tie up all the security guys ourselves and dress your client in rappelling gear? Not to mention that he ordered the death of a federal agent—me. And of course there's a dead body we're still trying to identify from the crime scene. Let's cut the shit right now. We know you were working with someone else and we know there was more they took from the safe. If you help us find whoever escaped we'll think about cutting a deal. And you better make a decision fast before one of your other guys talks."

"What kind of deal?" the lawyer asked.

"If he forgoes a trial, forty years with eligibility for parole."

There was a pause, then murmuring.

"My client is prepared to hand over evidence of the criminals involved in the robbery of Tatiana's Fine Jewelry a couple days ago. Video evidence. The same couple involved—a man and woman—are the same couple involved in the Prisock robbery. And this same man killed the dead man you found at the Prisock building. What will you give in exchange?"

There was a long silence, then, "If you give evidence that leads us to this alleged couple *and* they have the rest of the stash from the safe, we'll knock a decade off your sentence."

"Knock off fifteen years. With eligibility for parole."

"Fine."

"We want it in writing," Neely said.

"If you lie to us, you're getting forty years, no eligibility for parole."

The lawyer murmured his agreement.

Agent Moore spoke to someone else and Olivia heard the sound of a door opening, then closing. Then it was mostly silent with only the sound of rustling clothes and a chair scraping over a floor.

Roughly ten minutes later the door opened again. Then there was more rustling and murmuring, then, "This works."

"Talk," Agent Moore ordered.

"The name of the woman who stole the rest of the contents of the safe is Olivia Carter." He rattled off her address and other personal information about her place of employment. Then, "She'll claim she's innocent but I've got evidence of her committing the heist at Tatiana's. She worked with a man named Savage. The evidence against them is in a safe at..." He continued talking, rattling off the address and the code to the safe.

Before he'd finished Skye had moved into action and Colt, Brooks, and Savage spilled into the room. As if they'd been waiting outside it. Maybe they'd been trying to give her space.

It appeared as if Leighton still wasn't back. She hoped he was okay.

They all started talking about the game plan and who was going.

"I'm going. This is my mess too," she said into the murmur of voices. She couldn't let them do this by themselves. They'd all already given so much of themselves to this operation.

Everyone turned to look at her but she only had eyes for Savage. *Zac.*

He stepped toward her as the others started talking amongst themselves again. Taking her by surprise, he grasped her hands and pulled her close. "You're going to get on a plane and head back to Redemption Harbor with Brooks. You can't be anywhere near this evidence just in case the cops beat us there. You need to be in another state with an alibi. Brooks will go over everything with you."

"Zac—"

"No. We don't have time to argue. You have to go."

She wanted to resist but knew it would just waste time. Time they didn't have. "Please be safe. And don't get caught. If it looks like you will, just get out of there." Because she didn't want anyone getting arrested because of her.

Leaning down—and taking her off guard—he brushed his lips over hers. "I'll be a ghost." Then he was gone with Skye and Colt. Gage was apparently staying to provide technical support.

"You ready?" Brooks asked quietly, a hint of that cowboy drawl in his voice.

No, she wanted to say. Instead she nodded. "Yeah." Before they left she turned to Gage. "Will you keep me updated? Make sure..." She wasn't sure how to phrase it and felt weird even asking.

"I'll let you know what happens with Savage. But we're all very good at what we do. Your man will be fine."

Zac wasn't hers in any way that mattered but she nodded, her throat tight, and turned to Brooks. Crying wouldn't do anyone any good now. It was time to leave, time to get back to her daughter and Martina.

Soon it would be time to say goodbye to Zac. She just hoped she got the chance—and wondered if he would even care, or if he'd be glad to have her out of his life.

CHAPTER TWENTY-ONE

—I wouldn't say no to a nap.—

Zac stepped into the waiting elevator with Skye. Colt and Leighton—who'd joined them—were downstairs as lookouts and so far they hadn't seen anything out of the ordinary.

The address Neely had given the DEA had been the same address Agent Moore had texted Skye's burner with. Moore had also told Skye that she had maybe fifteen minutes to get what she needed before someone would be there. It was late afternoon and the sun would be setting soon. If they ended up having to make a break for it, it was a good time of day to do it. Always easier to blend in places after dark.

"Moore never acknowledged how he was set free or any of the events leading up to it," Zac said. "He kept everything pretty damn vague."

Back at the house he'd been eavesdropping on the live feed from the living room. And not once did Agent Moore acknowledge that he'd had contact with Zac or Olivia in the penthouse. As if they'd never existed. During another conversation he'd also told his boss that he'd escaped and then had to lie low after Neely had ordered him killed. But he'd given a very vague description of the man Neely had ordered to kill him. And he hadn't given Savage's name. Something Zac didn't think Neely knew. Moore had also been very careful in how he worded things in the recorded interview with Neely and his attorney. Not only that, Maxwell and Smith hadn't said a word about Olivia or Savage. Apparently Leighton had terrified them into silence.

"I know," Skye said. "He's smart. At this point I think we can trust him. If he was going to turn on us, he'd have done it by now. And if he tries later, how's he going to explain why he lied about so many things? No, he wants this win. He wants to bring down Neely. And Neely is about to prove himself to be a liar."

So whatever Neely tried to come back with after this point wouldn't matter. He'd be labeled a liar and no one was going to believe him over a DEA agent with no viable reason to lie. Savage nodded in agreement even if he didn't feel completely secure in Agent Moore's acquiescence to the whole situation. So far Heath hadn't breathed a word about Olivia either. Though Zac wasn't holding his breath the man didn't talk. He should have just killed him. Mark that down as one of his greatest regrets. Heath should be dead.

They'd beat Agent Moore's fifteen-minute time frame and were now leaving the downtown Miami condo complex with the evidence from the heist in hand. He planned to destroy it as soon as he saw what was on it. He needed to know that it was what Neely had said it was.

"Is what you said to Olivia true?" Skye asked.

"What?"

"When Neely was holding his weapon on you. Were you telling her the truth or were you buying time?"

He inwardly winced, hating that his entire team had heard his confession. "I really don't want to have this conversation."

"Too bad." Her voice was dry as she pressed the button for the lobby. "Cause you're gonna have it. Olivia is my friend and I adore both her and Valencia. So if you break her heart, I'm probably going to break your face."

Zac was pretty sure she was being serious. His lips curved up slightly as the elevator dinged and the doors whooshed open. "Trust me. If anyone breaks anyone's heart, she'll destroy mine."

Skye looked sideways at him but he wouldn't meet her gaze. Admitting to Olivia how he felt, actually saying the L word, had been hard enough. He hadn't been lying. He'd never said those words to a woman before. He hadn't thought he could actually feel them, *love* someone like he did her.

As they stepped out into the lobby, his gaze snapped to the three men and two women striding through the glass front doors. All of them had on blue jackets with DEA clearly embellished in yellow over the right breast pocket.

Zac reached into his pocket, wrapped his hand around the DVD. He'd wanted to view it first but he'd crush it now. As he did, Agent Moore looked over at him and Skye—made direct eye contact with Zac.

And looked away as if he didn't know him.

"Keep walking," Skye murmured low enough for his ears only.

Okay, then. Clearly Agent Moore wasn't going to betray them to his team.

Still, Zac wasn't going to fully breathe easy until they were outside. Pulse pounding, he headed straight for the lobby doors, his steps even and steady as the DEA agents barked orders at the woman standing behind the welcome desk.

Once in the fresh evening air, he looked at Skye.

She gave him a megawatt grin. "Let's finish this crap and head home."

Nodding, he broke into a jog as Colt pulled up to the front curb in an SUV. Skye jogged around to the passenger side as Leighton threw open the back door and scooted over for Zac.

"Was that the DEA?" Colt asked.

"Yep," Zac muttered.

"I'm going to die of a heart attack before I hit forty." Leighton strapped in as Colt steered into traffic. "I don't want to see any of them for a long damn time."

Yeah, no shit. "You're sure you're good with your contact?" Zac asked Leighton—who'd called in a huge favor to pose as the lawyer for both Maxwell and Smith. It had been the only way for him to get access to them. And it had been a hell of a risk.

"Yeah. I'm good."

"Let's grab some takeout after we make the drop off at the jewelry store," Skye said, pulling her cell phone out. "Anyone else in the mood for Italian?"

"I want Thai," Leighton said.

As the others talked about food Zac stared out the window, watching the darkening city fly by. On any other op he would have been putting in his own food order. The Corps had taught him a lot, and one of those things was that you ate when you could because you never knew when the next meal would happen. Or if it even would. Some things had stuck with him.

But the thought of food made his stomach tighten. He wanted to see Olivia, hold her, talk to her.

It was good she'd gone back to Redemption Harbor. Necessary.

But he still missed her. And he wouldn't rest until they'd cleared the air, until he knew he still had a shot with her. Because that whole house, picket fence and kid scenario he'd once thought was complete and utter bullshit sounded like the best damn thing in the world. But only if he had it with Olivia.

* * *

Gage looked up as everyone filed into the kitchen, takeout bags in hand. He had a lot to tell everyone but he was glad they'd brought food. He was starving. "Someone better have saved me something." Or he was going to be cranky.

"I snagged this before Skye could eat it," Savage said, dropping a brown bag onto the fold-out table.

This place was a dump but Gage wouldn't give up his current job to go back to the cushy—and boring as fuck—job he'd had in Seattle seven months ago. Working with his family, helping people, this was what his life had been missing.

"I would be offended if he wasn't telling the truth." Skye grinned and popped a fried shrimp into her mouth.

Colt brushed his lips over Skye's, uncaring that she was chewing, before leaning against one of the counters and opening his own bag.

"You guys drop off the jewels?" Gage asked.

Skye nodded. "Yeah."

"Good... I've broken the encryption on two of the flash drives." Leaning back in his chair, Gage linked his fingers together behind his neck and rolled his shoulders. "And before I lay everything out, I just want to prepare you. Some of this we need to give to the Feds. Some of it, however..."

No, better to just show them. Turning to his laptop, he pulled up one of the files.

He talked as he typed. "I've been digging deeper into Prisock. And they're exactly what they appear to be on the surface. But the safe Olivia's ex-husband targeted, that belongs to a man named Jarred Watson. Or belonged to. He's dead now, by the way."

"What, when?" Skye asked.

"Half an hour ago. Heard the address on a police scanner and it sounded familiar. It appears as if he was killed in a home invasion gone wrong. Considering the guy was killed by garrote wire, I'm thinking no. He was killed by Alexei Kuznetsov—or one of his guys more likely."

"The mobster we've been looking into?" Colt asked.

"Yeah. In a sec, I'll show you why I think he was killed by the guy." Kuznetsov was a piece of shit who ran a lot of drugs up and down the East Coast. Weapons and people too, and he'd been on their radar for a few months. "Heath was killed—he's dead too, by the way."

"What the hell, Gage?" Savage muttered, but he didn't stop eating. "Anyone else die while we were gone?"

"What? I'm just telling you what I discovered." Gage was glad that bastard Heath was dead too. He might not have said anything about Olivia—probably because he was too afraid of the Russians to say anything at all—but he might have tried later.

"Well don't just drop that information on Olivia. I'll tell her when we get back." There was a bite to Savage's words. Oh yeah, his friend was a goner for her.

Gage nodded. "I figured you'd want to."

"So how did Heath die?" Skye asked, her tone impatient. "And we're going to go back to Kuznetsov's involvement."

"Olivia's ex died during the prisoner transfer from the hospital. One of the DEA agents called Agent Moore while he was searching the condo you guys robbed. Gave him the bad news. It's the only reason I even know about it."

"Who did it?"

"Just another prisoner. Russian. And I think with some digging we'll find a link between Heath's killer and Kuznetsov."

Skye shrugged. "I'm surprised he was killed so fast, but it was bound to happen."

"Yep." He'd agreed to deliver the contents of that safe to someone and when he'd failed, they'd killed him. Now that Gage had seen said contents, he understood why. A man like Kuznetsov wouldn't have taken the chance that Heath talked, regardless. "So back to Watson. From what I've gathered he used to work in DC, sort of as a fixer, I guess. Someone powerful had a problem, he'd fix it. And he started gathering blackmail on said powerful people. About six months ago he moved to Miami and got a job at Prisock. And it appears his blackmailing days weren't over. Which brings me to why I think Kuznetsov is involved."

He shifted the laptop so everyone could see. "Is that..." Skye's eyes widened. "Damn."

"A standing US senator having sex with Kuznetsov's thirty-year-old, married-to-a-woman son? Yes. There's video too."

Skye grinned. "Holy shit. I remember that asshole. He based his whole campaign on what he considers 'family values.' This will destroy him."

"Exactly. But it's not illegal. Some of the shit I've found is very, very illegal. That, I think we should turn over to Moore and the DEA and some to the FBI. But anything like this..." He motioned to the picture on his computer. "I think we should save this as our backup. What we're doing... One day we're going to cross the wrong person or people. Maybe even get tangled up with the government. Hell, it almost happened with this job. We're *lucky* Agent Moore only cared about bringing down Neely and his crew and that the other players were willing to keep their mouths shut. We need some insurance as a get out of jail free card. Now, I know this might be—"

"I agree," Skye said at the same time Colt nodded.

Savage and Leighton murmured their agreement as well.

"I thought I might have to convince you guys."

Skye lifted an eyebrow. "Did you prepare an argument?"

"Maybe. Now you'll never know." He turned back to his computer and pulled up another image. One that made Skye toss her bag of food onto the nearest counter.

"Come on, man. Gotta give a girl some warning."

Colt snickered. "Someone finally made you lose your appetite."

"Why the hell would someone want another person to pee on them?" She shuddered and shoved her food even farther away as Gage closed the image.

"All right, so we're in agreement. We turn over anything that reveals illegal activities to Agent Moore? Everything else we take with us—and we keep backups."

Everyone nodded so he turned back to his computer. He still had five more drives to unencrypt. There was no telling what he was going to find.

CHAPTER TWENTY-TWO

—If he's the right guy, he won't leave.—

Savage moved quietly through Brooks's house, looking for Olivia. The sun wasn't even up yet, but he needed to see her. He and the others had recently arrived in Redemption Harbor and he'd gone straight to find her when they got to the ranch. But she hadn't been in her room. Neither had her daughter. Realistically he knew that they were okay but he wanted to see her with his own eyes. She'd quickly become an addiction and now he was on a mission at six in the morning.

When he stepped into the movie room, that vise around his chest eased the smallest fraction. A table lamp was on and Valencia was sitting next to her mom, some kind of tablet open in her lap, while Olivia was fast asleep, leaning back in one of the recliners. The little girl smiled when she saw him and then held a finger up to her mouth and told him to be quiet.

Slowly, the little girl eased her blanket off and slid off the recliner chair. Then she grabbed her processors from another chair, slid them on, and picked up a stuffed toy unicorn. Olivia shifted but instead of waking, curled up onto her side with a pillow clutched to her chest. Her long, dark hair covered half her face and she looked so peaceful. Yeah, he needed to let her sleep.

I'm hungry, Valencia signed.

I can make pancakes. He had no idea what possessed him to say that but he would certainly give it his best shot. How hard could it be?

But she smiled. *My mommy makes them like Mickey Mouse.*

I can do that. He hoped.

Still smiling, she fell in step with him as they left the room, clutching the purple and green animal. The horn was a rainbow of colors. *My mommy said you were on the trip with her and you helped my Nana.*

He doubted Olivia had told Valencia much but he nodded. *I was. And how's your Nana doing?*

Good. She tried riding horses yesterday but she wasn't very good. Valencia giggled at that. *She said she wanted to try again today.*

What about you?

She shrugged and answered audibly. "I think I like watching them and petting them more than riding. Maybe when I'm older I'll ride more."

He inwardly smiled. Olivia was right, Valencia sounded so adult. As they stepped into the kitchen he headed straight for the coffee maker while Valencia climbed up one of the bar stools and sat at the counter. She placed her unicorn in the chair next to her.

"My unicorn wants pancakes too," she said primly.

He laughed lightly. "I think I can manage that." He started the economy-sized Bunn coffee maker before moving to the stainless-steel fridge. "What do you normally drink in the mornings?" He figured before starting her breakfast he should get her something to drink. That seemed like something Olivia would do.

"Coke."

Frowning, he looked over his shoulder at her. "Really?" He might not know much about kids but that didn't seem right.

She giggled and shook her head. "No, I'm not allowed to have it except on special occasions. Milk, please."

"You're sneaky."

"That's what my mommy says." Her eyes lit up when she talked about her mother.

Something he understood. Whenever he thought about Olivia, it did something strange to his insides. "Your mommy is a special lady."

"I know."

After giving her milk, he found a container of shake-and-pour pancake mix and wanted to do a fist pump. All he had to do was add water. Hell yeah. He could do this pancake thing. Mercer was always cooking. How hard could it be?

Moving to the center island across from Valencia, he turned on one of the stove burners. "So, I know that you're missing your Thanksgiving play." Or…he assumed she was. Technically they still had time to get back. But Savage selfishly hoped they didn't leave. He wanted more time with Olivia. Valencia too.

"Yeah, it's okay though."

"I thought maybe we could put on a play for everyone." He started shaking the water and mix together. "I already asked your Aunt Skye and Uncle Colt." And he was definitely dragging Gage into it. He'd googled "turkey play" and come up with an actual script and everything. The costumes…he wasn't so sure about. Even if Olivia decided he wasn't worth the effort, he wanted to do this for her. For both of them.

Valencia's eyes widened. "For real?"

Nodding, he pulled out butter and scooped some into the pan. "For real."

"That would be awesome." She looked over as Brooks's dad walked in wearing jeans and a T-shirt.

He smiled warmly at the little girl. "Hey, kid."

"Good to see you, sir." Zac had practically grown up over here, spending most of his weekends at this estate. Douglas Alexander hadn't been here much though. He'd been a better parent to Brooks than Zac's own mother had been to him, but absent emotionally all the same. Brooks said his dad was making an effort now, however. Zac hoped Brooks gave the man a chance.

"You too, son."

"Mr. Alexander! The foal was born yesterday!"

"I heard that." He ruffled her hair absently before moving to the coffee pot and pouring himself a mug. "And you get to name her."

"For real?"

Douglas laughed lightly as he leaned against the granite countertop. "Yes, for real… You're cooking?" he asked mildly, raising an eyebrow at Zac.

Zac lifted a shoulder. "Giving it a shot anyway."

He snorted lightly. "So, you living in Redemption Harbor now too?"

Zac nodded. He wasn't sure how much Brooks had told his dad about their new venture with Redemption Harbor Consulting. "We're all back home." No need to explain who "all" meant.

"Looks like you've added more to your bunch too. I like that Skye. She's a pistol."

"That's one way to say it. So you moving back or just visiting?"

"Ah…moving back. Got divorced and figured it was time to return home. Got tired of Florida anyway."

Brooks walked in then, made a beeline for the coffee maker. "Got tired of Florida or that bi…" He trailed off after his dad cleared his throat sharply, and nodded at Valencia—who was watching them raptly.

"Hey, kiddo," Brooks said, smiling. "Your mom still asleep?"

She nodded. "We fell asleep in the movie room last night."

Right around then Martina walked into the kitchen and to Zac's surprise Douglas grabbed a mug and poured her a cup. "A little bit of cream, right? No sugar?"

Martina's dark eyebrows rose, but she nodded and sat next to Valencia, sitting the unicorn in her own lap. "Yes, thank you." She kissed Valencia's head, then she frowned at Zac. "What's that supposed to be?"

"Ah...Mickey Mouse." It looked more like a warped version of South America. He was pretty sure he'd added too much water because it was running everywhere.

Valencia giggled. "It's not very good."

"Valencia," Martina murmured, "that's not nice." But she laughed too.

Brooks's dad actually nudged him out of the way. "Watch a pro handle this." He pulled out a bag of flour and added some to the mix, thickening it up.

"I feel like I've walked into an alternate reality," Brooks muttered. "My dad's cooking pancakes."

Zac hid a grin because it was clear Douglas was trying to impress Martina. Which seemed...odd for the man Zac knew. He'd never seen the man try to impress anyone. Not even his last gold-digger wife who'd been a good thirty years younger than him. He seemed a hell of a lot different than the man Zac had known.

"Sit next to me, Mr. Savage," Valencia said, pointing to the seat by her. "I want to talk about the turkey play."

"Call me Zac," he murmured, pulling the seat out.

"Turkey play?" Olivia asked, stepping into the kitchen entryway, her jet-black hair down and around her shoulders in soft waves.

Wearing jeans and a loose T-shirt, she looked more rested than he'd seen her all week. The stress of the last few days was gone and all he could think about was kissing her senseless. After a long moment when her cheeks tinged pink, he realized he was staring at her. Clearing his throat, he stood and held the chair out for her. "I thought we could put on a play for Thanksgiving since Valencia is missing hers."

Olivia blinked, but sat in the chair. "I think that's a great idea." Warmth infused her voice as she wrapped her arm around her daughter.

Zac got her coffee and fixed it the way she liked—and felt like a randy teenager when their fingers brushed as he set it in front of her. He had to consciously think of things *not* Olivia naked and stretched out on his bed. Because getting a hard on now simply couldn't happen.

"Thanks," she murmured, her cheeks flushing that sexy shade of pink.

He just grunted and moved back to the counter with Brooks as Valencia started chatting about turkeys and costumes.

Zac forced himself not to stare at Olivia, but it was damn hard. As soon as he got a chance, he was getting her alone and talking. Because he wasn't letting her go without a fight.

CHAPTER TWENTY-THREE

—I may not be your first,
but I want to be your last everything.—

Zac knocked on the halfway open door to Olivia and Valencia's room. It had been two hours since breakfast and he was running out of patience. Olivia stepped out of the walk-in closet and smiled at him, blushing again.

Man, that blush. He cleared his throat. "You got a sec?"

She nodded and set a child's-size cardigan on the bed before stepping toward him. "Valencia's at the stables with Martina and Mr. Alexander. I think he's got a little crush on Martina."

Zac nodded. A crush indeed. The man was smitten, something he hadn't thought possible of the other man. Not that he gave a shit about that right now. He just wanted to talk to Olivia. *More* than talk.

"I just got a text from my neighbor," she said before he could speak, pulling her phone from her jeans pocket. She handed it to him.

He read it, gave it back. A local DEA agent had come by the house looking for Olivia, wanting to talk to her, and left his card for her to call him. "This is good. It's what we expected." After breakfast that morning they'd gone over what the next few steps would likely be. And the DEA would definitely want to talk to her. She just had to stick to the plan.

"I know." She wrapped her arms around herself. "I just want this all over with."

"When are you going to call the agent?"

Sighing, she perched on the edge of the bed, arms still tight around herself. He didn't like it. It felt as if she was closing herself off from him. That was unacceptable. "Soon, I guess."

"You want to go over what you'll say?"

She started to shake her head, then paused. "I'll tell them that my ex-husband showed up at my place wanting to talk to me about custody stuff. He's never shown any interest in our daughter but apparently changed his mind. But it turned out that my ex was the same old jerk. He just wanted to borrow money from me and maybe rekindle the past. When I told him no he got angry and hit me." She motioned to her face.

"Which your neighbors can corroborate."

"Yeah. So he left and then somehow knew I'd planned a getaway to Miami with my new boyfriend. Gage will make it look like he'd been stalking me."

Zac nodded as she continued.

"He confronted me again in Miami, demanded money or he'd make my life hell, would try to get partial custody of Valencia, even threatened her. So we decided to head back to Redemption Harbor where my daughter was staying with friends."

"The timeline works. You'll just have to sell it, especially when they ask you about Kyle Neely."

"I'll tell them I'd met the man before but didn't know him. He was just one of my ex-husband's associates, a man who actually scared me."

"They'll push you about the heist—both of them."

"And I'll feign ignorance. Act like I have no idea what they're talking about."

Zac nodded. "You've got a strong timeline to back up your version of events and an alibi for the second heist."

"One that's a lie."

"You'll make them believe it. And with an ex-husband who had no problem hitting his wife, it's not much of a stretch that he'd try to hurt you simply because he could, to make you and your new boyfriend look guilty of something you had no part of."

"Kyle's the one who tried to sell me out."

He lifted a shoulder. "Tomato, tomato," he said, making it sound like *tomayto, tomahto.* The only way this truly worked was if Agent Moore didn't turn them in for being part of the jewelry heist. So far it appeared as if he was holding up his end of the bargain. Probably because he was going to get a huge promotion from this. Taking down such a big crew basically by himself would help the man's career. "And Maxwell and Smith haven't said a word about you either." Whatever Leighton had said to them had done its job. They were going to get sentenced but it wouldn't be too bad, especially since they'd cut a deal and turned on Neely. They'd probably decided to just do their time and not get dead.

"Okay, you're right. I've got this." Tossing her phone onto her bed she raked her fingers through her hair. "Then hopefully my life will go back to normal."

"Not completely, I hope." He shut the door behind him. Because he wanted to be part of her future.

She stood as he did, eyeing him almost warily. Which just annoyed him. Was she really surprised by this?

"Savage—"

"It's Zac. You don't get to keep me at a distance anymore. We've seen each other naked and I've made you come multiple times." Blunt, raw words. Mainly because he wanted to see her cheeks turn pink again.

They did. She cleared her throat. "That's...fair. Look, I don't want to do this right now."

"Too bad. We are." They were finally alone and he needed to get some things out.

She jerked at his tone, her spine going ramrod straight. When she glared at him, he got hard. Because Olivia mad at him was fine by him. Mad, angry, turned on, happy, whatever. He just didn't want indifference or distance. He wanted her heat and passion. "Fine. What do you want to talk about?"

"Us." He closed the distance between them and cupped her cheek, rubbing his thumb against her soft skin. He'd never get tired of holding her, touching her. She wasn't pushing him away either.

For a moment she closed her eyes, leaned into it. He bit back a groan. Such a simple touch shouldn't affect him but it did all the same.

But just as quickly she shook her head and brushed his hand away. "Look. I know you said what you said because you wanted me to find that gun. I'm not going to hold you to anything. I'm—"

"Are you kidding me?" He kept his voice pitched low even though her words pissed him off. "I didn't say any of that because I had to. I said it because I meant it."

"How do I know you're telling the truth?" Her voice wavered slightly.

"You can't know anything for sure. But you can trust the man who caught you when you were three stories up and your rope was cut. The man who admitted his feelings for you in front of his whole team. Not because I was making shit up as a distraction. I've fallen for you, Olivia. I want a future with you."

She let her arms drop from around herself and laid one hand on his chest. Just that one touch and all the muscles in his body pulled taut. He wanted to feel her hands all over him, stroking and teasing. "Valencia and I are a package deal," she whispered.

"I *know.* And I want to get to know her, to be in *both* your lives. And I understand you can't just throw some man into her life but I'd like the opportunity to ease into it. To be there for both of you, to be more than your friend." He *did* want to be her friend, because he loved everything about her and who she was, but he wanted more. That whole package he'd always convinced himself was bullshit? He wanted it so bad he could taste it. But not with just anyone. Olivia was it.

Her eyes filled with tears and she wiped them away before he could. "Zac, I live in a different state."

"So? We try long distance and see where it goes from there. Then I'll move once we get to the point where long distance isn't working." Because he knew himself well enough that he couldn't live far from her for long. No, he wanted to be *in* her life, not on the periphery.

She sucked in a sharp breath.

He barreled on, needing to get all this out now. "Does that scare you? Because if this is about you not having the same feelings for me, then say it. I'll walk away right *now.* I know I screwed up with what I said to Brooks. But I'm owning it. You scare the hell out of me, Olivia. Not an excuse—just the truth." If she told him she didn't return his feelings, it would carve him up. But he'd rather know sooner than later. "Just don't push me away because of something stupid I said or because you're afraid of the future. Because that's a cop-out if you do. We deserve to be happy." Something he hadn't believed about himself for a long time. Until her.

She swallowed hard, watching him intently for a long moment. "I'm pretty sure that's the most I've ever heard you say at once."

Okay, she wasn't pushing him away. Slowly he reached out, grasped her hip. "Olivia—"

The bedroom door flew open and Valencia and Martina walked in. Martina's eyes widened slightly at the sight of them, then she just grinned. "Douglas and I are taking Valencia for pizza and to see the baby at Mercer's. I just wanted to get her another sweater. It's starting to get chilly." She picked up the cardigan from the bed and tucked it under her arm.

"Do you need extra batteries for her processors?" Olivia asked.

Martina shook her head. "I have everything. Don't worry about a thing."

"Mommy!" Valencia ran at Olivia, wrapped her little arms around her waist. "Nana said if I was really good we might get to go see a movie in town tonight. Can we go?"

"Absolutely." Olivia cupped Valencia's cheeks before kissing her forehead. "And you can have popcorn, before you ask."

Valencia smiled up at Savage. "You want to come with us to get pizza, Zac?"

He started to say yes when Martina clucked her tongue. "*Mi pequeña,* Zac and your mommy have to start on the script for the turkey play. We'll see them in a few *hours.* They'll go with us to the movies." Then the woman winked at him before hustling Valencia out.

"Did she just wink at me?"

Olivia's cheeks were full-on crimson now. "Yes. Yes, she did. She pretty much just told us we'd have a few hours to ourselves."

"I can think of a way to kill time," he murmured, only slightly teasing.

She cleared her throat. "Can we go to your room? Just in case they come back early."

Oh, hell. *What?* "Are you saying…"

She nodded.

His throat tightened and it took all his restraint not to just pick her up and carry her when he wanted to go straight into caveman mode. Grasping her hand in his, he tugged her out into the hallway. As they turned down the next one, Gage was coming out of his room.

The other man opened his mouth to say something, but Zac shook his head. "Unless something's on fire or it's an emergency, it can wait."

Gage just grinned as he looked between the two of them and saluted before heading in the other direction.

"Oh, he totally knows what we're doing," Olivia murmured as Zac pulled her into his bedroom.

"Do you care?"

"No."

"Good." Everyone in the house could know, for all he cared. That primitive part of him *wanted* every man here to know she was his. That she was off-limits.

He backed her up against the door and locked it as he crushed his mouth to hers. She hadn't actually told him she wanted a future with him but he was taking this moment at least.

They'd already proven they worked well as a team and he wanted to show her how good they could truly be together. Because he wanted everything from her.

Arching into him, she immediately grasped at the hem of his sweater and tugged it upward. Her fingers skated over his bare stomach as she lifted it up, up, up—he took over and jerked it over his head. His hands actually shook as he cupped her face, his mouth on hers once again.

All the military training in the world couldn't have prepared him for Olivia. Being calm and in control around her wasn't possible. When she grasped at his belt, he pulled back slightly, breathing hard. Keeping his hand over hers, he said, "Not yet." Because he needed to keep his clothes on for now. At least he needed to keep his dick covered.

He'd been waiting for this, for *her*, it felt like a lifetime. Who was he kidding? He'd never even thought someone like her existed for him. Olivia was this slice of heaven and he felt damn lucky to know her.

"You've tasted me. It's my turn." Her dark eyes glittered with hunger.

Groaning, he picked her up and carried her to the bed. He stretched her out underneath him, caging her in with his arms and body. "You'll get your turn—but I'm tasting you first. I need you to come before I'm inside you." And...that was when he realized he didn't have any condoms. "I don't have any protection." In Miami things had never gotten that far—because he'd been a dumbass, still trying to resist her.

She paused, pushing up on her elbows. "I'm on the pill. And I'm clean...it's been years."

"I am too. I was tested a year ago and I haven't been with anyone in...longer than that." He'd been all about the one-night stands for so damn long but that had lost its appeal long before his last abandoned job in Hong Kong. God, that seemed like a lifetime ago. Back then he'd never imagined working with his friends, making a difference like this—or meeting someone like Olivia.

Her eyes widened slightly. "Seriously?"

He nodded.

"Have you seen you?" She trailed a finger down the planes of his abdomen, making his muscles tighten and his cock kick against his zipper.

He wanted her mouth and hands all over him. "Right back at you, sweetheart." He slanted his mouth over hers again, teasing his tongue against hers. He wanted to devour her.

She touched him everywhere as they kissed, her fingers dancing over his back, his stomach, up over his chest and shoulders. It was as if she couldn't get enough of him.

Good, because he felt the same. He'd never been possessive before but when it came to her, it washed over him. Possessiveness and protectiveness.

He still couldn't get the image of her free falling down the side of that building out of his head. For the first time in years he'd felt true fear. The kind that sliced into a person with talons. He needed to erase that image, to mark her as his. If only for now. Because it would be a while before he could forget that.

Even though she said she wanted to taste him, he stripped her down, taking his time, unwrapping her like the present she was. First her jeans, then her sweater until she was in her lacy bra and panties.

Her breasts weren't more than a handful. Perfect for him. Only him.

Leaning down over her, he just tugged the cups down, not taking her bra off completely, and sucked one nipple into his mouth. Instead of teasing, working her up to it, he sucked on it hard.

She arched off the bed and wrapped her legs around his waist, making the sweetest moaning sound. If he hadn't still been wearing his pants, he'd have thrust inside her.

He rolled his hips against hers as she did the same to him. With her, he wanted to do more than just fuck. And he realized that was all he'd ever had. But with Olivia, it would be more.

Everything with her was more, *real.*

She dug her fingers into his back hard, holding on to him as if she thought he might stop. *Hell no.*

His cock pushed against the zipper of his pants but first he had to taste her again. He wanted that sweetness on his tongue when he pushed inside her.

She rolled her hips again, insistently, grinding against him.

"That feel good against your clit?" he murmured. The seam of his pants had to be hitting her there or close to it.

"You'd feel better." She slid her hands down his back as he moved to her other nipple, tugging and teasing.

When she started unbuckling his belt, he let her. He should keep everything off but he wanted to be skin to skin with her.

He hadn't been kidding—unless there was an emergency he didn't want to be disturbed. But the way things had been going, he didn't want to tempt fate. He'd give her foreplay but then he was going to be inside her before anyone could interrupt them. His entire body vibrated with the need to feel her tight sheath wrapped around him.

He shifted off her to shuck his pants. And when he knelt on the bed, his cock hard and at full attention, her eyes widened slightly as they had the first time she'd seen him. There was no hiding that he was a big guy all over. Nothing he could do about it. But he was going to make sure she was wet and ready for him.

Keeping his gaze on her face, he reached between her spread legs and cupped her covered mound. Even through the thin scrap of material he could feel her wetness.

Her gaze snapping to meet his, she rolled her hips into his hold. So he quickly discarded the panties and she slipped out of her bra. When she was bared completely to him, he froze for a long moment, staring at her sleek, smooth body. Her long, dark hair pillowed around her face as she watched him. He wasn't poetic by a long shot, but she looked like an angel.

His angel.

She reached for him, but instead of covering her body with his, of pushing inside her, he dipped his head between her legs. There was a driving need to taste her, one he wouldn't deny.

She let out a gasp as he flicked his tongue along her slick folds, but quickly slid her fingers through his hair. "Zac." When she moaned his name, he swore his dick got even harder, something that shouldn't be possible.

He dipped his tongue inside her. Just hearing his name on her lips did something to him. He'd always been Savage before her. Even with the one-night stands. Women seemed to like him because of his size, and expected him to be rough. Olivia saw him. Or at least it sure felt like it. She saw the man he wanted to be and didn't care about his past.

Zeroing in on her clit with his tongue, he applied enough pressure to have her shifting underneath him, the sweetest little moans leaving her mouth. Her breath was growing faster and harder the more he teased her. Sliding a finger inside her, he felt his dick kick again as her inner walls squeezed around him. Soon enough he'd be fully inside her. Quickly he added another finger, wanting her to be completely ready for him.

When she started squeezing around him, tighter and tighter, he knew she was close. Though he'd planned to taste her come, he eased his fingers out and climbed up her body.

Eyes heavy-lidded with hunger, she looked up at him. "In me, now."

That little bite to her words, the subtle demand, was enough to push him over the edge. Almost. He'd always been in control with women. But with Olivia, the woman owned and controlled him whether she realized it or not.

He teased her wet folds with his cock, groaning as he pushed deeper and deeper. As he thrust fully inside her, she gasped, her head falling back on a sigh of pleasure.

He nuzzled her neck as she adjusted to his size, kissing a path to that sweet spot behind her ear. Just feeling her tight body wrapped around his hard length and it was taking all of his restraint not to come. Something he'd never had a problem with before.

Reaching between their bodies, he didn't stop until he reached her clit. She dug her fingers into his back when he tweaked the sensitive bundle of nerves.

"So close, Zac."

He started moving inside her slowly, his balls pulling up tight at the sensation of being inside her. Her inner walls were so damn tight and he was close to falling over the edge.

Faster and faster he thrust while continuing to tease her clit.

He pulled back so he could see her face while she came. Her eyes were open ever so slightly, her breathing as ragged as his as she watched him. When he felt her inner walls start pulsing around him he knew she was close.

Her eyes fell shut so he crushed his mouth to hers as her climax started. She tightened her legs around him as her orgasm slammed through her, her inner walls clamping around him.

The thought of being able to come with her, to come inside her, pushed him fully over the cliff. Pure pleasure slammed out to all his nerve endings as he started coming in long, hard thrusts, over and over.

He completely lost himself inside her, the purest oblivion he'd ever experienced, until they both collapsed against the bed, breathing hard.

He wasn't sure how long they lay wrapped up in each other's arms and he didn't much care. He could stay here forever.

"I don't think I got to say it before," she murmured against his chest, breaking through the quiet of the room, "but I want to try this thing with you."

He slid a finger under her chin so she'd look up at him. He didn't want to have this conversation without looking at her face. "This thing?" he asked.

"A relationship. I want to see what we have together, even when I head home."

It didn't matter that she hadn't told him she loved him, this was a start. A very good one. He was going to show her that what they had together was something special, real. And worth holding on to. Forever.

CHAPTER TWENTY-FOUR

—One stupid mistake can change everything.—

Looking at the screen of his laptop, Gage was trying to ignore Brooks. Never should have confided in him.

"You can't hit on the new girl," Brooks muttered. Leaned back in one of the chairs in his office at the ranch, he crossed his arms over his chest.

"I'm not going to hit on her." Gage hadn't even met her yet. "I just wanted to do some background checks on her." Because he couldn't get that damn voice out of his head. He didn't bother glancing up from his laptop.

"You think Skye hasn't already done that? She knows the woman and she has a stellar work record."

Gage lifted a shoulder.

"You know what. I'll bet you that you can't get her phone number or find out more about her without using your computer."

Now he looked up. "What the hell are you talking about?"

"I mean, the only way you get to learn anything about her is if she tells you. If you look up a bunch of stuff about her, it gives you an unfair advantage and takes all the fun out of the chase."

"I'm not chasing her."

"Says the man obsessed with a voice."

"Why did I ever tell you that?" he muttered.

"It's a little sad." Brooks grinned, revealing a dimple that women seemed to love. Good-looking bastard.

Gage leaned back in his seat. "What kind of bet are you talking here? What do I get if I win?"

Brooks rolled his eyes. "Nothing from me, dumbass. But if you win, you get her number and get to know her. Do I really need to explain anything else to you? The birds and the bees perhaps?"

Gage started to respond when Brooks's dad knocked on the open door as he stepped into the entryway. It was weird having Douglas Alexander around, but he was different than the workaholic Gage remembered as a teenager.

"Son," he said, nodding at Brooks, who immediately took his boots off the expensive desk and straightened in his chair like a scolded kid. "I hear that there will be a DEA agent at the house in the morning."

Brooks pushed up from his chair and turned to face his dad. Leaning against the front of the desk, he nodded. "That's correct."

"Care to explain what's going on?" His dad leaned against the door frame, looking so much like his son it was clear they were related. Both had dark hair, hard builds and classic Hollywood good looks.

Brooks cleared his throat but launched into a brief explanation—leaving out some important details. But it was enough that the older man would be able to fill in the blanks.

Finally his dad said, "You want me to call one of my attorneys? Have them here as legal counsel for Olivia?"

Brooks shook his head. "No, but thank you. At this point having an attorney will make her look guilty or as if she has something to hide. She's going to go with the oblivious ex-wife role for now. And we've got our own attorney if necessary."

"Hmm." He nodded, but didn't move from his position. "I like what you're doing with this consulting company. You ever need anything from me, let me know."

Brooks cleared his throat and let out a grunted response that sort of sounded like a thank you.

Gage hid a smile. God, the relationship between these two was so awkward.

"So...most of the house is headed to town to see a movie. I'm going with Martina. Skye wanted me to ask you two if you wanted to go."

Brooks straightened the slightest bit. The stone-cold sniper was almost never uncomfortable but Gage knew how complicated his relationship was with his father. "Martina's not like the women you've been with in the past." There was an edge to Brooks's voice when he spoke about the older woman. No surprise—Brooks was simply like that when it came to any woman.

To Gage's surprise, the older man snorted. "Yeah, no kidding. It's why I like her. Really like her."

Brooks made a disbelieving sound and Gage could see this going badly fast so he stood from his seat. Before he'd opened his mouth, Douglas spoke.

"So when are you going to pull your head out of your ass and go after Darcy? It's time you started on a family and I'd like some grandchildren."

Okay, then. Gage looked at one of the expensive Monets on the wall, not sure what the hell else to do. He definitely didn't want to be here for this conversation—though he made a mental note of the name Darcy. Unfortunately Douglas was blocking the door and there was no easy way to extract himself from this slice of awkward hell.

Brooks started practically vibrating with anger. "Are you kidding me? Go after the woman you offered a few million if she'd leave me? This is why we can't ever have a normal relationship! You can never just leave well enough alone! And I don't buy this whole changed man attitude."

His father shoved up from the door, put his hands on his hips. "I did it to make sure she loved you and wasn't after your fortune."

"Yeah and how'd that work out?" Bitterness laced his voice. "Looks like you and I have something in common after all. Shitty taste in women."

Douglas gave him a strange look. "She didn't take the money."

A long, pregnant pause filled the silence and Gage really, really wished he was somewhere else right about now. He knew someone had hurt Brooks recently but his friend had never talked about it. Just said he was apparently a dumbass when it came to women because he had the same taste as his father. Maybe not, as it turned out. A woman who turned down a few million for him?

"What?" Brooks rasped out.

Frowning, his dad nodded. "How do you not know that? She told me to fuck off—though more politely than that. I always wondered why you let that one go. She was a real class act," he murmured, respect in his voice. "And I know she could have used the money too."

Another long silence expanded and Gage was about to just make a break for it. This was way too much emotional stuff for him.

"Son, I'm sorry, I thought you knew that—"

Brooks didn't respond, just stepped past his father and muttered something about going riding.

"Don't end up an old fool like me," Douglas said to Gage. "If you ever have kids, don't meddle in their lives. You'll have a lot fewer regrets." Shaking his head, he stepped back out of the office.

Gage collapsed back into his chair and texted Brooks even though he didn't expect a response. Not right away at least. Brooks could go off for days alone if he wanted to.

After shutting his laptop off, he headed downstairs to find the others. Brooks was right. He wasn't going to do any research on their new hire. Hell, what was he thinking anyway? He couldn't date anyone he worked with—it was just asking for trouble. Besides, once Nova, aka "the voice," got a look at Leighton or Brooks he wouldn't stand a chance.

CHAPTER TWENTY-FIVE

—You can't logic your way through emotion.—

Zac gently squeezed Olivia's hand, ready for this interview to be over. They sat across from Agent Torres and Agent King, the team the local DEA had sent out to talk to the two of them—but mainly Olivia, it seemed. "Routine questions about an ongoing investigation" was exactly how they'd worded it.

Almost everyone was out of the house except Brooks, who was in his office. Since he owned the estate, he wanted to be nearby. After all, Olivia was staying here with Zac, her new boyfriend, at his friend's estate for the Thanksgiving holiday. It appeared as if the agents believed that story. Or at least they weren't throwing cuffs on them yet.

Thankfully everyone else had made themselves scarce getting ready for the "turkey play" later tonight. Everyone but Zac. No, he was sitting right next to her and holding her hand like the concerned boyfriend.

Boyfriend seemed like such a stupid word for what they were—though he wasn't quite sure what they were at this point. He knew he loved her and that she cared for him. But after last night she hadn't said she loved him back. He wanted to be okay with that, to be patient—but it still cut. In a way he hadn't been prepared for.

Agent Torres, a Hispanic woman in a pantsuit, stood from her seat on the couch, nodding once at her partner. "Thank you for being so cooperative. If we have any questions, we'll follow up."

Following suit, Olivia stood. "I'll be here through the end of next week then I'll be headed home. But you have my contact info."

Both agents nodded and murmured niceties before she and Savage walked them out. Once he shut and locked the door behind them, she buried her face against his chest. He pulled her close, savoring the feel of her in his arms. Where she belonged.

"How did I do?" she mumbled against his pecs.

He kissed the top of her head lightly. "Perfect. And considering Agent Moore didn't come himself, I think we're in the clear. Those were just two Redemption Harbor locals doing their job. The evidence against you is destroyed, they have Neely in custody and have enough to put him away for a very long time. And the Miami PD haven't called us in for a lineup or questioning for the jewelry store heist, so that tells me the DEA has literally nothing on us. Neely just looks like a big liar at this point."

"I have a feeling since all the jewels were returned to the store, the Miami PD has closed that case." Olivia's voice was wry.

"No kidding." The cops wouldn't waste their time with the case anymore.

As far as Neely went, Zac didn't think the man would last that long in prison. He'd gotten involved with Heath, and inadvertently some very dangerous Russians. The Russians would want to clean house and Neely was a problem for them since it was clear he had no problem talking.

She pulled back slightly to look up at him. "Did you notice how carefully they watched me when they told me Heath was killed?"

"Yeah. You appeared surprised though." Not overly wrought, but still shocked.

"I'm just glad it's over." She laid her face against his chest, turning her cheek into him.

"Me too," he murmured. "When you leave next week...I'd like to set up a time to come visit you guys. I'll stay at a hotel." He didn't want to put her in an awkward position with Valencia.

"Actually," she said, looking up at him again, "you could stay with Martina if you'd like. And when Valencia stays with her we can have grown-up time."

He grinned. "I like the sound of grown-up time. And now you need to prepare for the show of your life." Her cheeks flushed in that way that pushed him over the edge, making him smile even bigger. "Not that kind of show, pervert."

"Oh my gosh, the play! What time is it?" she asked.

He glanced at his watch. "Five, which means I have one hour until curtain call."

"Thank you for doing this for Valencia. It's incredibly sweet."

He didn't know how to respond because he didn't want her gratitude. He just wanted her. Leaning down, he kissed her again, teasing his tongue against her own with a barely leashed hunger. He wanted to push her up against the door and thrust inside her over and over until they were both spent.

Then do it again.

Somehow he forced himself to pull back. Mainly because he didn't want to get caught by a six-year-old. "I've got to go get ready." He leaned his forehead against hers, willing his cock to go down. It was definitely going to take time.

Laughing lightly, she reached between their bodies and rubbed her hand over his hard length. "Tonight, you and me..." She squeezed gently.

"You're going to pay for that." He stepped back, groaning at the discomfort.

"I hope so," she murmured.

For a moment he was tempted to say screw it all and throw her over his shoulder and head upstairs—until he heard the pitter-patter of little feet. "Shit, distract her. Tell her I'll meet her outside by the pool in a few minutes."

Olivia pulled him down for a quick kiss before hurrying from the foyer, her light laughter trailing behind her. And he found himself smiling. Something he'd been doing a hell of a lot more of since her.

* * *

"I don't know how you guys did this so quickly," Olivia murmured as Skye sat next to her—in a turkey costume made from poster board, glitter, felt and a bunch of other crafty stuff.

And she still looked like a badass.

"Martina took over," Skye said, laughing. "She's a little scary."

Olivia snorted and picked up her glass of white wine. "Coming from you that seems like high praise."

Out on the huge patio where the production had been put on, little twinkle lights were everywhere, crisscrossing over the pool, giving it a fairy-tale feel. The fountain was lit up and someone had added orange and yellow candles over pretty much every flat surface. It was a gorgeous night with stars splattered overhead in every direction, the air was crisp and cool and she was with people she loved. But she couldn't seem to relax, to turn her mind off. She wasn't even worried about the whole DEA situation, though she probably should be. No, she was worried about Zac and their future, whatever that may be.

"So, I looked into some of the schools around here and one of them has an incredible Deaf and Hard of Hearing program," Skye said in that blunt way of hers.

Olivia glanced at her friend. "Way to be subtle." She'd actually done some research on her own, but wasn't going to tell Skye that.

She lifted an eyebrow. "Has anything I've ever done been subtle?"

Olivia just smiled and glanced over to where Zac was talking with Mercer and Mary Grace—and holding their baby. Just seeing that gave her all the feels. She wasn't sure she wanted to analyze why either.

"Martina seems to be having a great time here too," Skye continued, nodding to where she was talking to Douglas and Colt's dad, who both seemed to be vying for her attention. And Martina was definitely eating it up.

Not that Olivia could blame her. Both men were attractive and seemed nice. It had been a long time since Martina had even dated anyone and she deserved to be happy. "Yes, she definitely likes it here too," she murmured. And so did Valencia. Right now her daughter was standing in front of Leighton, Brooks and Gage, telling them something that must be very important. She was switching back and forth between talking and signing, all her movements animated, making her braids swish back and forth. To give them credit, they were listening intently and nodding as she talked.

"And if you guys ever move here you have a huge extended family now."

"Skye—"

"I know it's too soon for that kind of talk. I'm just planting little kernels in your head for *when* it gets to that time."

"When?"

Skye looked over at Zac. "Girl, yes, *when.* He'll move for you no doubt. And I'll throw him a going-away party if it ever gets that far. But you'll be happier here and you'll have a better support system."

"All right, Dr. Phil."

"Take it from someone who almost lost everything and everyone—having that support system makes life better. Easier in a way I never imagined was possible. Ever. It's not weak to need people... Plus I miss my freaking niece. And you need to give me another one soon."

Olivia nearly choked on her wine. Coughing, she set it on the little glass table next to the swing-bench they were sitting on. "Have your own if you want one so bad."

"Um, no. I will be the fun, cool aunt. But this," she said, motioning to her middle area, "will remain baby free. So what's holding you back with Savage?" she asked abruptly, switching subjects as if it was a normal segue.

"Why do think I'm holding back?"

"Because I see the way he looks at you—and you and I are similar, whether you believe it or not."

At that moment Savage looked over at her and it was like little butterflies just took flight inside her, all wild and out of control. She thought of the way she'd teased him before the play, how she'd *really* wanted to drag him upstairs and have her wicked way with him—and how terrified she was of truly letting him in.

"I need to talk to Zac. Will you keep an eye on Valencia?" she asked Skye, even though she knew everyone here would be watching her daughter. But if she specifically asked Skye, she knew the woman wouldn't let Valencia out of her sight.

"Of course."

Before she'd even pushed up from her seat, Zac had handed the baby to Mary Grace and was heading Olivia's way. She sidestepped a table of snack food and was in his arms as if it was the most natural place to be. She really did love him.

He loosely placed his hands on her hips, looking down at her in a way no man had ever looked at her. With complete love and adoration.

And it scared the hell out of her. How could this be real? How could *he* be real? She knew she loved him, but saying the words out loud scared her.

"I like your construction paper turkey hat." Laughing, she reached up and touched it.

He caught her wrist and brought it to his mouth. Tingles raced through her as he oh so gently brushed his lips against her skin. There was nothing overtly sexual about it but the brief contact had warmth rushing between her legs. "I'll wear it later if you like it so much," he murmured, making her laugh.

"Can we sneak into the kitchen for a minute?"

"I'm going to need more than a minute."

Warmth infused her cheeks, as it so often did around him. "Ha, ha. I just wanted to talk to you in private."

Suddenly serious, he nodded.

"Are you ending things with me?" he asked as he shut the door behind them. He pulled the hat off and set it on the closest countertop.

"What—No!" How could he think that? "I love you. I know I haven't said it yet, but I do. I love you so much that it scares me." She placed a gentle hand on his chest when he went to pull her into his arms. "I've got to say this so just let me get it out... What I feel for you doesn't even come close to what I had with my ex. Not even in the same stratosphere of emotions. Or anyone for that matter. I've never been in love until now. And for so long it's just been Valencia, Martina and me. We've been a team and it's worked. The thought of letting you in and then losing you…it shreds me up inside. It might sound lame but I've just been struggling with the idea of giving in to the wonderfulness of you, of *us*, and then losing it."

"You think I don't have those fears?"

"You do?" The tension in her chest started to ease the tiniest bit.

"I've never felt this way about anyone. Other than my grandmother and brother, and the family I choose," he said motioning outside, "I've never let anyone else in. And I'm scared that Valencia won't like me or want me to be with you. And the thing is, I'd understand. I don't know that I'm good enough for you guys." She made a scoffing sound but he continued. "I'm also afraid that you'll move back home and decide this was all just lust but nothing more." He scrubbed a hand over the back of his neck, looking truly stressed for the first time since she'd met him.

And she wanted to wipe all that away. "Zac." She wrapped her arms around him and went up on tiptoe. She'd had no idea he had the same fears as her. He seemed invincible, like nothing could faze him. "I love you and that's not going away. Distance won't change it."

"Would it be too much for me to come stay the week you guys get back?"

"I already asked Martina and she said her guest room is ready."

"Really?"

"She adores everyone here, and since you helped save her and helped keep me safe—and sane—and came up with the idea for the Thanksgiving play, I'm pretty sure you can do no wrong. She might even bake for you."

His eyes lit up at that. "Really?"

"Yep. I won't," she said, laughing. "I don't have that skill but Martina will bake or cook anything you want."

Leaning down he brushed his lips over hers, and as he started to deepen it, the back door flung open. Valencia raced at them and as Olivia bent down to pick her up, her daughter flew past her and jumped into Zac's arms.

He seemed a little stunned but easily picked her up, a giant smile on his face as he held her close.

Olivia still had some fears because hey, she was human. But this man had stolen her heart when he'd come up with the plan to do the turkey play. That was the kind of man worth fighting for…worth everything.

She knew, in a bone-deep way, that he was it for her. The real deal. Time or distance wouldn't change it. Zacharias Savage was definitely part of their future.

EPILOGUE

—This is the year I get everything right.—

New Year's Eve

"Dude, chill. She's going to know something's up." Skye not so softly nudged Zac in the ribs as she came to stand next to him by the fountain.

"I'm not doing anything." He looked over at Olivia, who held Valencia on one hip as they talked to Brooks's dad about something. Valencia had been determined to stay up until midnight but judging from the way her eyes kept drifting shut, he didn't think it was happening.

"You keep patting your pockets like they're on fire," Colt said, joining them. He wrapped an arm around Skye's shoulders and kissed the top of her head. "You look insane."

Skye snorted. "What are you doing over here by yourself anyway?"

"Giving myself a pep talk," he muttered, only slightly embarrassed. These were his people. They'd seen him at his worst.

They both laughed as Skye said, "She's going to say yes."

He was pretty certain of that too but there was a part of him, the little boy inside him that didn't fit in anywhere, that didn't feel worthy. Who was terrified she'd say no. That the past month and a half had been this fantasy he'd convinced himself of. Or what if she thought it was too soon? They'd gone at warp speed since meeting each other but it felt right on every level. And what he felt for her wasn't something he would second-guess so he didn't see the point of waiting any longer. Plus, he wanted to lock her down. And he gave zero fucks if that made him a caveman. Olivia was his.

Instead of responding to Skye, he muttered something about going to put Valencia to bed before heading over to his girls.

His girls.

The first time Valencia had made that comment his heart had stopped in his chest. But they *were* his girls. And he wanted to take care of them and protect them. Martina too. They'd become his family faster than he could have imagined. He wanted it official.

"Hey, sweetheart, let me take her to bed," he murmured as he reached them.

Olivia gave him a grateful smile and Valencia didn't argue about not being tired as he gathered her into his arms. Instead she laid her head on his shoulder, and just like every time before, his heart grew. He hadn't even realized he had this much love to give. Hadn't thought he was capable of it.

But these two... He wanted to be a better person because of them.

"Make sure you're back in time for the countdown. I want my New Year's kiss." Olivia winked at him before turning back to Douglas.

It didn't take long to find the guest room in Brooks's house that Valencia and Olivia had claimed as their own for the night. Of course he hoped Olivia would stay with him for a few hours before daybreak.

Over the last month and a half he'd traveled to see them as often as possible. Everyone had juggled jobs around so he could take a lighter load but that couldn't last forever. He wanted to live in the same city as Olivia, wanted to wake up to her face every morning. And he wanted to claim her so the world knew she was his—and he wanted the world to know he belonged to her. Because she completely owned him.

"Zac," Valencia murmured sleepily as he pulled back the fluffy comforter. "Gotta tell you something." She latched onto the stuffed unicorn in the bed and pulled it against her chest.

He laid her down and slipped her shoes off. She'd be sleeping in her party dress tonight but he helped her take off the thick jacket Martina had insisted she wear, much to her annoyance. "What is it?" he asked, pulling the covers up to her chin. Then he grabbed the blanket at the end of the bed and unfolded it. The heat was on but he wanted to make sure she was warm enough.

"I know it's not New Year's yet but I made a wish."

He didn't know if that was an actual thing, making a wish on New Year's, or if it was something she'd come up with. He'd quickly learned that she had a big imagination and liked to tell stories. "Whatever it is, I hope it comes true." If he knew what it was and could make it happen, he most definitely would.

"I made a wish that you'd be my daddy." Her eyes drifted closed as she curled on her side, unicorn held tight against her.

His throat tightened as a swell of emotion overtook him. "I hope that comes true too," he whispered, even though she was already asleep. One of her processors had already fallen off so he picked it up from the pillow then slid the other one off as well and set them on the nightstand.

A soft gasp from the doorway made him turn to see Olivia standing there. She'd worn a lacy black dress fitted to all her curves—unfortunately covered up most of the night because of her coat. The coat was off now and he just drank her in.

"Zac." She stepped into the room, her eyes wide. "What did you just say?"

Crossing the short distance to her, he dropped down on one knee and her eyes got wider. "I want to spend the rest of my life making you and Valencia happy." And he couldn't wait a second longer. He pulled out the small jewelry box, his palms damp as he opened it. "Olivia Carter, will you marry me?" His heart pounded in his ears as he waited all of a millisecond before she threw her arms around his neck.

"Yes," she whispered, brushing her lips over his as he slid the ring onto her finger. "Yes, yes, yes."

Standing, he lifted her into his arms and carried her from the room and took her next door, to his own guest room for the night. "I don't care where we live," he said, setting her on her feet. "As long as we get to wake up to each other every morning." And he wanted to be there for Valencia for all the day-to-day stuff, like taking her to school in the mornings. He would hate leaving his job but he thought they might be able to work something out where he did contract work. Most of their jobs were out of town anyway.

"Well I care." She wrapped her arms around his waist. "We both love Redemption Harbor, and more importantly I love you. I've been looking into a school Skye recommended and I've already done a tour." She blushed slightly. "I didn't tell you because I wanted to get as many details as possible in case you ever did propose."

"In case." He snorted. It had been a foregone conclusion for him.

Smiling, she held her hand out and finally looked at her engagement ring. "This is gorgeous, Zac. Two carat, French cut basket setting with a platinum band. Incredible clarity."

He laughed lightly. "You really do know your diamonds."

She flushed slightly as she met his gaze. "Force of habit—I really wouldn't care what you gave me as long as we get married."

He did know that and it made him love her even more. "I might have had a little help." He'd asked Skye to help him ring shop—and she'd laughed and pushed him in Mary Grace's direction. That had been the smart decision.

"Well it's beautiful and I love it."

"I love you."

She beamed at him, so much joy in her expression. "If it works for you, I can have Valencia registered for January. We'll just have to figure out living arrangements—because your place is too small."

"She won't mind switching schools midyear?" He'd planned to move into things a lot slower, but only because he thought that was what *she* would want. He'd move in with them today if possible.

"Not at all. When you're not around she's been begging to move here. She wants to be around you, her aunt and uncle and her 'new family' as she calls everyone—and the horses."

He snorted at that. "My lease is almost up." He lived in a "sad single guy" condo, as Olivia had once called it. Since moving to Redemption Harbor he'd been consumed with work and never home. He hadn't bothered putting up any art or decorations. Sad was probably an understatement.

"So...maybe we can rent for a little bit, while we look for a place to buy?"

He nodded, crushing his mouth to hers because he couldn't not kiss her any longer. He needed her naked and underneath him. Now. There was a lot they'd still have to figure out but the important thing was, she'd said yes.

And he was never letting her go.

—The End—

Thank you for reading Savage Rising, the second book in my all new Redemption Harbor series. If you don't want to miss any future releases, please feel free to join my newsletter. Find the signup link on my website:

http://www.katiereus.com

ACKNOWLEDGMENTS

Thank you never seems enough, but here goes; As always, I owe a big thanks to Kari Walker. In addition to all the behind-the-scenes work Sarah does, I also owe a HUGE thank you to Sarah for answering all my questions about the Deaf culture. Thank you for taking the time to beta read and offer so much wonderful insight. Any mistakes in this book are my own. Once again, thank you to Jaycee for a stunning cover. Julia, I'd be lost without your editing skills! Thank you to Joanna Moreno for the translation help. Carolyn Crane, thank you so much for your insight as well! For my wonderful, wonderful readers, thank you for all the emails and private messages about this new series! Starting a new series is a scary thing and you all have let me know that I made the right decision with launching Redemption Harbor, a series that's been running around in my brain for years. As always, thank you to my family for putting up with my crazy hours. And, of course, thank you to God.

COMPLETE BOOKLIST

Red Stone Security Series

No One to Trust

Danger Next Door

Fatal Deception

Miami, Mistletoe & Murder

His to Protect

Breaking Her Rules

Protecting His Witness

Sinful Seduction

Under His Protection

Deadly Fallout

Sworn to Protect

Secret Obsession

Love Thy Enemy

Dangerous Protector

Lethal Game

Deadly Ops Series

Targeted

Bound to Danger

Chasing Danger (novella)

Shattered Duty

Edge of Danger

A Covert Affair

Redemption Harbor Series

Resurrection

Savage Rising

The Serafina: Sin City Series

First Surrender

Sensual Surrender

Sweetest Surrender

Dangerous Surrender

O'Connor Family Series

Merry Christmas, Baby

Tease Me, Baby

It's Me Again, Baby

Mistletoe Me, Baby

Non-series Romantic Suspense

Running From the Past

Dangerous Secrets

Killer Secrets

Deadly Obsession

Danger in Paradise

His Secret Past

Retribution

Paranormal Romance

Destined Mate

Protector's Mate

A Jaguar's Kiss

Tempting the Jaguar

Enemy Mine

Heart of the Jaguar

Moon Shifter Series
Alpha Instinct
Lover's Instinct
Primal Possession
Mating Instinct
His Untamed Desire
Avenger's Heat
Hunter Reborn
Protective Instinct
Dark Protector
A Mate for Christmas

Darkness Series
Darkness Awakened
Taste of Darkness
Beyond the Darkness
Hunted by Darkness
Into the Darkness
Saved by Darkness

ABOUT THE AUTHOR

Katie Reus is the *New York Times* and *USA Today* bestselling author of the Red Stone Security series, the Darkness series and the Deadly Ops series. She fell in love with romance at a young age thanks to books she pilfered from her mom's stash. Years later she loves reading romance almost as much as she loves writing it.

However, she didn't always know she wanted to be a writer. After changing majors many times, she finally graduated summa cum laude with a degree in psychology. Not long after that she discovered a new love. Writing. She now spends her days writing dark paranormal romance and sexy romantic suspense.

For more information on Katie please visit her website: www.katiereus.com. Also find her on twitter @katiereus or visit her on facebook at:
www.facebook.com/katiereusauthor.

Made in the USA
Las Vegas, NV
10 August 2021

27922700R00156